Printed in the United States of America on acid-free paper
First Edition

Cover design by Catherine Hopkins
Typeset by Sandi Stancil

Library of Congress Cataloging-in-Publication Data

Forrest, Katherine V., 1939–
Murder by tradition / by Katherine V. Forrest
   p.   cm.
   ISBN 0-941483-89-4 : $18.95
   I. Title.
PS3556.O737M84   1991
813'.54--dc20   90-21994
                                                  CIP

MURDER BY TRADITION

KATHERINE V. FORREST

NAIAD
1991

BOOKS BY KATHERINE V. FORREST

CURIOUS WINE

DAUGHTERS OF A CORAL DAWN

AMATEUR CITY
A Kate Delafield Mystery

AN EMERGENCE OF GREEN

MURDER AT THE NIGHTWOOD BAR
A Kate Delafield Mystery

DREAMS AND SWORDS

THE BEVERLY MALIBU
A Kate Delafield Mystery

MURDER BY TRADITION
A Kate Delafield Mystery

Acknowledgments

The professional and personal support I received during the writing of this novel is especially meaningful. I am deeply grateful . . .

To the Third Street Writers Group, respected and highly talented colleagues who have become, over the years, my trusted friends:

> Gerald Citrin, Montserrat Fontes, Janet Gregory, Jeffrey N. McMahan, Karen Sandler; and newcomer Vicki P. McConnell.
> Added thanks to Jeff and Gerry for vital moral support.

To Michael Nava for advice on several legal intricacies, and for his honest friendship and the inspiration of his own work.

To Barbara Grier, an editor's editor, for her advice, for her clear perception of this novel and all my work.

Most especially to Detective Supervisor Mary F. Otterson, Madison, WI. For the incalculable value of her advice, her patient communication of the realities of police work. For her precious friendship over the years. For her own integrity which more than anything has helped me understand the essential truth of Kate Delafield and has given me Kate's reality.

MURDER BY TRADITION

KATHERINE V. FORREST

PART I

— 1 —

Detective Kate Delafield drove down Third Street, past five black-and-whites clustered beside an expanse of yellow police tape fluttering in a mild breeze. She parked the Plymouth around the corner on Harper Avenue. Detective Ed Taylor, yawning audibly, climbed out of the car and stretched; he knew from many past investigations how deliberately she preferred to approach a crime scene. Pulling her notebook from her shoulderbag, Kate recorded the date, Feb. 4, 1989, the time, 7:35 a.m., and the temperature, approximately fifty-five degrees in the

city of Los Angeles. She strode back around the
corner, Taylor dawdling in her wake.

At this early hour on a Saturday morning, auto
traffic moved smoothly along Third Street, slowing
only momentarily at the site of the police activity.
The block was devoid of pedestrians. She walked
past a liquor store occupying the corner of Harper,
its vertical neon sign reflecting down the two
intersecting streets. Then came Indigo Restaurant,
Minassian Rug Company, a Christian Science
Reading Room, John Atchison Beauty Shop, a
laundry. Then Tradition.

The mid-block restaurant, its taped-off perimeter
patrolled by Felix Knapp and Chris Hollings, was
scarcely wider than a storefront. Kate nodded to the
two officers, pleased with the positioning of police
tape which would help to keep media coverage well
back from the crime scene.

Taylor ducked under the tape; Kate moved past
it and looked in the window of the adjacent
business, Andria's Hole in the Wall — a
contemporary clothing shop with garments in its
window that she would not wear to a Halloween
party. Next came Mariana Custom Cleaners. Then a
small office building, and on the corner of Sweetzer
Avenue, a mini-mall with a half-dozen shops. Across
the street a 7-Eleven dominated a matching
mini-mall. The next building was Taj Soundworks,
then a vacant storefront, a shop called Objects,
Pacific Printing, Classy Nail, a yoga center, and
Banner Packing.

After recording all of this in her notebook, Kate
walked back to Tradition and past the tape to study
the restaurant.

White shutters decorated the lower half of the front window, tapestry curtains the top half. A small puff-shaped canopy, dark blue, sheltered a door, the window in the door decorated by tapestry matching the curtain in the larger window.

Sergeant Fred Hansen, with Taylor beside him smothering another yawn, stood sentry in the doorway, watching her, one hand resting on his gun belt, the other clutching a clipboard.

She nodded. "Morning, Fred."

Hansen returned her nod. "How are you, Kate?" Somberly, he consulted his clipboard. "Victim's Edward Ashwell Crawford, white male, goes by Teddie, T-e-d-d-i-e, according to his partner." He gestured behind him. "Nice little neighborhood restaurant with takeout, catering, too." His stolid expression softened. "Nice little business. Wouldn't mind having it myself." The softness was replaced by impassiveness. "Except for what's in the kitchen. Real scenic in there. His partner slid all over the place getting to the victim to see if he was still alive."

"Great," muttered Taylor. He unbuttoned his plaid jacket, tugged on its sleeves, shoved his hands in his pockets.

Kate recognized Taylor's fidgeting as preparation, a bracing for what awaited them. "Anything else?" she said to Hansen with a brusqueness that came out of her own tension, a familiar tightening inside her, a necessary girding.

Hansen shook his head. "The partner's too freaked out, couldn't get much out of him." He gestured to a black-and-white parked off to the side of the yellow police tape; a figure sat in the rear, his bowed head in his hands. "Pierce and Swenson, Foster and Deems are canvassing but everything on the street's closed except the 7-Eleven. There's an alley behind the restaurant, we're working the neighborhood over there. The victim's been dead a few hours, I'd say. Some of the mess is drying."

"Thanks, Fred," Kate said.

Hansen opened the door of Tradition.

A counter with an old-fashioned ornate cash register occupied the front of the long room. A refrigerator display case along the adjacent wall was empty of its usual contents, but neat tags in script lettering announced what had been planned for the case: lemon pasta with herbs, grape leaves, chicken breasts dijon, shrimp salad, vegetable bouquet.

Visible in the murky depths of the room were eight small tables on a faded Oriental carpet, with tablecloths and delicate wrought iron chairs with tapestry-covered seats. On the walls three impressionist prints of nature scenes seemed dream-like in the shadows.

Taylor, glancing around, scratched the bald spot at the back of his head, pulling his lank blond hair back over it. "Very frou-frou," he pronounced.

Kate liked the place, its gentility amid the prosaic commerce of the street. She suspected that it attracted loyal customers who appreciated the unpretentious charm. She moved to the counter and stooped down to read a card in a small wicker basket.

TRADITION
Catering for the Discriminating

She stood up straight. Squaring her shoulders, she walked toward the doorway behind the counter. Standing on the threshold she took in the scene in one encompassing glance that included the ceiling, then carefully focused her gaze.

The kitchen was compact, with a double stainless steel sink and Formica-topped counters, a built-in refrigerator — all surrounding a large table for food preparation. Immaculate, Kate thought. She would trust anything prepared in here. She lowered her gaze slightly, examining the room in patterned sections like a camera lens. The cabinet and walls were pristine white, except for a considerable area near the sink where a design of bright red arcs and splatters extended several feet high on the wall. Low on the wall was a smear of red as if a hand had swiped at the stain.

"This guy can't have an ounce left in him," Taylor grunted from behind her in the doorway.

She lowered her gaze to the polished tile floor. Blood had pooled into the channels between the white tiles for several feet around the body of Edward Ashwell Crawford. Other individual puddles and trails of blood defiled the floor, as well as bloody footsteps, several of them skid marks where someone had slid through the gore. The dead man's black pants clung wetly to his legs. Patches of white skin were visible through a torn and shredded shirt fouled crimson and plastered to his body; only from a portion of the collar could Kate tell that the shirt had been white. Teddie Crawford's arms were crossed over himself as if to staunch the blood draining from his body. His dull brown stare was fixed on the ceiling.

"Swiss cheese," Taylor said. "Somebody turned him into fucking Swiss cheese."

"You never realize how much blood the body holds," Kate murmured.

"One hell of a good-looking young guy," Taylor offered.

Wondering how he could tell, Kate looked more closely at the body. The head lay in a pool of blood, and the tousled hair, dark and thick, was saturated with it; the face, bleached out, was measled with red droplets. Even so, the head and its features were finely made. Long eyelashes thickly fringed the staring dark eyes, the nose was patrician, the mouth, even in the slackness of death, was sensuous, the torso slender and well-formed. The bloodied hand nearest to Kate had long tapered fingers. In a scene of such carnage, she was amazed at Taylor's perception. "Yes," she agreed. "Very good-looking."

And gay. She sensed it with gut-deep certainty.

She craned her body over the threshold, studying the dead man's hand which was nearest to her; it was turned palm down, the little finger angled unnaturally. She needed to get more information from this room, and quickly. She said impatiently, "Not a damn thing we can do till the coroner and the technicians get here. We can't even go in."

Taylor pointed at the maelstrom of blood and bloody footprints. "How can anybody mess this up?"

"Let's not make it worse," Kate said flatly. As the D-3 on this case, she was in charge; essential crime-scene decisions were hers. "We need Shapiro and Napoleon Carter here before anybody else goes in."

"See that?" Taylor was pointing to the table.

A piece of glass glittered under the fluorescent light; a powdery residue coated its surface.

"Coke," he said.

She shrugged. "Probably."

"A party that got out of hand," Taylor said. "Way out of hand."

"Maybe," Kate said, staring at the dead man's fixed gaze, knowing she was being irrational as she hoped that this beautiful young gay man had not lost his life in a party that had gotten "out of hand."

— 2 —

"My whole life's in that place," sobbed Francisco
Caldera. "It's gone, it's nothing without Teddie . . ."

The rail-thin Latino was slumped sideways in the
back seat of a black-and-white, feet dangling out of
its open door, arms crossed in a clutching of his own
body. Kate stood beside the squad car with Taylor.

"When was the last time you saw him?" she
asked. With difficulty she kept her gaze focused on
the grief-ravaged young face turned up to hers. After

a single glance at Taylor, he had not taken his eyes off her. Even the knowledge that this man was a suspect, that killers often exhibited as much or more grief as anyone else, did not diminish an almost compelling need to soothe him, to stroke his thin, fine-textured dark hair.

"Last night," he said, brushing away tears. "We closed up at eleven."

"Was that as usual?"

He shook his head. "Big catering job tonight. We made marinades, sauces . . ." He lifted a hand, dropped it into his lap in a gesture of futility. He wore a white cotton jacket over a lime green shirt; his pants were gray and voluminous.

Kate asked, "Who left first?"

Briefly he closed his eyes. Moisture glistened on his dark lashes. "He did. Gloria picked him up." At Kate's questioning look he added, "Gloria Gomez. His roommate. They have an apartment over on Crescent Heights."

A female roommate. Kate felt no shift in her certainty that Teddie Crawford was a gay man. And that Francisco Caldera was a gay man also. Possibly the female roommate was a lesbian. She said, "Where did they say they were going?"

"Malone's. A bar in West Hollywood." He added in bitter self-reproach, "He wanted me to go. But me, I had to get some sleep. I go to that bar with him, he might be alive . . ."

Kate thought about Joe D'Amico at the crime lab and his constant gossip about the gay bars in West Hollywood and Silverlake; she didn't recognize the

name of this one. Could it be new? Or perhaps not a
gay bar? She asked casually, "Does Malone's have a
particular clientele?"

"A mix. Gloria likes it. She was seeing some new
guy she wanted Teddie to meet."

So Gloria Gomez apparently was heterosexual.
And Malone's Bar attracted an assortment of sexual
orientation and ethnicity, judging by Gloria Gomez's
affection for it.

"This Gloria," Taylor said. "How'd she get along
with Teddie?"

"Like he was her brother. Everybody loved
Teddie."

"Somebody didn't. Tell us what happened to him
last night."

Warily eying Taylor, Caldera shook his head.
"After he left here — I don't have clue."

Kate observed Taylor with weary annoyance. His
knee-jerk behavior toward men in any way distinct
from himself was always heavy-handed assertion of
authority. Francisco Caldera might have been born
and bred in middle-class American culture, but he
was Latino, and that was all Taylor saw.

Taylor said, "You actually see Gloria Gomez pick
him up?"

"She honked from the alley. She drives a Honda
Civic, I know the horn."

Hitching her pants to put a foot up on the floor
of the squad car, Kate leaned over to be closer to
Francisco Caldera, a hand not quite touching him.
She said gently, "Tell us when you got here this
morning and what you saw."

"I came in the place about seven o'clock —" His
dark eyes awash and fixed on Kate, again he crossed

his arms over his chest in an effort to control his
shudders.

"Which door?" Taylor was busy writing.

"Through the alley door like always. I saw Teddie
. . . lying there. I had to see if . . . I ran to him, I
slipped all over the place . . ."

He lowered his head and sobbed. He pointed a
tremulous finger at his white Nikes. "It's
Teddie's bl . . . it's Teddie's bloo —" He dissolved
into gulping sobs.

Taylor asked, "Did you touch him?"

"I don't remember, sir." The voice sounded as if
it were bubbling up through water.

"Turn him over?"

Caldera shook his bowed head. "I was so scared,
I got to the phone and then the police came."

"Why were you scared?"

Taylor's voice was mild, but Caldera jerked his
head up. "I never saw anybody dead before. It was
Teddie. My friend, the best friend I ever —" Another
paroxysm of tears.

Taylor said, "You knew why this happened to
him, that's why you were scared, right?"

Jabbing tears off his cheeks with his fingers,
Caldera stared at him. "Man, what are you *talking*
about?"

Taylor, Kate conceded, was asking good questions.
But she entered the conversation. "What can you tell
us about his associates?"

"He knew everybody. All up and down the block.
Everybody in the neighborhood where he lived.
Everybody."

"His family," Kate said, "what do you know about
them?"

He slumped further down in the seat, a hand across his eyes. "Joe and Margaret will just . . ." He shook his head.

"Joe and Margaret," Taylor said, writing in his notebook.

"An aunt and uncle. They raised him. They live in a trailer park in Lancaster, but Teddie sees — saw them every chance he . . . got. God . . . he's *dead.*" Again he burst into tears.

Kate watched him with an emotion she recognized from witnessing bereavements and having gone through her own. People were either sheathed by shock and behaved calmly, almost normally, as she had, or they were swallowed up by agony. Difficult as it might be to witness, agony at least meant that grieving was already in process, and recovery closer.

"I'm sorry," Kate said. "I know this is very hard for you. But we need to get information as quickly as we can to find out who did this." She asked, "Did Teddie have enemies? Anyone at all you can think of?"

"No. Not a soul. I tell you, everybody loved Teddie."

"Everybody's got enemies," Taylor stated.

Caldera answered with quiet dignity: "Not Teddie.'"

"Who was his girlfriend?"

"Girlfriend?" Caldera looked at him. "Teddie was gay. We're both gay."

There it was. Kate marveled at Francisco Caldera, at the ease of it. She asked, "How did the two of you get along?" Before Caldera could answer she rephrased the question more bluntly: "Were you lovers?"

"Never happened." To Kate the tone carried a strong vibration of regret. "He was more than a partner, he was like a brother. We both put everything we had into this place. But he was the one who really made it work. I can't do anything without him."

Taylor said, almost idly, "You're both young guys. How'd you get the money to start up?"

"My money. But he had the brains. Teddie was born knowing how to do this. And he charmed the customers, the business was just starting to —"

"Okay," Taylor said, "how'd *you* get the money?"

"Insurance."

Kate, although she surmised what was coming, waited along with Taylor.

"A friend died, okay?"

"I'm sorry, Mr. Caldera," Kate said into the silence.

Caldera shrugged. "Call me Francisco. And I've lost many friends . . . many."

"Francisco," she said, and smiled at him. "Did Teddie have a lover?"

His face softened as he looked at her. "Nobody serious. Not since Carl."

"Tell us about Carl," she said.

He shrugged. "Nothing to tell. He's been history over a year now."

Taylor said, "Where can we reach him?"

"He's in the book. Carl Jacoby, in Silverlake. But he didn't have anything to do with this. He broke up with Teddie when he tested positive."

"Teddie tested positive?" Taylor's voice was suddenly animated.

"No, Carl did."

"Your friend Teddie gave it to him," Taylor said. "Right?" He gestured so imperiously at Tradition that Kate had to resist looking around at the restaurant. She stood with her back to it, as if to block out images of its blood-drenched kitchen.

"No, Teddie was negative."

Taylor shook his head. "I don't get it."

"Carl was freaked at the idea he could've given it to Teddie. So freaked he checked right out of Teddie's life." He was looking at Kate as he spoke. "It happens. You test HIV-positive, you look at everything differently. Everything."

Criminalist Napoleon Carter and his team had arrived, along with blood spatter expert Charlotte Mead and photographer Ted Carlton. As had Shapiro, Wilshire Division's photographer.

Kate said, "We'll have more questions later, Francisco." Then she asked quietly, "How old was Teddie?"

"Twenty-three," he said, and again began to sob.

Every angle and dimension of Tradition had been photographed. The body of Teddie Crawford, no longer strobe-lit, would nevertheless lie on the floor for hours longer, Kate knew; Charlotte Mead and Ted Carlton would now begin work in this room that in the awakening warmth of the day was filling with the rich coppery scent of blood.

"Ed, Kate," Charlotte Mead barked from beside the double sink.

Kate smiled at the tall, lanky, blue-smocked woman. They had worked together on other homicides when blood spatter analysis was necessary. Charlotte Mead was brilliant at her difficult, painstaking, eccentric profession.

"Come on over here, you two," Mead commanded. "Hands in your pockets, you touch anything, you own it. Ed, you watch where you put those elephant feet." She indicated a route that skirted the gore on the floor.

Taylor stepped over the threshold. "Believe me, you're gonna see a real twinkle toes." He stuffed his hands in his jacket pockets, as did Kate — routine safeguarding of a crime scene; he and Kate would not touch anything, even accidentally. But Kate also understood that a deeper concern underlay Taylor's caution: the dead man was gay, and this room was awash in blood.

"Your assailant's been cut," Mead told them. "See this nice single round drop of blood?" She pointed with her pen at a red globule on the counter near the sink. "We got a swimming pool on the floor but this drop's all by itself. So it hardly came from the deceased. And over here, blood's on one of the faucet handles. And on this bar of soap. No question we'll find blood in the drain. Your man tried to clean himself up."

Mead's weathered face was sharp with eagerness, her professional interest whetted by a crime scene only minimally despoiled. All too frequently, police presence — hands and feet altering evidence — cast ambiguity onto the reconstruction she was required to create for the benefit of a jury.

Kate looked at Charlotte Mead with deference and a touch of envy. Her expertise — and that of all the criminalists — was the one purely impartial aspect of a homicide investigation. Mead was on the side only of her scientific findings, and her testimony in court could be the despair of the prosecution just as well as it could the defense. The best course of action always was to find out exactly what she knew.

Kate said, "Anything else you can tell us right now?"

Mead indicated the wall and cabinets behind the corpse of Teddie Crawford. "There's a castoff pattern." With her pen she described an arc corresponding with a faint pattern of red droplets rising high up on the white surfaces. "Your man threw blood in the act of stabbing. His own blood. No question he's cut. Check the hospitals and clinics."

"We'll get right on it, Charlotte. No sign of the weapon, I take it."

"Come on, Kate. He'd put his pecker back in his pants, wouldn't he?"

"Just checking, Charlotte." Kate grinned at her. A familiar tenet among law enforcement professionals held that multiple stabbing was a form of sexual pathology.

Mead's blue eyes fastened onto the body on the floor. She shook her head. "Look at him, just look at him. Such a beauty."

Kate joined Mead's contemplation of Teddie Crawford. Twenty-three years were all he had

known. The rest had been taken from him. What
else was important?

"You be real careful in here, Charlotte," Taylor
said. "The guy's gay, you know."

Kate looked at him balefully.

Charlotte's voice, her face, were impassive.
"Careful is my life, Ed."

Gloria Gomez had arrived at Tradition, Hansen
informed Kate and Taylor.

"Take her to the station," Kate ordered. "Ed and
I will be along shortly. Fred," she added, "call us the
minute the coroner gets here." She wanted to be
present when Teddie Crawford's body was moved.
She was grateful for Charlotte Mead's information;
knowing the killer was wounded narrowed the field
of suspects significantly.

The media, both print and visual, had assembled
along with a sizable crowd outside the yellow police
tape protecting Tradition, the crowd and the
television cameras settling in to wait for that hushed
moment of drama when the wrapped body of Teddie
Crawford would be rolled out to the waiting coroner's
van.

Lieutenant Bodwin had also arrived, and entered
Tradition accompanied by Kate and Taylor, who
briefed him. Silent, his craggy face expressionless, he
observed the kitchen from the doorway. He would be
dealing with the press.

"Charlotte says our man's wounded, Lieutenant,"
Taylor told him. "We need somebody to get right on
checking hospitals and clinics."

"Yes, well, it seems pretty fucking stupid for him to go to a hospital, doesn't it," Bodwin said, turning his back on the room where the crime lab team worked.

"Good thing so many of them are pretty fucking stupid," Kate said agreeably. She knew he understood that criminal impulses and behavior had little to do with intelligence. His remark had been reflexive, rooted in his unforgiving resentment of Charlotte Mead. Mead, who observed no niceties of status and would take on Chief Daryl Gates if it meant preserving the sanctity of a crime scene, had repaid the lieutenant's assertive entry into one such scene by isolating his fingerprint on an item of evidence and then spreading the report throughout the department.

"I'll take care of assigning someone," Bodwin said, and left to face the television cameras.

Gloria Gomez, in black jeans and a white cotton knit sweater, her shoulder-length dark hair disheveled, looked younger than her twenty years. Her delicate, almost childlike hands lay tightly clasped on the Formica-topped table in the interview room.

"I need to see Teddie," she whispered, her eyes dull black with shock. "I . . . can't do anything with how I feel till I see Teddie."

Kate nodded. "I understand," she said. Seeing Anne had been so absolute a requirement that she had disregarded every attempt to dissuade her from viewing what was in the burned out wreck on the

Hollywood Freeway. She added, "But that won't be possible for a while."

For Gloria Gomez, seeing Teddie Crawford would not happen for days, if it happened at all. There would be further violation of Teddie Crawford's body at the autopsy. Then his next of kin — presumably Joe and Margaret Crawford — would determine what happened to him next. His face appeared minimally damaged, and clothing would conceal the devastation done to his body. Depending on the Crawford family's burial beliefs, Gloria Gomez might have her wish in the form of an open casket funeral.

"Gloria," Taylor said, "we know this is hard. But try your best to talk to us. When did you last see Teddie?"

Kate flicked a glance at Taylor. He was being as considerate to Gloria Gomez as he had been impersonal with Francisco Caldera.

"Last night . . ." The young woman faltered.

"Last night," Taylor said, leaning back, crossing an ankle over a knee, his casual posture an attempt to relax her. "Tell us about that."

"I picked him up at Tradition like I said I would —"

"Where was Teddie's car?"

"He doesn't — didn't have one."

"What time did you pick him up, Gloria?"

"Right at eleven. We went to Malone's like we planned."

"Anybody with you?"

She shook her head. "I had a late date with Paul. I wanted Teddie to meet him."

"What's Paul's last name?"

"Lopez . . . Paul Lopez. Teddie liked him —

bought both of us beers . . ." Her gaze seemed
unfocused.

Kate thought of Aimee, remembering the
homicide investigation of only two months before, the
horror of Owen Sinclair's death reflected in Aimee's
unfocused eyes. She needed to call Aimee, to tell her
she would be tied up indefinitely on this new
investigation. And, she ordered herself, she needed to
eliminate extraneous thoughts and concentrate on
the brutal murder of this gay man and the
important work required of her right now in this
room.

"He can't be dead," Gloria Gomez said to Kate.
"There's no reason . . ."

"No, there isn't any reason at all," Kate said
quietly. "I'm very sorry."

"The guy he met . . . did he . . ."

Kate exchanged a swift glance with Taylor. "What
can you tell us about that?"

"Not much. Teddie met this guy. They left
together."

Kate recognized in the matter-of-fact voice the
deep calm of shock. "What was his name?"

"Lyle . . . Miles . . . something like that. I'm not
real good at names . . . I didn't hardly exchange
word one with this dude."

"I take it you didn't care for this dude," Kate
suggested.

"Teddie likes a different line of men than me,
macho-types." The attempt at a grin distorted into a
grimace. "Yeah, I didn't like him. I can't exactly tell
you why."

"What did he look like?"

"Muscle-bound. The type that wears a tight T-shirt and sticks out his chest like a rooster, you know?"

Kate nodded encouragingly. "That's what he was wearing? A T-shirt?"

"Yeah. A black one. Under a bomber jacket."

"What color was the jacket?"

"Dark . . . dark brown. Maybe black."

"Do you remember about his pants?"

"Jeans."

"Regular jeans?"

"Oh yeah, I remember now, that's one of the things I didn't like about him. His jeans. Real faded. Ladders in the knees. People that buy clothes to make them look poor make me sick."

Her voice shook with a vehemence that Kate recognized as misdirected emotion. She made her own voice calm as she asked, "Dark hair? Blond?"

"Blond. Thin stuff, you know? Be bald in no time."

Kate nodded. "His eyes, do you remember what color?"

She pondered. "Maybe blue."

"How old do you think he was?"

She shrugged. "Older than Teddie. Maybe thirty? He had a moustache, I can't figure men with face fuzz too well."

"Neither can I," Kate said with a smile, adding another note on her legal pad. Gloria Gomez showed every sign of being a very good witness. "His moustache, was it thin? Medium? Thick?"

"Thick. With guys, the thinner the hair, the thicker the moustache. Right?"

Again Kate smiled. "Would you recognize him if you saw him again?"

"Yeah. Sure."

Kate turned to a new page. "Gloria, tell us everything you remember about last night at Malone's Bar."

The young woman sighed, and sat up in the metal chair. "We went in, the place was crowded, and Paul, he's at a table. I introduce Teddie, he goes to the bar to buy us some beers. I see him right away talking to this dude. Then Teddie comes back and sits with us, but I see he's still staring over at the bar, I kidded him a little bit."

Taylor looked up from the pad on which he was scribbling notes. "Paul knew Teddie was gay?"

"Sure. Paul was kidding him too. Like, saying he'd buy the next round of beers but maybe Teddie'd like to go get them."

"And did he?" Taylor asked.

"Yeah. Yeah, he did. He stopped to talk to the dude again." She leaned forward, arms crossed, the small hands clasping the inside of her arms. "He walked the beers back to the table, said he'd be back with us later. I didn't pay much more attention, Paul and I were rapping, but all of a sudden Teddie's at the table with this dude, saying he'll get himself home." The hands were again clenched tightly together, the knuckles and fingertips white. "Teddie shook hands with Paul, he . . . kissed me goodnight. I told him to be careful. But I didn't mean about . . . I never thought . . ."

Kate asked, "Did this man speak at all?"

"Yeah, I don't remember what he said."

"Did he have any sort of an accent? Anything you remember about his voice?"

Pulling at the ends of her hair, she reflected. "Uh uh."

"Gloria, will you help us out? Work with a police artist in putting together a picture of this man?"

"Yeah. Sure. Anything."

Kate said, "Tell us a little about Teddie. How you met, how you ended up sharing an apartment."

"We were in a psych class together at Cal State L.A. a couple of years ago. We helped each other out, we hit it off, we stayed friends. He and Carl split, I lost my roommate, Teddie moved in. I'm in school full time, I need all the help I can get with the rent."

"How do you support yourself?" Kate asked.

"I work nights at the Cineplex at the Beverly Center. Sometimes I help out at Tradition if they get in a bind, but I really don't like that kind of work. My brothers, they're helping with my bills, to get me through school. I'm going for my chemistry degree. Six more quarters and I'll have it," she said in the tone of someone on an unshakable course.

Taylor asked, "When did you know Teddie was gay?"

"One look." She smiled briefly. "So many gay men are gorgeous, it's the first thing you think when you see a really good-looking single man. Teddie, we talked a few minutes, I knew — and it was never a secret anyway. Teddie was proud he was gay."

"Proud?" Taylor looked up from his note-taking.

"Yeah. Proud." The dark eyes focused on Taylor had lost some of their dullness. "You got some problem with that?"

Taylor shrugged. "Some people do. Did he pick men up all the time?"

"The other way around. Teddie was . . ." Staring at Taylor, Gloria said, "Okay, he was a queen. A flirt. He was beautiful, a flashy dresser, he was smart and funny, guys came on to him all the time. But he was careful, too. I mean, I bugged him about it. You worry about every gay guy you know these days."

Taylor leaned toward her. "He much of a drinker?"

"Uh uh. He'd drink a beer now and then. Wine. He gave me a bad time anytime I drank in front of him."

"He take anything else?"

Kate knew he was thinking of that piece of glass in the kitchen of Tradition. *A party that got out of hand,* Taylor had said. *Way out of hand.*

"You mean dope?" Gloria Gomez was indignant. "Give me a break."

Taylor said disarmingly, "Lots of people take a toot once in a while."

"Yeah, and I don't see why you people make such a freaking deal out of it. But Teddie didn't. Not even a joint."

"You can't be sure about that," Taylor said with clear skepticism.

"I'm sure about Teddie," Gloria Gomez said. "Case closed."

"Gloria," Kate said, "tell us about Teddie." She felt seared by the image of Teddie Crawford on the

blood-soaked kitchen floor of Tradition. She needed
to see something else.

"The sweetest guy . . . my best friend. Francisco,
he's so good a cook he's magic, and Teddie, he
always brought food home from Tradition." Gloria
Gomez said softly, "I'd come in from work, from
school, there was always food. He'd do my laundry,
anything to help out. Teddie always took better care
of other people than he ever did of himself."

"What other people?" Taylor asked. "Who besides
you and Francisco?"

"Everybody. With me, guys come and go like ping
pong balls. But Teddie, he seemed to stay friends
with everybody he knew. Even ex-lovers. His friends
dying and he never gave in to the dying, you know?
The guy — he's just amazing. I always told him so,
told him every day . . ."

She was smiling fondly, in reminiscence, and
Kate saw in her dark eyes the depth of the grieving
to come. Gloria said, "Mrs. Sheffield down the hall.
Eighty-seven years old, Teddie looked in on her
every day, took her trash out for her — she's crazy
about Teddie. Joe and Margaret, the way he cared
for the two of them. Teddie was . . . Teddie
was . . ."

"A saint?" Taylor suggested.

Gloria Gomez looked at him and closed her
mouth, her lips narrowing.

As silence accumulated, Kate decided to conclude
this interview, if for no other reason than to gather
more information from other sources. "Paul Lopez,"
she said. "Where can we reach him?"

Gloria Gomez pulled an address book out of a
cloth shoulderbag, opened it to a page, handed the

book to Kate. Kate recorded an address on Hobart
Avenue in Hollywood and a phone number.

There was a tap on the door of the interview
room. Taylor climbed to his feet, excused himself. A
moment later he signaled to Kate from the doorway,
then disappeared.

She rose. "Gloria, we'll set you up to work with
our artist. And we'll need you to sign a statement."

As Kate walked out of the interview room with
Gloria Gomez, she glimpsed Taylor in the homicide
unit of the Detectives Squad Room, in conversation
with assistant district attorney Bud Sterling. Sterling
Silver, he had been nicknamed, for his successes in
court. Could this highly experienced prosecutor be
taking on this case?

"Detective Delafield," Gloria Gomez said as they
approached Records and Identification. Kate turned
to her. The young woman's eyes were coal black in a
face that seemed bleached of color. "You're gonna get
this motherfucker."

Kate nodded. "I'll get him."

"Two messages," Taylor told Kate as she
approached her desk in the Detectives Squad Room.
"A suspect —" He checked his notebook. "Kyle
Jensen, caucasian, blond. At Hollywood Presbyterian.
Being treated right now in ER, cuts on his hands.
They'll keep him, we got two uniforms on the way.
And Hansen says Everson's at Tradition."

"Good," Kate said. "We'll go there first. What
about Bud Sterling?"

"He heard about the case."

"So I gathered. Did you tell him we may have a suspect?"

"Yeah. I told him everything we know so far."

"What did he say?" She was exasperated by his phlegmatic responses.

He shrugged. "He says he'll follow up."

"I've always wanted to work with him." Slinging her purse. over her shoulder, she tried to transmit some part of her own zeal to him. "Let's go get him a good case, Ed."

As Taylor climbed into the Plymouth, he grumbled, "I don't see why the hell we have to go back to the crime scene. We got a live suspect."

"He isn't going anywhere," she answered, sliding in behind the wheel. "I want to hear what Everson has to say. We haven't really looked at the scene. Or been near the body."

"Autopsy's Monday."

"You'll have to attend, Ed. I've got court, the Weldon prelim. Anyway, we need a good look at everything right now — before we question this suspect."

"You want to count the knife cuts on this stiff or what? What's to see?"

"His hands," Kate said, threading her way through the police vehicles in Wilshire Division's parking lot.

"Why? So what if he's got defensive wounds? Or doesn't? We know what happened."

Her patience was running out. "Okay," she said. "Why don't you tell me what we know happened."

"The same tired shit. Teddie picks this guy up,

they come back here, snort coke, Teddie wants to get down to screwing and the guy turns Teddie into his personal dart board."

"The same tired shit," she echoed contemptuously.

"Come on, Kate. They live like that, they ask for it."

Kate sped down Venice Boulevard. Be cool, be calm, she ordered herself. But the torrent of anger felt cleansing. "So Teddie Crawford meeting somebody in a bar and dying for it is tired shit. So Florence Delgado walking down La Brea at night and dying for it is tired shit. The day that taking murdering creeps off the street becomes tired shit, I quit."

"What is *this* shit? I'm a cop, you're a cop. Why are we having this conversation?"

She bit off her words: "Because you think Teddie Crawford deserved to be killed."

"Goddammit, nobody deserves to be killed. But some people fucking ask for it. You know it, Kate."

"Right," she snapped. "Justifiable homicide. The victims being tired shit and all."

"The victims being *dumb* shit," Taylor said heatedly. "The victims —"

"Deserve what they get, is what you're saying. You got it all figured out, Ed."

"For chrissakes, Kate. I didn't make the world. I don't see you with any smart answers."

"I don't have any." The curtness of her dismissal was directed at herself. Taylor was no less a blockhead today than he had been in the seven years they had worked together. What point was there in arguing with him?

The crowd had thickened in front of Tradition.

Soon they would have what they were waiting for:
the coroner's van was parked in front.

Kate pulled the Plymouth into the same parking
place on Harper Avenue that she had used that
morning. Still seething over her encounter with
Taylor, she strode down the block, Taylor in her
wake, and pushed her way through the crowd.

Everson, arms tidily crossed over his tweed
jacket, stood beside the kitchen sink talking with
Charlotte Mead.

"Christ, it smells like a stockyard in here,"
complained Taylor from the kitchen doorway.

"Charlotte's perfume," Everson said.

"Right," Charlotte Mead growled, looking up from
her clipboard. "Eau de stockyard."

Grinning, Kate made her way into the room. She
liked this deputy coroner; his personal fastidiousness
seemed ludicrous in context with the carnage of the
crime scenes he visited, but it reflected his diligence.
"How are you, Walt?"

Everson gestured to the floor. "Better than him."

"When'd he get it?" Taylor asked.

"Not before one this morning," Everson said. "Say
between one and three."

Kate asked, "He have any defensive wounds?"

Everson nodded. "Rigor's almost complete, but I
can give you a bit of a look."

Taking a fresh pair of latex gloves from his bag,
Everson snapped them on and hunkered down beside
the body of Teddie Crawford. Kate and Charlotte
Mead crouched at his side, Taylor leaning over.
Everson grasped Teddie Crawford's left arm with
both hands, and with effort managed to turn it
slightly. In the palm of the bloody hand a gash was

visibly incised. Everson repeated the process with the
right hand. Its palm was also slashed, the little
finger almost severed.

"Classic defensive wounds," Everson said.

"His hands need to be bagged," Taylor said.

"Thank you, Ed," Charlotte Mead said. "We dolts
at the crime lab are happy to know that."

Kate allowed herself a scant moment to enjoy
Taylor's discomfort. "No watch, no jewelry," she
mused, examining Teddie Crawford's hands and
wrists. "Walt," she said, rising to her feet, "did you
notice a wallet?"

"Nope, but knowing you were coming, I didn't
turn him." He leaned over the body. "Move back."

Grasping Teddie Crawford by the shoulders,
Everson pulled him over onto his side. The hands
and arms, stiff from rigor, did not move, but blood
from multiple wounds on the dead man's back
poured onto the floor in crimson gushes. Kate stared,
startled, disoriented. If Teddie Crawford was still
bleeding, how could he not be alive? Her mind
flashed to a death investigation five months ago, a
three-month-old baby left for several hours in a car
on a hot September day while the parents shopped.
She herself had lifted the baby from the car, a tiny
blonde girl still very warm to her touch, and formula
had bubbled from the baby's tiny rosebud of a
mouth. Kate had thought for a wild hopeful moment
that the baby was reprieved, that somehow the clock
had turned back to change events, that the
pronouncement of death was wrong. The coroner
later told her that what she had seen had resulted
from the cooking process still at work in the baby's
body. And the blood now gushing from Teddie

Crawford's body resulted from its collection against open stab wounds in his back. Then or now, there would be no reprieve.

"The guy who did this must have been going for the record," Everson muttered, crouching down and studying the punctures as blood pooled into fresh formulations on the floor. "Probably close to forty wounds all told." He patted the pockets of the blood-soaked pants, sliding his gloved hand into each one. "Nothing," he said. Gently he lowered the body back into its previous position, stood, snapped off the wet red gloves and dropped them into a plastic sack. He addressed Kate. "We take him?"

"He's yours." The coppery odor in the room was overpowering, clinging to her nostrils, penetrating her clothes. Her corduroy jacket and gabardine pants had just been to the cleaners; they would need to go directly back.

As Everson picked up his tape recorder and began dictating, Kate turned to Charlotte Mead. "Anything else you can tell us?"

Mead placed her clipboard in her sample case. "Nothing you can't see. None of the blood, except for the cast-off pattern, is more than thirty-seven inches off the floor. Your man got the decedent down and that was it."

Kate pointed to the wall, at a pattern of wavy vertical lines close to the floor. "That's an odd looking pattern."

"Not if you know what it is," Mead said with only a trace of tartness. "The decedent never got off the floor but he was all over the place while he was being stabbed. Got his hair soaked in his own blood on the floor, banged his head up against the wall."

Criminalist Napoleon Carter came in to tape paper bags around the hands of Teddie Crawford. Two attendants from the coroner's office began the process of wrapping the body in a new white sheet which would afterward go to the crime lab for separate analysis. Then came the placement of Teddie Crawford in a body bag, loading the zipped black bag onto a stretcher. Finally he was wheeled out for the edification of the waiting crowd and the television cameras.

Kate examined the room. All surfaces had been dusted for fingerprints, the piece of glass on the counter collected for analysis of its powder residue.

"Here's our weapon," Taylor announced, pointing to an oak knife block on the counter between the stove and a microwave. "Or where it used to be, I'm betting."

Kate examined the knife block. Seven of its eight apertures were filled. The handles of the knives had not been dusted; they were rough-textured plastic that would not hold a print. With a thumb and forefinger placed carefully on the haft, she pulled out one knife after the other. A cleaver and a serrated blade filled the top of the block; the rest of the well-used knives were arranged in order according to length, and all were clean. The empty slot was between a six- and a ten-inch blade.

"We need to collect the knife block," she said.

She and Taylor inspected the contents of the cabinets and refrigerator. Basic foodstuffs were neatly stocked, as was an assortment of cooking utensils; nothing seemed out of place or in any way unusual.

"Let's go talk to our suspect," Kate said.

— 3 —

The day was fast winding down, the hazy city washed by orange-gold from the dying sun. As Kate and Taylor drove eastward through spotty Saturday afternoon traffic toward Hollywood, upscale Santa Monica Boulevard mutated into shabby mini-malls, food stands, used car lots, film labs, an occasional porn theater, auto repair and plating shops — many of the businesses with retractable metal bars across their fronts.

In a treatment room at Hollywood Presbyterian Hospital, a thin, bearded young man in hospital greens stared impatiently as Kate and Taylor extended their badges and identified themselves. "Yes, all right," he said, "I'm Doctor Mercer."

Kate said, "You treated a man named Kyle Jensen for cut hands. We need to ask you some questions about that."

"Can't tell you a thing," the surgeon replied curtly. "Medical information is confidential. As you know."

"Yeah, we know," Taylor said. His tone was matter-of-fact. "So you tell us now or we subpoena records and you sit in a courtroom hallway two days waiting to testify. How did he cut his hands?"

The surgeon's narrow shoulders moved in a slow, weary shrug. "I never talked to you, agreed? He says he cut them on an open ham tin."

Kate said, "And did he?"

Mercer shrugged again. "Could be. Open ham tins are so lethal they should carry labels."

"What are his wounds?"

"Severe lacerations, both hands. In lay terms, the web between the thumb and the forefinger on the right hand —" He held up his own hand in demonstration, "— incised to the bone. Another minor laceration on the outside edge of the palm. Less trauma to the left hand — a palm laceration and one inside the thumb. Minor cuts on all the fingers."

"Could they be knife wounds?"

"Certainly."

Taylor asked, "Defensive wounds?"

"Could be, yes. Very deep, though. If he was in a knife fight, it was the fight of his life, he really tore up his hands. The stupid prick's got the pain threshold of a bull. Couldn't understand why we wouldn't just slap on a bandage. We had to refuse treatment unless he checked in for surgery."

Kate asked, "Any other cuts on him?"

"Not that I saw."

"Blood on his clothes?"

"He came in with his hands wrapped in bloody towels. I didn't see his clothes." He crossed his arms and said with finality, "Check with Nurse Donnelly."

"We'll want you to hang onto those towels," Kate said.

"Check with Nurse Donnelly," he repeated.

"We need to talk to him," Taylor said. "What pain meds is he on?"

"The anaesthetic was local, he's had antibiotic, and Tylenol with codeine. We'll give him a prescription when we release him tonight."

Kate said, "In your medical judgment, is he in any way impaired to talk to us now?"

Mercer checked his watch. "He had pills more than an hour ago. Take your best shot." He strode toward the door. "Remember, you owe me. Keep me out of that goddamn hallway."

"Right," Kate said. But if Kyle Jensen was Teddie Crawford's killer, Dr. Henry Mercer would indeed be in that hallway.

The gown-clad young man sitting up in the hospital bed was alone in his semi-private room. Impassively, he listened to Kate identify herself and

Taylor, looked over their identification, and tersely
answered Kate's question: his full name was Kyle
Thomas Jensen, he lived at 1699 North Western
Avenue in Hollywood.

Kate scrutinized him. Muscular, with thinning
sandy-blond hair hanging down his neck, a light
stubble on his cheeks, a thick moustache that
accentuated rather than concealed sensuous, slightly
bow-shaped lips, he was a possible fit for Gloria
Gomez's description. And his first name, Kyle, was
close enough to Lyle and Miles, the names she had
mentioned. But thus far he also fit the picture of
innocence: he looked polite, a little puzzled, a touch
annoyed.

Propping a foot up on the bedside chair, Taylor
flipped open his notebook. "How old are you, Kyle?"

"Twenty-seven. Why?"

Kate asked, "How are you feeling?"

Jensen glanced at his bandaged hands as if to
judge their condition by appearance. "Okay." His
eyes, pale blue, diamond-shaped, met Kate's; they
were unreadable. "What's this about?" His voice was
a high-pitched huskiness.

Taylor replied affably, "We like to check out
people who come to emergency rooms with major
injuries. How'd you cut your hands, Kyle?"

"This is a major injury?" He waved both hands.
"It's just a dumb-shit accident."

"Needing surgery means pretty bad cuts. Tell us
about it."

Jensen shrugged his broad shoulders. "I took out
the garbage. Slipped, took a header, cut my hands

on a ham can. That's it." The twitch of his lips was rueful. "Those things are damn sharp. I bled like a pig."

Kate nodded. He was very convincing. "Where was this?"

"The apartment building. Out back."

"Anybody see you?" As Jensen shook his head, Kate continued, "When did this happen?"

"This morning . . . maybe about eight."

"When did you get here?"

"I guess maybe ten or so."

"You were injured enough to need surgery, Kyle. Why'd you wait till ten o'clock?"

"Hey, I didn't know how bad off I was till I got here. I wrapped up in towels, the bleeding stopped. My girlfriend, she freaked out, she brought me here." He poked at his hospital gown with a bandaged hand. "These bozos feed you bullshit. They make you check in just to get your money."

"What's your girlfriend's name, Kyle?"

"Shirl. Shirley Johnson."

"She live with you?"

"Sure."

"Where do you work?"

"Why? What the hell *is* this?"

"Routine," Taylor said. "We just need to make sure you're not shitting us, you're not protecting somebody who did this to you."

"Yeah, well I'm not — and I don't know what the hell that doctor did to me but right now I need another pain pill."

Kate said casually, "We do have a few more

questions, Kyle. We understand you'll be released
this evening. Why don't we have a car pick you up
and take you to the station, then home?"

He shrugged, lay back on his pillows. "Yeah,
sure. Anything to get this bullshit over with."

Kate approached the patrol officer outside Kyle
Jensen's room. "He see you, Dale?" she asked,
indicating the closed hospital door with a motion of
her head.

The thin young officer shook his head, grinned.
"Nope."

Kate said, returning his grin, "Make sure he
doesn't."

"You got it."

"And check with Nurse Donnelly about the
condition of his clothes when he came in. Have her
hold onto the towels his hands were wrapped in."

"You got it."

Without comment, Taylor accompanied her down
the hallway to the elevator. He knew as well as she
did that despite Gloria Gomez's description and the
incriminating evidence of Kyle Jensen's cut hands,
there was insufficient probable cause to arrest or
even hold him, much less get a search warrant to
obtain his bloody towels. Jensen had done them a
favor by his willingness, undoubtedly unwitting, to
come to the station to answer further questions.
Either he believed their story that they routinely
checked out major injuries at hospitals, or he was
confident that he would not be linked with a

homicide, or he felt that cooperation was his best option. Or, he was simply innocent. She and Taylor had much more work to do. She needed to be well prepared for the next meeting with Kyle Jensen.

* * * * *

Sixteen-ninety-nine North Western Avenue was close by, a five-story brick building on the corner of Hollywood Boulevard, its facade crisscrossed with corroded fire escapes, its red brick coal-dust-grimy from decades of air pollution. Across Western a similar building of stucco was freshly painted pink, a banner on a fire escape proclaiming *Se Rentan Apartamentos.* Across litter-strewn Hollywood Boulevard was a seedy store named Bargain Saver, a billiard room, a hamburger stand, a pawn shop.

The small lobby of the apartment building was tracked with dirt and reeked of cooked cabbage and onions. Junk mail littered the cracked gray tile floor under a row of mailboxes identified by names on slips of paper jammed into crevices or fastened on with tape.

"A palace," Taylor muttered.

"We've seen worse," Kate returned.

"Like I said, a palace."

His tone was curt — more indication to Kate that he detested his involvement in this case. Screw him, she thought. He would do his job as he was supposed to. She would see to that.

He was inspecting the mailbox for apartment 209, its identifying piece of cardboard held on by a piece of electrical tape. Two names were scrawled on the

cardboard: *K. Jensen* and *B. Dayton.* He said,
"Wasn't the name of the alleged live-in girlfriend
Shirley Johnson?"

"Let's check out back," Kate said. "See if there's
any sign of the alleged ham can."

The cracked and broken cement at the rear of
the building was strewn with newspapers and shards
of glass and junk food wrappers. A battered
dumpster squatted at the edge of the alley; Taylor
raised its misshapen lid. "Fucking shit," he said as a
stench distilled from rotting garbage and alcohol
fumes engulfed them. The dumpster was less than a
quarter full.

"Call in for a photographer while I look around,"
she told him. "Priority. We'll need gloves," she added
as he trudged off. "And an inventory sheet."

"Fucking shit," he repeated.

She got down on one knee to examine the cement
around the dumpster. Meticulously, she inspected the
path she and Taylor had taken from the apartment
building's rear door. When Taylor returned a few
minutes later, she pointed down at the cement, its
fractured surfaces scoured and baked by years of
wind and sun. "From his story, the severity of those
cuts, there should be blood marks."

Taylor grunted assent. "Let's check out the
alleged girlfriend. I'm betting she's as make-believe
as the ham can."

The young man who answered the door of
apartment 209 wore only skin-tight stone-washed
jeans. Looking at the well-muscled torso, hairless
save for a dark column extending down from the

navel, Kate thought of Aimee's female loveliness with
a renewed sense of self-certainty. No male chest held
any allure for her beyond objective admiration.

"I'm Detective Delafield, LAPD," she said. "This is
my partner, Detective Taylor."

The young man glanced at their identification
with an impatient heave of his naked shoulders.
"Yeah, so what?"

Kate said, "Is Shirley Johnson here?"

"Shirl?" He stared at her, his hostility dissolving
in surprise. "What the hell you want with Shirl?"

"A few routine questions," she replied. "Is she
here?"

"Nah." He leaned against the door jamb. "Maybe
later."

He's got a rap sheet, Kate's intuition told her. He
had relaxed too visibly at their apparent lack of
interest in him. She said, "Does Shirl live here?"

"Nope."

"Has she ever lived here?"

"Nope."

"Where is she?"

He replied with a shrug.

Kate said, "May we know your name, sir?"

"Sir? Geez, what a sweetheart of a cop. Dayton,
Burt Dayton. What you want Shirl for?"

Kate said, "May we talk somewhere other than
this hallway, Mr. Dayton?"

"Mr. Dayton, yet. Okay. But like I said, Shirl
ain't here." He stepped away from the doorway to
allow entry.

The   sagging   sofa   and   armchair   were

mustard-colored, the carpet dirty gray and thread-
bare. The lampshade on the single table lamp was
stained yellow-brown.

"Take a load off," Dayton said, throwing himself
onto the sofa.

Taylor propped himself against the adjacent wall;
Kate remained standing. She said, "Does Kyle
Jensen live here?"

Dayton's dark eyes flashed to her. Warily, he
nodded.

"Did Shirley Johnson take him to the hospital
this morning?"

He rubbed an index finger around his lips as he
contemplated her. The lips were thick, fleshy;
sensual for the narrow sharpness of his features. "So
what if she did?"

Taylor said, "How did Kyle cut his hands?"

"I don't know. Oh shit," Dayton uttered in
disgust, realizing that he had already said too much.
"Shit," he said.

"We need to know," Taylor said, pen poised over
his notebook. "How did he cut his hands?"

"Shit, man, I don't know."

"When did it happen?"

"Dunno."

"Burt," Taylor said with elaborate patience, "do
we need to haul you in for something so dumb as
finding out how Kyle cut his hands?"

Dayton pointed to Kate. "I like her better. She
calls me Mr. Dayton."

"Mr. Dayton," Taylor said, unperturbed, "when
did you find out about his hands?"

Crossing his arms over his chest, Dayton
slouched down into the sofa, spreading his legs wide

open. Kate had always disliked such a posture in either men or women, its impudent flaunting of genitalia. Dayton said reluctantly, resentfully, "This morning."

"What time?"

"Early. Why? What's up?"

"What time, Mr. Dayton?"

"Early. Dunno what time, I coulda cared less." Looking at Taylor he conceded, "It was still dark out."

"Mr. Dayton," Kate interjected. "Why don't you just tell us about it?"

"What's to tell? I was asleep, okay? He comes in the bedroom, wakes me up, says he hurt his hands. They're all wrapped up, he wants me to help him out of his clothes. So I do it, okay? This morning he has me call Shirl. She comes over, looks at his hands, takes him to the hospital and that's all I know. Okay?"

"Let's take this one step at a time," Kate said. She moved to the armchair, gingerly positioning herself on its grubby arm. Before this day was over, she reflected, these pants might be too far gone to even go to the cleaners. Propping her notebook on her thigh, she said, "He came into the bedroom. How many bedrooms do you have?"

"This is the White House or something? One." He gestured behind him. "We got extra beds."

You had to mention the beds, Kate thought. God forbid anybody should think you're queer. "He told you he hurt his hands. How did he say he did it?"

He looked at her, his gaze vigilant. "This is big trouble, right?"

She returned his gaze. She and Taylor had to be

exceedingly careful. If Kyle Jensen was a viable suspect, it was possible that he had not acted alone, that this man was an accessory. "Mr. Jensen's injuries are quite severe," she said. "We're making routine inquiries. How did he cut his hands?"

"Said he fell, cut them on some kind of a can." His thick lips turned down in distaste. "I didn't ask for a blow by blow, ya know?"

Didn't you now, Kate thought. "Tell us what you saw when you looked at him."

He shook his head. "Nothin'. I didn't look, didn't see him. Not then. He said don't put a light on, I'd toss my cookies." He shifted uncomfortably. "He knows blood makes me puke, okay? He was so sticky wet, I almost lost it anyway. And when I went in the bathroom and washed my hands, saw my hands . . . yuchhh, holy Jesus." He sat up, crossed his arms over his chest, closed his eyes and pulled his legs together.

Kate felt persuaded, if not convinced, that Burt Dayton had had nothing to do with the murder of Teddie Crawford. "You said you helped Mr. Jensen take off his bloody clothes. Where are those clothes now?"

Burt Dayton raised a hand, and without looking, pointed in the direction to the left of Kate.

Adrenalin surging through her, Kate stared at a black plastic garbage bag, its top tied with a yellow strip, sitting on the far side of the closed apartment door.

"Kyle said throw it away," Dayton continued. "Me, I wouldn't touch it if a garbage truck drove up the stairs to pick it up. What if the bag busted open?"

Thinking about Charlotte Mead and the tests she could run on this cache of what might be uncontaminated crucial evidence, Kate released an inaudible breath.

"Kate?" Taylor said.

She looked at him, her mind racing, knowing he was questioning the legalities here, knowing she must not make a mistake.

They did not have a search warrant. In any sort of felony trial, much less a homicide trial, any violation of Fourth Amendment rights could mean the release of a defendant, no matter how compelling the evidence of guilt might be.

She and Taylor had properly identified themselves and had been invited into this apartment. Without a search warrant they could conduct a search beyond this room only with Burt Dayton's permission, but in any event they could not remove anything from the bedroom that Kyle Jensen shared with Burt Dayton. This room, however, was a common area into which they had been lawfully admitted, and potential evidence had been pointed out to them and was in plain view. She said quietly to Taylor, "Get an evidence bag. And check on that photographer."

"This is some kind of really deep shit," Dayton muttered as Taylor left the apartment.

Kate said placatingly, "We often have to do far more than necessary just to be thorough."

"Christ, don't tell Kyle I said anything or he'll fucking kill me."

"If there's no problem, then there's no problem. Right?" Kate said. As Dayton puzzled through this platitude, she asked casually, "Is he that much of a hothead?"

"He's okay. Unless you do something that pulls his cork."

"Does he get his cork pulled very often?"

He looked at her and did not answer. She had, she sensed, just run out of cooperation.

"Where can we reach Shirl? We need to talk to her."

"Dunno."

"Where does she work?"

"Dunno."

"What's her phone number?"

"Ask Kyle."

"How long have you known Kyle?"

Studying her, again he circled his lips with an index finger. "Long time. We came out here together."

"From where, Mr. Dayton?"

"Pittsburgh."

"Really." She made her tone conversational. "I understand that's a nice town."

"A dead town. Dead and buried. Here is where it's at."

She kept her gaze on his face, wondering how this fleabag of a place could be better than what he'd left. She asked, "Then you've been lifelong friends with Mr. Jensen?"

He contemplated this question as if it were a new concept. "Yeah. Maybe. Off and on. We do our own thing, but he's okay, you know? Whatever this is about, he's clean."

As Taylor returned to the apartment with a large evidence bag, Kate asked, "What about you, Mr. Dayton? Are you clean?"

"I got no problems," he said, watching Taylor bag the black plastic sack and begin to fill out the evidence seal.

Kate said casually, "Okay with you if we take a look around, Mr. Dayton?"

"No way. And knock off that Mr. Dayton crap. No way, lady. You want anything more outta me, I think I'll check it out with a shyster."

"That's certainly your privilege, Burt." Getting to her feet, she pulled a card from her notebook. "Maybe Kyle doesn't have to know how we got the bag of clothes. You were supposed to throw them in the dumpster, right? If you see or hear from Shirl, have her call us, okay?"

He got up, took the card, tucked it in the back pocket of his jeans. "Yeah." He almost smiled.

Ted Carlson photographed the interior and exterior of the dumpster and the area surrounding it. Then Kate and Taylor donned plastic gloves.

Kate removed her jacket, handed it to Carlson. Steeling herself, she turned to Taylor. "Give me a lift up."

"Christ," Taylor grumbled. "Christ knows what's in there. These days you'll catch Christ knows what."

"It could be worse," she said, more to herself than to him as he locked his hands together and she

fit her foot into the brace. "The city picked up the
garbage no more than a day or two ago —" She
vaulted up and into the dumpster.

She landed on shifting mulch and staggered,
grabbing the edge of the dumpster to catch her
balance. Determinedly ignoring the stench, telling
herself the germ potential couldn't be fatal — could
it? — she surveyed the refuse in which she stood
shin-deep.

The gleam of silver caught her eye and she
immediately fished out the object and passed it up
and over to Taylor.

"What the hell," he said. "A *wheel* . . . from a
fucking *wheelchair*."

"Seems like it," she said, unable to even
conjecture why such a thing would be in here.

Grateful for the nicety of several closed trash
bags, she first passed these out to Taylor for
separate inventory, then methodically dispensed to
him every solid object she put her gloved hands on.
He laid out the trash on the concrete around the
dumpster: liquor and wine bottles and beer cans and
foil dinner trays and cardboard cartons and
newspapers. Finally, only a layer of refuse remained,
sloshing around her shoes: chicken bones, potato
peelings, egg shells, coffee grounds, rotting fruit,
other unidentifiable food remnants. Bracing her
hands on a corner of the dumpster, Kate scrabbled
awkwardly up and out.

While Carlson photographed the dumpster's
emptied interior, she and Taylor laid out the
contents of the bags. She took it upon herself to
inspect several sanitary napkins, identifying the
rust-colored stains as menstrual blood. She was

surprised to see four broken hypodermic needles — that they had been thrown away. Dopers risked AIDS transmission as much through their unwillingness to buy new needles as through ignorance — they did not hesitate to inject their bodies with broken needles.

"Wonderful stuff," Carlson said as he photographed from his blue-jeaned knees the array of debris. "Maybe I'll enter these shots in competition."

"First prize," Taylor muttered.

While Carlson packed up his gear, Kate and Taylor threw all the garbage back into the dumpster. They had not been quiet or discreet about any of their activities. Several people had peered down at them from windows, but no one had so much as inquired what they were doing.

Taylor snapped off his gloves, tossed them into the dumpster. "So much for the alleged ham can," he growled.

— 4 —

Kate's apartment was empty. A few dust motes spun in the slants of greenish-yellow light allowed by branches of the scotch pine guarding the living room window. The faint smell of damp earth reached Kate: Aimee had watered the plants. She smiled. That Aimee did not actually live here was becoming more and more a technicality.

Kate checked the answering machine. From its unblinking light Aimee had picked up the message about the homicide investigation that had been set into motion by the early morning call from the watch commander.

Kate walked into the bedroom, pulling off gun belt and clothing as she went. Looking at the unmade bed and its configuration of pillows, she remembered the dark tangle of Aimee's hair over the pillow that morning, the bow-shaped curving of her body under the blanket she had pulled up to her ears in slumberous protest when Kate had taken her warmth from the bed.

She and Aimee had made love last night, as they had every night during this, their first month as lovers. Even knowing that much of Aimee's passion came from sheer youthful vitality, that much of her own passion was fueled by Aimee's newness, her beguiling beauty, her frank eroticism, she luxuriated in memory — the intimate caresses that had awakened her from sleep in the heart of last night, the renewed fire of their lovemaking . . .

Kate turned away from the bed.

You can't divide your focus, she castigated herself. You need to think about Teddie Crawford, nothing else. If Kyle Jensen is Teddie Crawford's killer, tonight may be your one clear shot at him. You need to piece together what happened at Tradition, you need maximum preparation. No distraction.

She stuffed her discarded clothing into a plastic bag and then tossed the bag of clothing into the depths of the closet. She felt empathy for Burt Dayton's revulsion at the contents of that other plastic bag; she was beginning to sense a seeping contamination from the death of Teddie Crawford

unlike anything she had ever experienced. At least
that other plastic bag now resided in Charlotte
Mead's care. Mead's test results would by themselves
establish certain incontestable facts.

Setting the taps scalding hot, she stepped into
the shower, the scent of Aimee's lilac shower gel
invading her senses. Quickly shampooing her hair,
she mulled over the facts of this homicide case,
searching for obvious loose ends. She had assigned
officers to interview the residents of Teddie
Crawford's apartment building, and Carl Jacoby,
Teddie Crawford's former lover, as well as Margaret
and Joe Crawford. She and Taylor would go next to
Malone's Bar. For now that was all she could do.
Until she confronted Kyle Jensen . . .

Briskly toweling dry, she glimpsed her body in
the steam-shrouded mirror. She really should gain
back some of the weight she had lost in the first
weeks of experiencing Aimee. In her fourth decade of
life, a degree of huskiness seemed better suited to
her five foot-eight inch frame than the leanness of
her youth. As usual during the fast-moving early
stages of a homicide, she had no appetite for food.
She had not eaten today — but she needed to, for
the sake of her own efficiency.

She munched on a piece of cheese while she
selected fresh clothing. Authoritative clothing,
specifically for her interview with Kyle Jensen. Black
pants, a simple white blouse, simple black wool
jacket. She had just buttoned her jacket over her
gun belt when she heard Aimee's key in the lock.

"I'm here," Kate called. Walking into the living
room, she watched Aimee toss her leather jacket into
an armchair, admiring her body in jeans and a

maroon pullover. Would she ever become accustomed to her beauty?

"I have to run," she said, edging toward the door, resisting the urge to take Aimee in her arms and know again for just a few moments the actuality of her. But that would be too radical a distraction . . .

"I heard about it on KFWB." As if sensing Kate's need for remoteness, Aimee remained where she stood and crossed her arms. "You changed your clothes," she observed, the blue-violet eyes surveying Kate's body. "Kate, this killing's really bad, isn't it."

Aimee had come to know why Kate was sometimes compelled to change her clothes during the process of an investigation. Kate understood that Aimee admired her, viewed her profession with something close to awe, but that a component of that awe was the sort of dread fascination accorded by most people to morticians. What Kate told her about her cases, past or present, she sanitized. "A stabbing," she summarized, for her own sake as well as Aimee's.

"Yeah," Aimee said, stuffing her hands in the back pockets of her jeans. "The dead guy's gay, Jennifer actually knows him. She's been in that restaurant, what's it called, Tradition?"

"Yes," Kate said. Jennifer and Cheryl, whom Kate had never met, were current roommates of Aimee's in the condo they all shared in Brentwood.

"You arrest anybody?"

"We're checking out a suspect."

"Kate, you gotta get this gaybasher."

Gaybasher. Somehow she had not thought of Teddie Crawford's killing as a gaybashing.

Aimee asked, "Will you be back tonight?"

"I think so. I'll let you know if I can't. Will you
be here?"

Aimee's gaze drifted down Kate's body. She
smiled. "Sure."

Kate let herself out of the apartment. *Gaybasher.*
She felt shaken by the word. She buried her
inchoate emotion. She would exhume it later for
examination, when she was able to.

She turned her thoughts back to Aimee, but
briefly. When she came home she would make love
to Aimee. She would need to.

Malone's Bar, near Formosa Avenue and the
former Samuel Goldwyn Studios — now Warner
Hollywood Studios — on the eastern edge of West
Hollywood, stood out from its neighboring nondescript
storefronts. The clapboard front, freshly painted
white, was a virtual inducement, Kate thought, for
the legion of sprayers layering graffiti over the city.

Inside the bar, its length at least three times
that of its width, the usual beery-acid-ether smell
invaded her nostrils. But she liked the place. The
room felt comfortable, dark and cool and well-used,
even though it contained few patrons on this
Saturday afternoon — three Latinos at a table
silently drinking Dos Equis from the bottle, a fat,
gray-haired man hunched over the bar watching
television, and a young man sitting alone at a table
reading a newspaper through a curtain of straight
dark hair hanging over his eyes.

The bartender, a small man of perhaps fifty,

wore a brown leather apron over a sport shirt and pants. From the sharp-eyed glance he cast over Kate and Taylor's identification, his cautiously neutral face when he looked up, Kate surmised that he had seen police badges more than a few times.

She said, "Were you working here last night?"

"Sure," the man answered in pure tenor tones. "I'm Jimmy Malone, it's my place, why wouldn't I be here?"

Irish as Paddy's pig, Kate thought, smothering a smile. "Do you know a man named Teddie Crawford?"

The reaction was unguarded astonishment: rounded lips and rounded blue eyes. The bartender quickly recovered himself. "Can't say I do," he said.

"Of course you do," Kate said quietly. "And you need to talk to us. Teddie Crawford was killed last night."

Jimmy Malone's jaw worked soundlessly for a moment. "Teddie? *Teddie?*" The tenor tones were even higher. He slapped both hands on the bar and stared aghast at Kate. "Teddie's *dead*? He was in here just last night." He said in a stunned whisper, "He's *dead?*"

The other bar patrons, Kate noted, were looking on in alert curiosity, nothing more. She said to Jimmy Malone, "Was Teddie a regular here?"

Malone moved down the bar, Kate and Taylor following, out of earshot of the other patrons. "Just semi. A great guy. A terrific guy." He shook his head, his eyes teared with shock.

"He came in last night," Kate said. "Tell us about that."

Malone shook his head as if to clear it. "What's
to tell? Gloria and him came in, sat at a table with
a guy I pegged as Gloria's."

"Why?" Taylor asked.

"Teddie likes Godzilla-types. Ever since he broke
up with Carl. Does Carl know about this?"

"You get a lot of gays in here?" Taylor inquired.

Malone looked at him. "I don't ask. Or care. I
welcome everybody. Even you."

Feeling like cheering, Kate grinned at Malone.
"And did he meet Godzilla here last night?"

"He did. The usual. Muscles, jeans, hair, leather
jacket — you know the type."

"What's this Godzilla's name?"

"That I don't know."

"Ever see him before?"

"I have. A few times."

"How long has he been coming in?" Kate asked.

The bartender pondered. "Maybe a month, six
weeks."

"This Godzilla, he cruise guys in here?" Taylor
asked.

"Can't say I noticed that he did. Older men come
here, very quiet types. So any cruising's pretty quiet
stuff, you know."

Some older gays, Kate knew from Joe D'Amico,
went to such bars as the Gold Coast or the
Gauntlet; they did not frequent a big dance and
cruise bar such as Rage, or stand and stare bars
like Micky's or Motherlode. And the older, very quiet
types mentioned by Jimmy Malone were undoubtedly
closeted and would seek ambiguous bars like
Malone's . . .

"Mr. Malone," Kate said, "has there been recent gaybashing in the neighborhood?"

"Call me Jimmy. Cops haven't been in about it." He looked at her gravely. "The men talk about it."

She nodded grimly, understanding him. Closeted men often did not report gaybashing; they could not afford to. And bars such as Malone's would be prime hunting ground. She said softly, "Describe Godzilla."

Writing in her notebook, she led Jimmy Malone through a description that had points in common with Gloria Gomez's report of the man Teddie Crawford had left with. Remembering the piece of glass on the counter in Tradition, she sent up a trial balloon. "Jimmy," she said, "we have information about illegal substances being used in here."

"For sure not," he bristled. "What is this, now?"

"Jimmy," she said, hardening her tone, "my partner and I haven't the least interest in conducting a narcotics investigation. None. We're looking into a homicide. Period. But if we find out you've withheld any information connected to this case, you'll be up for obstruction."

Malone raised his hands. "Look. Nobody I see deals in here. Nobody. But I don't control the world. Fellows come in, they pop a pill right along with their beer. What am I supposed to do? I go in the john after I close up, there's empty baggies all over the place. What am I supposed to do?"

"Did you observe Teddie Crawford or any of the people he was with take anything?"

"Teddie, Gloria, never. I don't know about anybody else."

Taylor asked, "What about the john? Did Teddie or Godzilla use the john?"

"Yes," Malone answered immediately. "They went in together."

Kate nodded. She knew from Maggie Schaeffer, the Nightwood Bar owner who had become her close friend, that good bartenders were observers who did not miss a thing. "Jimmy, tell us what you know about Teddie Crawford," she said.

He shook his head. "A charmer. Flashy dresser, too good-looking, but you couldn't help liking him." Jimmy Malone's eyes moistened again as he spoke. "He'd prance in here like a leprechaun, talk to everybody, he knew everybody. I tell you . . . well, I just liked him."

"Thank you, Jimmy." Kate gave him one of her cards. "If you remember anything else you think might help us, call me."

"That I'll do," he said sadly, tucking the card in a pocket of his apron.

— 5 —

A message lay on Kate's desk in the Detectives Squad Room: Shirley Johnson had called at 7:05 pm, left no number, would call again. Kate issued instructions that she be notified immediately when that next call came in. Kyle Jensen had been transported to Wilshire Division by Officer Dale Morrissey, and was waiting.

Kate preceded Taylor into the small, blue-walled interview room with its acoustic tile ceiling and Formica-topped table. Jensen, his back to them, looked thoroughly bored as he lounged in one of the metal chairs, legs outstretched and ankles crossed, bandaged hands resting on his thighs. He wore navy blue sweatpants and dingy jogging shoes; sandy-blond hair hung not quite to the collar of a gray sweatshirt that outlined the musculature of his shoulders and arms.

Kate studied the dressings on his hands. The right hand was entirely swathed, while a thinner bandage covered the palm and thumb of the left, with tape on the fingers. Were these the hands that had plunged a knife over and over again into the body of Teddie Crawford?

Gaybasher. Kate's unwilling mind became an echo chamber for the word. Looking away from Kyle Jensen, she gripped the cold metallic back of a chair.

If you have ever been objective and professional, be that now. If this man is a killer, his conviction will hinge on your professional conduct in this room right now.

"How you doing, Kyle?" Taylor asked cheerfully, unbuttoning his jacket, pulling out a chair and settling himself into it.

"I'm okay, man," Jensen answered, his gaze drifting over Taylor. "Goddamn waste of a Saturday, I just want to get home."

Kate took refuge from her tension in an uncharitable assessment of Taylor's apparel. He too had gone home after the rummage through the dumpster, and had changed into brown pants and a blue-yellow plaid jacket over a canary-yellow shirt and blue-patterned tie. By this time she knew that any time Taylor's attire coincided with her own view that clothing should reinforce one's stature as a police officer, it was purely by accident.

"Kyle," she said, to draw the young man's gaze. She had remained standing, and used her height to look down at him. "We tape-record interviews as a matter of routine. Any problem with that?"

The light blue eyes fixed on hers were expressionless. "No problem, I'm cool."

Naive cool, she thought, making herself comfortable at the table. Kyle Jensen lacked the hard-won smarts of a career felon — the criminal history check on him had come up negative — and in all probability he also lacked knowledge of both the capabilities and limitations of police work. Burt Dayton, on the other hand, had two priors, both in Pennsylvania, one a 1987 for shoplifting, sentence suspended, the other a 1988 for bad checks, sixty days plus probation, the jail time impetus, probably, for his decision to leave for California.

"What's your situation with pain medication?" she inquired. "Feel well enough to talk to us?" She knew from Head Nurse Donnelly at Hollywood Presbyterian Hospital, via Officer Dale Morrissey, that the pain medication given Kyle Jensen would allow questioning.

"Yeah." Jensen waved his hands. "This wasn't brain surgery, you know."

"Pretty serious, though." Her tone was sympathetic. "Ever had a serious injury before?"

"Nah." To her surprise, the diamond-shaped eyes filled with regret. "If Dad could see how okay I was with this . . . I didn't have a war to fight like he did, you know. All I ever heard was how he got his ass blown off in Korea, how it was two days before they could get him out and he never said shit about the pain."

"I was in Korea too," Taylor said, grinning. "Got my ass shot at, but not off."

"Dad really did get his ass shot off," Jensen said, grinning back at Taylor. He brushed his left posterior with the undamaged fingers of his left hand. "One side of him all gimpy, looked funnier'n hell. Grenade blast took off a pretty good-sized chunk. Dad took out the slope-head shit that did it, though. Two more besides."

"Right on," Taylor said.

Repulsed by this exchange, Kate was nonetheless pleased by its tenor. To have either herself or Taylor establish rapport with this suspect would be an advantage, and Taylor appeared to be succeeding in that. Taylor said conversationally, "Your dad live in California?"

Jensen shook his head. "Been dead five years and two months. Lung cancer."

"Sorry," Taylor chorused with Kate.

With the fingertips of his left hand, Jensen fished a pack of Marlboros from a pants pocket. Taylor took the pack, shook out a cigarette, handed it to Jensen, lit it for him. "Dad got lung cancer from the goddamn steel mill," Jensen said, the smoke he expelled through his nostrils partly dissipated by his thick moustache. "The goddamn smelter, not cigarettes."

Sure, Kate thought, imagining how that moustache must reek of smoke. She pushed the ashtray toward him. "Steel mills — I take it you're from Pittsburgh." When he nodded she followed up, "How long have you been in L.A.?"

He studied the cigarette he held between the taped thumb and middle finger of his left hand. "I

guess . . . more than a year now. Took off last
January."

He knew to the month how long his father had
been dead, yet had to reflect over how long he had
lived here . . . She asked politely, "You still have
your mother, I hope?"

"Maybe *you* hope — I don't. Yeah."

His tone closed this off as a topic of conversation.
She asked, "What do you do, Kyle?"

He sat up a little straighter. "Deliver for Green
Haven. Know them?"

"Can't say I do."

Taylor said, "Aren't they landscapers for rich
people?"

"Yeah. Yeah, man." Jensen turned to Taylor, the
high pitch of his husky voice amplified. "They do
lawns, plants, even trees — I mean *big* trees. I
deliver shit you wouldn't believe. Arabs buy up these
Beverly Hills mansions, the sand niggers rip out
everything. Green Haven comes in and next day
there's this perfect lawn and palm trees and hedges
and rose bushes like it's been there a century
already. Unreal, man. Movie stars do it, too. I was
at Warren Beatty's house once. He was doing this
party . . ."

He trailed off, watching Kate write on her legal
pad. "Look, what do you want from me? I just want
to get the hell outta here."

Kate felt a coiling tension. "Let's get a few
standard questions out of the way," she said. She
took his name, address and phone number again,
and his date of birth.

"Ever been arrested?"

"Nope."

"What hours do you work at Green Haven?"

"Days. I work days. Why?" The tone had grown distinctly hostile.

Kate selected her words. "We're checking out a serious incident that occurred last night. Before we can say any more about it, or ask you any relevant questions, we need to tell you what your rights are."

His shrug was impatient. "I watch TV, I know all that shit."

"We need to tell you anyway, Kyle." Taking a card from her pocket she read him his Miranda rights. "You can decide at any time to exercise these rights and not answer any questions or make any statement," she concluded. "Do you understand each of these rights as I have explained them to you?"

"Yeah. What bullshit."

"Having these rights in mind, are you willing to talk to me and Detective Taylor now?"

"Yeah. What bullshit," he repeated.

His ignorance of the power of his constitutional protections, typical of most citizens, was to her and Taylor's benefit, and his arrogance would enhance their advantage. He had apparently lost awareness that his words were being recorded, a not uncommon occurrence during interrogations. She would not remind him. She tucked the card back into her pocket and said pleasantly, "Now tell us again how you cut your hands."

Jensen's sensuous lips became distinctly bow-shaped as they curved slightly upward. "You keep your part of the deal first. What's all this about?"

"A young man was stabbed last night in West Hollywood."

Instantly he said, "That's got nothing to do with me."

"How did you cut your hands?"

His chest and shoulders moved in a visible, if inaudible, sigh. "Like I already told you, I took out the garbage this morning. Tripped, took a header, landed on an open ham can. That's it."

"What time was this?"

"Like I told you, this morning, about eight."

"Anybody see you do it?"

"How the fuck should I know? Sorry," he said, softening his irritation. "Not that I know of."

"What did you do after you fell?"

"What do you mean, what did I do?"

"Did you bleed?"

"What am I, made outta wood?" He shook his hands at her. "Shit yes, I bled."

"A lot?"

"Like a fucking pig."

Obviously he was no longer concerned with the niceties of language with her. She said, "So, what did you do about the bleeding?"

His nose twitched, apparently from an itch caused by his moustache; he pawed impatiently at it. "Wrapped my hands up in towels."

"When was this?"

He stared at her. "A week later. For chrissake lady, right away. I was *bleeding*."

"Then you bled right away, as soon as you were cut?"

Continuing to stare at her, he said with deliberate slowness, as if communicating with a simpleton, "Yeah, I always bleed as soon as I'm cut."

"So you bled down at the dumpster?"

"Yeah."

"You bled on the ground?"

"Sure."

"In the hallway, on the way to your apartment?"

For the first time he looked at her warily. "Well, hey, I don't remember it all that well, I was, you know, I was pretty pissed off, I don't remember exactly how I bled, who would?"

She pursued him. "Did you bleed on the floor of your apartment?"

"Dunno. I guess."

"Did you get blood on your clothes, Kyle?"

"Yeah. Some." His tone became hostile again. "Why do you need to know all this shit? Who got killed, the pope?"

Kate stopped to write down his exact words, then asked, "Did you change your clothes?"

"Sure."

Kate pointed to his hands, the cigarette held awkwardly because of the bulk of the bandage. "If you had your bleeding hands wrapped in towels, how'd you manage to change clothes, Kyle?"

There was no hesitation. "Shirl helped me."

"Shirley Johnson, right?"

"Yeah."

Kate finished making another note on her pad. "Where can we reach Shirl?"

"What the fuck for?"

"Is there some problem about her verifying what you've told us?"

Again Jensen pawed at his moustache. "You people fuck around for no reason. You got my phone number, right?"

"Yes. What's her number?"

"That's her number."

"You're saying she doesn't have a phone?"

"I'm saying that's her number."

"Are you saying Shirl lives with you?"

"Yeah. I told you before. Yeah."

"Where were you last night, Kyle?"

His eyes, glittering pale blue ice, traveled from her to Taylor and back again. "You're trying to fuck me over, the both of you."

"Where were you last night?"

He sat up at the table. "With Shirl." The husky tones were forceful.

"Where?"

"At her place."

"I thought she lived with you."

He shrugged. "Yeah, well, sometimes she does."

She said commandingly, "What's her phone number, Kyle?"

For a moment he contemplated the corner he had backed himself into. "I ain't gonna tell you," he said. "You can just fucking lay off her."

"How long were you with her last night?"

He shrugged again. "All night."

"Can she verify that?"

"Maybe not." He grinned at Taylor. "Maybe I fucked her brains out."

Recognizing this as a diversionary tactic, Kate sat back, confident that Taylor would now pick up the interview.

Grinning back at Jensen, Taylor reached to the

ashtray, snuffed out the cigarette that Jensen had smoked down to the filter. "So okay, you were with Shirl last night. Did you leave at any time?"

"Nope." Jensen shook another Marlboro out of the pack, stuck it in his mouth.

Taylor lit the cigarette. "You feel okay? Anything you need?"

"I'm okay, man." Smoke streaming from his nostrils and through his moustache, Jensen surveyed the room. "You oughta pipe music in here."

Taylor looked at Kate and rolled his eyes. He asked with ironic politeness, "Any special kind?"

Jensen knocked ash from his cigarette. "AC-DC, Poison, White Snake, stuff like that."

"My youngest son is nuts about Metallica," Taylor offered.

"Yeah, they do real good shit."

Kate was looking at Taylor in wonder. He grinned back at her. "Kyle," she said, picking up the questioning again, "did —"

There was a knock at the door. Taylor got up, left the room, returned a moment later. "The call you've been waiting for," he said.

Shirley Johnson. Kate walked from the room, then hurried to her desk and picked up her phone.

"Ms. Johnson, this is Detective Delafield —"

"Yeah. Burt Lancaster talked ta me, I figured I oughta call."

"Burt Lancaster," Kate said, confused.

"Yeah, you know, Burt Ding Dong Dayton." The woman on the phone sounded as if her mouth were stuffed with cotton. "Lissen, whatever you got Kyle

for, it's got nothin to do with me, unerstand? Burt
Lancaster phones this morning, says Kyle cut his
hands real bad. So I come over and take the jerk to
the hospital cause Burt Lancaster don't drive."

Kate could hear chomping, the distinct snapping
of gum. The woman continued, "Burt Lancaster's a
jerk too. I unerstan not havin a car, but can you
believe livin in this town and not bein able to
drive?"

"Hard to imagine," Kate said, enjoying Shirley
Johnson, gum chewing and all. "Ms. Johnson, what's
your relationship with Kyle Jensen?"

"*Relationship?* Uh oh." The snaps of gum
resembled the back-firing of a car. "What's he tellin
ya?"

"You're his girlfriend, you live together off and
on."

"*What?* The asshole. The *turd,*" she shrieked,
adding a furious punctuation of gum snaps.

Grinning as she made notes, Kate asked, "What's
the truth of the matter?"

"We went out *once.* Okay, twice. I been over to
his pigsty *once* before today. He calls me, I talk to
him, but I ain't inerested. Somethin weird about
him."

"But you went over this morning to help him
out."

"Yeah, well, what can you do?"

"I know what you mean," Kate said. She liked
this woman. "Other than today, when was the last
time you saw him?"

"Two, three weeks ago."

"You didn't see him last night?"

More gum snaps. "Nope. Me and Monica went to this movie, rotten movie, lemme tell ya —"

"Did you help him change his clothes this morning?"

"Fuck no. You kiddin?" The chewing sounds ceased. "Burt Lancaster says this is serious shit. That right?"

"It could be, yes," Kate said. "I'm not at liberty —"

"Hey, I don't even wanna know. I'll check things out later with Burt Lancaster."

Some instinct nudged Kate into a curiosity question. "Why do you call him Burt Lancaster?"

"Walks around with that naked chest of his stickin out, thinks he's gonna be an actor, the dipshit. Struts like he's Bruce Willis. Kyle, he's a muscle-builder, so he struts too. You ask me, those two guys strut for each other."

Kate understood this last remark to be in the same vein as the observation that women dressed for each other, but she found it interesting. "You've been very helpful, Ms. Johnson," she said. "Would you give me your phone number and address? We'll bother you as little as possible."

"Yeah, okay. Kyle's a turd, but I hope he's not in bad trouble."

Kate returned to the interview room fortified by her contact with Shirley Johnson. As she took her place at the table, Jensen was still talking about music. Taylor greeted her in mute relief.

It was time to get to the guts of this interrogation. "Kyle," she said, and waited until he turned to her. She asked without preamble, "Ever been in a bar named Malone's?"

Jensen's gaze moved away from her, upward, to contemplate the acoustic tile of the ceiling. "It don't ring a bell," he said.

"How about a bartender named Jimmy Malone? Know him?"

"Nope."

"That's odd," she said. "Because he claims to know you."

He shrugged. "I ain't responsible for what some nut claims."

"Do you know a man named Teddie Crawford?"

Still gazing at the ceiling, Jensen shook his head. "Don't ring a bell."

"Ever been in a restaurant called Tradition?"

"Can't say I have."

"Do you know Burt Dayton?"

His glance at her flashed away; he returned his gaze to the ceiling. "Bullshit. This is just bullshit."

Her fingers tightened on the pen she held; she felt tension clamp onto every muscle in her body.

Everything they had learned so far pointed to this man. He fit the description of Teddie Crawford's late night companion. He had transparently lied about how he had cut his hands. He had no alibi for the time when Teddie Crawford had been killed.

But no one had directly identified him. Any competent lawyer would discount the fact that she and Taylor had found neither a ham can nor bloodstains. And so what if Jensen had no alibi? Scientific evidence had yet to be developed that would place him at the crime scene. So they had

nothing on which to hold him. As Taylor would put
it, they had diddley shit.

If she did not break him down right now — or if
it occurred to him to exercise his right to terminate
her questioning or to insist on the presence of a
lawyer — they had no option but to release him
until they could accumulate sufficient evidence to
arrest him. As if this murder suspect, this drifter,
would hang around waiting for an arrest.

She reminded herself of the first rule of
interviewing criminal suspects: *Make them believe
you know everything.*

"Kyle," she snapped, "stop playing games."

He did not respond.

"You think Detective Taylor and I were playing
games while you sat in your hospital bed all day?
You can't be dumb enough to believe you could be
out in this city last night and have nobody
remember you. You were in Malone's and we know
it. You met Teddie Crawford there and we know it.
You left with him and we know it."

She got to her feet and paced beside the table,
halting to stare down at him. "You say you cut your
hands on a ham can. There is no ham can. You say
you immediately bled. There is no blood."

He said nothing.

She lowered her voice. "But there *are* the bloody
clothes you wore last night, Kyle. We have them.
Bloody clothes to match the blood at the scene. All
as evidence against you."

She played her final card. "The call I just took?
Shirley Johnson. You said she helped you change
your clothes this morning. She says she didn't. You
said you were with her last night. She says you

weren't. She hasn't seen you in weeks. You've got no alibi, Kyle."

"Kyle," Taylor said in a tone that was all the more telling for its gentleness, "you're dead meat."

Still communing with the ceiling, Kyle Jensen said, "You got the wrong guy. I didn't kill anybody."

Kate exchanged a triumphant glance with Taylor. She said quietly, "That's the second time you've mentioned somebody being killed. Who said anybody was killed?"

His gaze jerked to her. "You did. You —" He clamped his mouth shut.

"We never told you anybody was dead," she said. "But you've just told us that again. You said it because you know it — because you know it better than anybody."

She glanced at Taylor. His nod was almost imperceptible, but it buoyed her; her tension was almost unbearable.

She took a deep breath, expelled it in pistol-shot words: "Look at me, Kyle."

Standing over him, she stared down into the pale blue eyes. "Everything you've told us is a lie. You've got one chance left. The truth, Kyle. Tell us right now what went on between you and Teddie Crawford last night. The truth is the only thing that can possibly help you. It's the only hope you have."

As seconds of silence passed, Kate walked back to her chair, sat down. There was nothing more she could say or do.

"I got a question." Jensen turned to Taylor. "I want to ask a question."

"Sure," Taylor encouraged him.

Kate watched in prickling suspense, knowing that

Taylor, too, understood that Kyle Jensen hovered on the brink of revelation.

"This is just a for instance." Jensen's husky voice was scarcely audible. "For instance you get into it with somebody and you're trying to protect yourself and they end up dead. Then what?"

Taylor said, "Depending on what went down, maybe a case can be made for self-defense."

"Like . . . meaning what?"

"Kyle," Kate said, entering the discussion to prevent Taylor from saying anything that even faintly smacked of a deal or an offer, "if you were acting to save your own life . . ." She reached to him, touched his arm lightly, briefly, as if to add the final push to a tree ready to topple. "If you were acting in self-defense you could be cleared."

His eyes met hers, slid away. "Yeah, well, that's what I did."

She said slowly, deliberately, "What did you do?"

"The dude came at me. I had to take care of myself."

"Meaning what, Kyle?"

"I took him down. To make him stop."

She closed her eyes for a moment, dizzy with the release of tension. Struggling to control a sudden convulsion of emotion, she said, "Tell us about it."

He slumped in his chair, crossed his bandaged hands on the Formica-topped table, stared down at them. "Malone's yeah, okay, I met him there. Yeah, okay, he had some coke, we scored a couple of lines. Real good stuff. He says he's got more back at his restaurant. So I say okay, let's go. We get there and the place is all closed up, you know? But I figure what the hell — and like a dumb shit I go in with him."

His voice dropped. "He comes at me with a knife, a big motherfucking knife. Man, I was scared shitless. Even when I got the thing away from him he didn't back off an inch. I cut him, I had to, he fought like hell. I lost it, I just fucking lost it. I didn't know if the dude was alive or dead, I just got the fuck outta there."

Gaining control of herself, Kate spent time over her shorthand notes until it was plain that nothing more would be forthcoming. "Kyle," she uttered softly. Her objective now was to have him view her as an ally, to have him talk as much as possible. "We need to understand how you got yourself into this mess. Let's take this one step at a time. When did you first see him?"

He said earnestly, "He came in with this Mexican chick, I was looking at her, not him. Next thing he's at the bar getting some beers. Then he's back at the bar and we're shooting the shit, he says do I want to go to the john, he's got real good coke."

She was interested in his insistence that he had looked at Teddie Crawford's female companion, not Teddie Crawford. And she was intrigued by his voluntary admission of sharing cocaine. In her experience, such an admission was tactical: See how forthcoming I am when I don't have to be — why would I lie to you about anything else?

"So you went with him to the john," she said.

"Yeah. He rolls up a bill and we score the stuff."

"How many lines?"

"Two."

"Two each? Or altogether?"

"Each."

"Anybody see you?"

He shook his head. "We were in a stall."

"Let's back up. When he first came up to the bar, what was said?"

"He said how're you doing and I said just trying to get fried, how about you, friend. He just grinned, said he'd drop off the beers and be back."

"Did he introduce himself?"

"Said his name was Teddie."

"Just that?"

"Yeah. Just that. I said my name was Kyle. You got a problem with that?"

"Of course not, Kyle. I'm just trying to get a complete picture of what happened. He came back and then what?"

He shrugged. "We got into the usual shit, what we did for a living, all that. He was nosey, wanted to know a lot of stuff about me. I told him I like to go to the beach and work out and ride around on my bike — I'm a dirt biker. You know, just shit like that."

"What did he tell you about himself?"

He cocked his head as he reflected. "Not a whole hell of a lot, now that you mention it. Mostly he yakked about his restaurant."

Making rapid notes, she asked, "What did he say?"

"How hard he worked but he liked it, and his partner was the best thing that ever happened to him, and the catering part was really starting to take off. He told me some stories, funny stuff he saw at parties he worked."

"When did you leave the bar?"

He shrugged. "Late, I don't know, before last call."

"Did you talk to anybody else while the two of you were there?"

"Nope."

"When you left with Teddie, how did you get to the restaurant?"

"I took us. On my bike."

"You went directly to the restaurant?"

"Yeah. No, wait a minute, I stopped at the 7-Eleven on the corner to get some smokes."

"Did you both go in?"

"Yeah."

"You mentioned you were uncomfortable that the restaurant was closed, you said you were a dumb shit to go in. Why did you think that, Kyle?"

He shifted on his chair. "Nobody was around, I didn't like it. I hardly knew this dude."

She looked him over, wanting him to notice her scrutiny of the breadth of his chest and shoulders, the dimensions of him. She asked, "Why did being alone with a much smaller man concern you?"

"Hey, lady, it didn't. Not till he pulled the shiv. That's when I saw I was a dumb shit."

"Let's go back a minute. You arrived at the restaurant. What door did you go in?"

"Back door. We came in through the kitchen. I took my jacket off, he right away lays out lines of coke, we score it."

"Then what?"

"I get this big tour. He tells me about every stupid thing in the place. Like napkins — how he got a hundred of 'em, a dime apiece, from some

fancy French restaurant that went belly-up. Then we
go back in the kitchen and finish off the rest of the
coke."

"How much altogether from when you got to the
restaurant?"

"Three lines."

"Each?"

"Yeah, he was really wasted."

"And you? Were you wasted?"

"Nah, I was high, that's all."

"Then what?"

"He picks up the knife. Comes at me."

"Come on, Kyle," Taylor interjected. "Let's stop
shitting around. Tell us why the knife, what he
wanted."

Jensen turned to Taylor, looked at him carefully.
"I'm guessing you already got it figured out, man."

"Maybe," Taylor said equably. "But you're the guy
that has to tell us what and why and how."

Jensen shrugged, shook a cigarette out of his
package of Marlboros. Taylor lit it for him and said
with quiet command, "Tell us, Kyle."

Jensen exhaled smoke through his nose and
moustache with an audible snort. "He was a fag,
man. He wanted to suck my cock."

"Okay. What did he say, what did he do? You
want to help yourself, you gotta tell us the detail
how you got into self-defense with him."

"Makes me sick, man."

"Sure, I know." Unbuttoning his jacket, Taylor
leaned back on two legs of his chair and hooked his
thumbs under the straps of his shoulder holster.
"But you gotta help yourself here."

Kate listened to this exchange in disgust. Taylor would say that he was playing on Jensen's homophobia to keep him talking, but she knew better.

"First I knew what he had in mind," Jensen said, "we were in the restaurant part, I'm looking at these fucking ten-cent napkins. He puts his hand here —" He brushed his upper right arm and across his chest, "feeling me up."

"What did you do?"

"I was cool. Stepped away. But he comes at me again and skims his hand down over my crotch, tells me he likes the look of my basket. That's when I say I'm not gay, not interested."

"What did he do then?"

"Just laughed, he says no problem. Says come on in the kitchen. So we go in there, do the one last line. Then he gropes me again, says I don't have to do anything, just let him suck my cock. I push him away, tell him I'm getting the hell out of there."

"I bet. Then what?"

"He yanks a knife out of this rack, stands there holding it." Jensen squeezed his eyes shut. "I can see him plain as day. 'You do my coke, I do you,' he says to me. 'That's how it works.' And I'm staring at that knife, I could vomit on him, I'm scared shitless."

"Take us through the rest of it," Taylor said softly. "Everything you remember. One step at a time."

"I turn to pick up my jacket, see him relax a little bit. I figure I can grab his wrist, get the knife away from him. Instead he jerks the knife so I catch

it in my hand. He yanks it out, comes at me, I
catch it in my other hand, knee him in the balls.
We go down on the floor."

He sighed, stubbed out his cigarette. "I don't
remember nothing more till he stopped fighting,
stopped moving. I got over to the sink, grabbed some
paper towels, turned on the taps, saw I was cut bad.
I grabbed a couple of dish towels, wrapped myself
up. I got the fuck outta there."

Kate asked quietly, "Was he dead?"

He did not look at her. "He didn't move. I heard
some . . . sound."

She said, keeping her tone even, "When you were
describing him coming at you with the knife, you
said you could see him plain as day. How was he
holding the knife?" She stood up, away from the
table. "Show us."

He got up, positioned himself in front of her. "He
was about here. And the knife was like this." He
held a bandaged hand up at shoulder level. "The
blade was stuck right out at me."

"Yes," Kate said. "You said you were staring at
it. Was the cutting edge up or down?"

"Up. I could see how sharp it was."

"Okay, I'm Teddie." She assumed a stance
mimicking holding a knife at shoulder-level. "You try
to take it away. Show me."

"Okay." He reached for Kate's wrist with his
right hand. "But he moved and I grabbed the knife
instead." She made a stabbing motion at him;
bandaged palm up, he pantomimed closing his hand
over the imaginary knife. "Then he slid it out and
cut me." She slid the "knife" out. "He tried to stab
me —" She raised the "knife" again. He grabbed for

it with his left hand. "He slashed my other hand. I kneed him." He grinned at her. "I won't show you."

"I appreciate it," she said, managing to grin in return. "Then what? You said you both went down. How did that happen?"

He looked at the floor as if picturing the events. "I knee him, he buckles, lands on top of me, takes me to the floor. We're fighting like hell for the knife. That's all I remember."

"Sit down, Kyle," she said. Reclaiming her own chair, she waited until he was settled in and Taylor had lit another cigarette for him. "Did he cut you anywhere else?"

"Nope."

"Any bruises or marks?"

"Nope. He fought like a fucking cat, tore at my clothes, my hair . . ."

"What happened to the knife?"

"Took it with me."

"Why?" she asked. She remembered Charlotte Mead's words: *He'd put his pecker back in his pants, wouldn't he?*

"Fingerprints," he said.

She nodded. But his fingerprints at the crime scene, in the absence of related evidence forming a path to him, would prove useless unless they were on file in the criminal justice system. She guessed he might not know that. "What else did you take, Kyle?"

"I had some butts in an ashtray. Drank out of a glass. I tossed the stuff into one of those green plastic garbage bags. I was so freaked I even took my paper towels."

Remembering that Teddie Crawford's body lacked

any jewelry, she reminded herself of that first rule of interviewing criminal suspects: *Make them believe you know everything.* She said, "You took a few other things, Kyle."

"Yeah, well, I don't know why I did. I didn't keep any of it."

She caught Taylor's glance; his eyes glinted in appreciation. She said to Jensen, "Describe what you took."

"I don't know what kind of watch it was."

"Describe it the best you can."

"Black strap, black face, gold numbers."

"And?" she said insistently.

"The pinky ring was just . . . a gold ring."

The deputy coroner, she remembered, had not found a wallet on Teddie Crawford's body. "What else, Kyle?"

"A dinky little fruity wallet."

"Did you take the money out?"

"No," he said.

He was playing the odds that they would not find that wallet, she guessed. Making a note to double-check with Gloria Gomez and Francisco Caldera about what jewelry Teddie Crawford wore as a matter of routine, she thought of the blood-drenched kitchen in Tradition. Of the man seated in front of her tracking footprints through the blood as he gathered up evidence of his presence. Of him looting Teddie Crawford's body while the young man groaned and bled away the last moments of his life.

She did not believe that Teddie Crawford — the Teddie Crawford she had come to know from her interviews with the people in his life — had threatened Kyle Jensen with a knife, demanding sex. Far more probable was the scenario that Teddie Crawford had been the one defending himself, from a hate-filled gaybasher.

Gaybasher. The word reverberated in her.

She looked away from Kyle Jensen, knowing that while she could control her voice, she could not conceal the naked loathing that might be on her face. She said evenly, "What did you do with the stuff you took?"

"Tossed it. An alley. Don't ask me where. I just tossed it."

She did not believe him, but she let it pass; she would find that green plastic bag. Back in control again, she looked at him. "How did you get home?"

"On my bike." He raised his hands. "They really didn't hurt very much. Not till this morning."

She nodded. Cuts could be like burns, with the nerve endings temporarily numbed. "A few more questions, Kyle. Beyond what you've told us, did Teddie make other sexual advances toward you?"

"Nope."

"What were you doing in Malone's?"

He sat up. "What do you mean, what was I doing? Having a few beers. Like you do in a bar."

"Do you go there all the time?"

"Shit no. I just found it. It's quiet, I like the place."

She asked, "Have you ever been in the Gold Coast or the Gauntlet?"

"No," he said, belligerent.

"How about Rage?"

"Never."

"Micky's or Motherlode?"

He glared at her. "Why are you asking me about fag bars?"

"Have you been in any of them?"

"What the fuck is this? You calling me a fairy?"

"Have you been in any of them?" she repeated.

He half rose, shoved his face toward hers. "I'm not a faggot. I'm not a goddamn butt-fucking faggot."

She looked into his eyes, into bottomless rage. "You left Malone's with a gay man."

"I'm not a faggot." The husky voice was a seething fury. He swallowed, sat back, obviously struggling for control. "Lady, you're really pissing me off. I didn't *know* he was a faggot. I didn't know till he groped me."

"You couldn't tell at the bar?"

"Shit no. I can spot fags with the best of them, and the man didn't act fruity with me."

"Okay," she said. He relaxed visibly. "We'll need to go through this one more time, Kyle." His relaxation became slumping dejection. "Then we'll have a statement for you to sign, and we'll book you."

"*What?* Book me? You said —"

"We'll book you for homicide," she said, feeling a small measure of satisfaction. "Our job is to investigate, to gather information. The degree of responsibility for what you did is something for the court system to determine."

"That's not what you told me, man," he accused Taylor.

"It's right down the line what we told you," Taylor said.

"Fuck. The fuck you did, man."

"So we'll book you," Kate said, "then place you in a detention cell."

He held his head between his bandaged hands. "I need a pain pill. Fuck."

— 6 —

Kyle Jensen, his confession signed, had been officially arrested, and incident to that arrest had been booked, strip-searched and incarcerated, had had samples drawn of his blood and urine, as well as hair follicles taken from his head and crotch — all of this to his profane displeasure. On Monday he would be arraigned and assigned a public defender. And he would remain in jail, Kate was reasonably sure, until the disposition of his case; bail of any amount appeared beyond his resources.

She walked into the Detectives Squad Room, Taylor at her side, and dropped into her desk chair, feeling as if her bones had turned into quick-melting plastic.

Taylor propped a hip on the edge of her desk, crossed his arms, and gazed down at her. "That's the best goddamn interrogation I've ever seen you do, maybe the best I've ever seen, period. Nobody else in the department could have pulled that confession out of him. We had diddley shit and you nailed him, trussed him up like a Thanksgiving turkey. Partner, you were great."

Smiling her thanks, warmed by his appreciation, she felt — knew — that she had been like an athlete in a peak performance, she had extended herself fully, used every ounce of her training, experience, instincts, knowledge, courage. She felt expended, spent.

"I figure a plea bargain, involuntary man-slaughter," Taylor said.

"You're not serious," she said, gaping at him, realizing that she did have something left in her: astonishment.

"I hope we *get* involuntary. He draws a public defender that takes it to trial, he could even get off. "Hey," he said as she stared at him, "figure it out for yourself. Teddie Crawford made a pass at another guy, backed up his cock with a knife. A jury's looking at this red-blooded normal guy, they'll figure Jensen freaked out and just lost it, that's all."

"*Just lost it?*" With effort she lowered her voice. "Look Ed, I know juries are capable of anything. But we throw in the towel and take manslaughter? This

red-blooded normal guy let himself get picked up by
a gay man, he robbed him, he hacked and *mutilated*
him to death."

"Hey, I'm on your side — sure the guy should do
time," Taylor said, spreading his hands. "And maybe
a jury's gonna buy it. But I say Jensen's story hangs
together just enough. I say a jury's gonna look at
Kyle Jensen and see a regular guy who got freaked
out by a cock-sucking fag."

"Let me ask you something, Ed." She was
amazed by the calmness of her voice, the coherency
of her words. "*Why* do men freak out over gay men?
*Why is calling another man homosexual the ultimate
insult? Why* are gay men so completely disgusting to
other men?"

He pinched the crease in his brown pants
between his thumb and forefinger, pulled at it.
"Come on, Kate. The shit they do to each other is so
up-chucking putrid you can't even think about it."

She could see his tension and discomfort. She
pushed on. "Why not? Please do your best to tell me,
Ed," she said. "I really want to know."

"Jesus, Kate." He looked at a spot somewhere
over her head. "What's to tell? They aren't men.
They're faggots." He raised a hand, waved it limply.
"Mincy little faggoty fake-men."

"That doesn't answer it. And not all of them are
effeminate. Look at Rock Hudson," she argued,
wishing she could name other virile but closeted
movie stars made known to her by gay friends Joe
and Salvatore. "Some of them are really masculine."

"Rock Hudson was a pervert, not a faggot. All
those masculine-type guys are perverts. They use the

faggoty men like some guys use sheep or a piece of liver."

She could hardly wait to pass on this piece of wisdom to Joe and Salvatore. "Ed, so what if somebody's a mincy little fake-man? Some people grow to be over seven feet tall. Some people —"

"Some people are freakish, but they're still men or women. Faggots, they want to be fucked, so they turn themselves into women. If you're a real man, then you aren't a woman."

She chose her words. "Ed, what you just said — do you realize, do you have any idea how much it shows utter contempt for women?"

His face acquiring a florid cast, he got up from her desk. "Hey, Kate. With all due respect — don't tell me how men feel about women. I'm a normal guy, I been married twenty-three years to a woman who's very happy about it. You don't understand. I don't expect you to. Just drop it."

Here it was again, his unspoken judgment that being a lesbian rendered her invalid — an outsider, a misfit. "Ed —"

"Do me a huge favor, Kate. Drop it. You're a great detective, a terrific partner. Let's not get into this other crap with each other, okay?"

Cold fury gathered within her. "Then you do me a favor too, Ed. I intend to put together the best possible case for Kyle Jensen spending the rest of his unnatural life in the cage where he belongs. What he did was not manslaughter. It was murder."

She watched in escalating rage as Taylor stood with his arms crossed and his legs spread, his face closed. "Monday I'm in court, so I need you at the autopsy." She snapped off the words. "The favor is, do only what you need to do on this case. Let me do the rest, and stay the hell out of my way."

"It'll be a pleasure, not a favor." He made a tiny, ironic bow, and turned his back on her. "With your approval, I'll leave you to sweep up and I'll just take myself on home to Marie."

Kate let herself into her apartment at 2:30 a.m., her mind still churning over details of the Teddie Crawford homicide and her anger at Taylor. She had dictated her preliminary report for transcription, then reviewed the reports generated by the patrol officers at the crime scene and by the detectives assigned to interview people peripheral to the crime. The interviews she would follow up as a matter of routine. And necessity. She had felt currents of the officers' homophobia in the terseness and the brevity of some reports that dealt with gay male associates of Teddie Crawford.

A search warrant was in the works for Kyle Jensen's apartment and his dirt bike; the bike would be impounded for lab analysis. Again she reassured herself that so far she had done everything possible to facilitate the district attorney's evaluation of the case.

Taking off her jacket, she noticed light glowing palely from the bedroom. Aimee must have fallen asleep waiting for her. Kate tossed the jacket over the back of a chair, removed her gun belt and took out the Smith & Wesson, shook the bullets out of the cylinder, placed the gun and ammunition in a table drawer. Now that Aimee spent so much time in the apartment, safeguarding the gun had become routine, just as it had with Anne.

Aimee was awake, sitting up against pillows under the narrow beam of a reading lamp, wearing the white silk sleeping shirt Kate had given her, a book in her lap. Kate loved her in the shirt, the white a backdrop for the rosy hues of her skin, the dark sheen of her hair, the blue-violet of her eyes.

"Welcome home, Detective Delafield. Did you get him?"

Aimee's voice was languid, she looked charmingly sleepy-eyed. Kate stood gazing at her with pleasure. And want. "Yes," she said. "Arrest and confession."

Aimee put her book on the night table. "Tell me."

"Tomorrow." She added gently, "I need to not talk about it tonight, okay?"

"Okay. Do you have to go in tomorrow?"

Kate sat on the side of the bed, took her in her arms. Warmth from Aimee's body radiated into her hands, seemed to flow up her arms and under her breastbone. "Yes," she said. "Early." Officers had been assigned to safeguard the search warrant site, and she would be advised when the warrant was ready so that she could be present for the search. She was certain that the green plastic bag Kyle Jensen claimed he had tossed away would be found in either the apartment or the bike's storage compartment. "Couldn't you sleep?" she murmured, wanting right now to know only the silkiness of Aimee's hair against her face. She inhaled an amalgam of shampoo, face cream, ineffable female scents.

Aimee nestled her head on Kate's shoulder. "I

dozed a few hours. You have to be too tired to move. Come sleep in my arms." Her lips touched Kate's neck, moved upward in drifting softness across her cheek, her arms sliding around Kate's shoulders.

Kate kissed her. The lips under hers were a soft welcome, parting for her tongue. Kate momentarily savored the delicate flesh between, and then Aimee's tongue met, sweetly stroked hers.

Aimee eased her lips from Kate's. "You need sleep, not this."

Kate's arms tightened. "No. I need this." And once more Aimee's lips were under hers, parting for her tongue.

Some moments later, Kate released Aimee and said thickly, "Let me shower."

Aimee had begun to unfasten Kate's clothes. "Baby, just get in bed."

She could not. Her need to shower was absolute. "I'll only be a minute."

For the third time since her day had begun she cleansed her body with scalding shower spray. The heat seemed to expand the tumult of her need for Aimee. Wrapped in a towel, she returned to the bedroom.

Aimee's reading light was extinguished, the vertical blinds open; the room was a silver wash of moonlight. Again Kate sat on the side of the bed, marveling at the gift of beauty this young woman had brought into her life, luxuriating in the sight of breasts covered by the silk shirt that glowed ivory in the silver light, the eyes and cheekbones sculpted from shadows.

Then other eyes, blankly staring eyes, intruded

into Kate's vision. Shaking her head as if that would dispel the images, she grasped Aimee's arms.

"Easy, baby . . ." Aimee's hands skimmed her shoulders. "Your back's still damp," she murmured, and undid Kate's towel and pulled it up around her shoulders.

Kate slid her hands around Aimee's back, lifting her body up into her own, acutely aware of the fit of Aimee in her arms, the configuration of the breasts and body against hers, the murmur in Aimee's throat as Kate enclosed her in her arms. She brushed a hand down over Aimee's thighs, heard the intake of breath, felt tension in Aimee's body.

"All day," Aimee whispered. "I thought about you . . ." Her arms encircled Kate's shoulders.

"I need to hear that tonight." She would answer that want, and perhaps some of her own need.

Breathing the scents of Aimee's hair, she slid her hands under the silk shirt, around her waist. Caressing the soft flesh of her stomach, she moved her hands slowly upward, filling them with the exquisiteness of Aimee's breasts, the nipples blossoming in her palms. Aimee, head back, eyes closed, sighed.

"I need to hear you," Kate said again. She heard the urgency in her own voice.

"You will," Aimee murmured.

Kate drew the shirt up over Aimee's head, Aimee raising her arms to aid her, the down on her arms outlined by moonlight. Kate ran her palms along her arms, over her shoulders, her throat, cupping her face. She kissed her throat, exploring until she felt the pulse beat; she pressed her lips hard against it.

Aimee uttered a sound, a vibration under Kate's mouth.

Kate lowered herself onto her, groaning with the bliss of Aimee's warm nakedness everywhere melding into hers. Kissing her, she pushed a thigh between Aimee's legs, her kiss increasingly passionate. But Aimee's soft warm hands slid down her back, and Kate took her mouth away, groaning again, and buried her feverish face in the cool pillow next to Aimee's head in surrender to the gentle caressing.

But somehow the scent of the pillowcase held hints of copper, and memory of a bloody room, and the smell in that room filling up her nostrils. She felt a vibration in her own throat from a sound that was like a sob, and raised her face blindly from the pillow.

Aimee's arms gripped her body. "Kate . . ."

Kate's mouth possessed hers, her tongue thrusting into her; Aimee's body thrust up into hers in equal power. Kate's hand clasped between Aimee's legs, the hair wet on her palm, the interior a velvety yielding to her fingers; she sank fingers in to the hilt.

Her mouth came to Aimee's breasts, captured a nipple. Tantalized by the faint salt taste she sucked each nipple in turn, she moved her fingers strongly in the creamy wet, greedy for more of the ecstatic gasps. She would gorge on this feast of a woman, feed herself till she burst.

She moved down Aimee's body, not quickly, breathing her, inhaling her, pressing her mouth into her, her tongue grazing the down-dewy skin. Her hands gripped firm curving hips then slid up inside smooth thighs, clasping and feeling the tender flesh as she spread the thighs fully open.

For a long moment she breathed in a woman smell that seemed to go beyond woman to creation itself. Then she claimed the woman, sucking her into her, and stroked and drank the satiny wet, dimly aware of thighs shuddering against her face, of thrashing on the bed, of muffled cries, of stillness, of soft moaning.

She raised herself. Aimee's supine body lay in strips of moonlight from the vertical blinds. An image of another body, slashed, splashed with blood, filled her vision.

She clasped Aimee's hips, pulled her across the bed, out of the moonlight, and again buried her face between her thighs. She sucked and stroked and fed again, the hips imprisoned in her hands sometimes undulant, sometimes shaking; she drank until she was spent, until the wet seemed like endless salt tears.

She lay exhausted, Aimee's body in her arms an inert, shapeless weight. "Baby," Aimee breathed, "let me . . ."

"I'm okay . . . Aimee . . . I needed . . ." She could not continue.

And then Aimee was asleep, and Kate finished her answer from a place so dark and so desperate that it would forever exist in silence: *I needed to feel alive.*

— 7 —

Kate passed through security at the downtown Criminal Courts Building, and rode up in a crowded elevator to the fifteenth floor offices of the District Attorney of the City of Los Angeles. In the blue-carpeted, simply furnished outer office, she waited while the receptionist announced her to Deputy District Attorney Linda Foster.

From the few facts she had picked up from her contacts in the DA's office, she did not feel optimistic about this prosecutor. Linda Foster's six-year career had begun, as had most DDA careers, with a probationary period at an outlying court; for eighteen months she had prosecuted misdemeanor cases and handled felony prelims in Compton. Then had followed a standard one-year stint at the Eastlake facility for juveniles.

All the action was downtown of course, and she had been assigned here as a DDA-1 three years ago. She was now a DDA-2 and, except for a few assault with a deadly weapon cases, had been buried mostly in drug enforcement — little felonies, as they were referred to — because, according to several of Kate's sources, Foster had a habit of saying exactly what was on her mind, not a good idea in view of the man who was currently the elected District Attorney.

Wryly, Kate remembered her hope of having Bud Sterling prosecute this case; instead, in testimony to its status, it had been assigned to the low woman on the totem pole, one who had never even tried a homicide case.

"Kate? Linda Foster. I've heard about you, it's good to meet you."

Murmuring her own automatic pleasantry, Kate shook the cool, firm hand extended by a thin, frizzy-haired young woman in a tailored black skirt and jacket.

"So. Come on back to the office." Linda Foster turned and marched briskly off, Kate following.

Kate felt at home in the warren of utilitarian cubicles assigned to the deputy district attorneys, the worn anonymity of the cramped offices, the work-laden desks. This place always held for her the same weary yet not unpleasant ambience of entrenched bureaucracy and never-ending paperwork as did her own Wilshire Division.

In her windowless box of an office, Linda Foster
kicked off her pumps, flung her well-cut jacket onto
a bookcase stuffed with case files, dropped her body
into her desk chair. "Feel free to make yourself
equally comfortable," she told Kate, reaching to a
shelf behind her desk to plug in a Farberware coffee
percolator.

Smiling, Kate sat in the flimsy metallic chair
across from her. "I'm okay. I have to conceal my gun
in public, so I'm used to wearing a jacket."

"That's a bitch."

Kate surveyed Linda Foster with casual but acute
attention, trying to evaluate the slender young
woman as a jury might view her. She was in her
mid thirties, and the sandy blonde frizz was a
distinctly contemporary hairstyle. Stylish oversize
rose-tinted glasses framed gray-green eyes intense
with impatient intelligence. Her makeup was light,
the delicate mouth barely lipsticked. Simply cut
clothing and minimal makeup did not conceal Linda
Foster's femininity, but, Kate reflected, most women
could more easily exaggerate their femininity than
understate it. She wore no wedding ring; Kate had
learned that she was divorced, had a seven-year-old
son, and lived with a college professor.

Kate sensed rather than saw a strain of
toughness in Linda Foster, a trait common to good
female attorneys, but a double-edged sword. Many
male cops and judges, resigned to the legally
mandated presence of women within their ranks,
disdained more forceful women attorneys as cutthroat
castrating killer bitches. Kate did not doubt that
certain members of juries held the same opinion.

Foster blew a strand of frizz from her forehead,

propped one nyloned foot on a corner of the desk. "So. This is what I know. Kenneth Pritchard's a volunteer public defender."

Kate nodded. "I know a Kenneth Pritchard, but the last I heard he was a corporate insurance lawyer."

"Insurance? God, what a bore. This guy's from Butler, Steele and Simon, the snotty firm for upper-class felons. So he's slumming, he's a cowboy riding into town to defend the disadvantaged and downtrodden."

Grinning, Kate asked, "And you're not?"

Foster shrugged. "Sometimes the disadvantaged and downtrodden deserve to be. I already know from the case reports we'll have a pre-trial motion for dismissal on the grounds the cuts on Jensen's hands prove self-defense. A motion to quash Jensen's confession on whatever procedural bullshit Pritchard can concoct, aside from claiming Jensen's pain pills impaired his ability to know what he was saying. Thanks to your excellent work, that shouldn't fly a foot."

Kate nodded. "Thanks. Good," she said. So far she was pleased with what she had heard.

"So then they plea bargain. Involuntary, is my guess. What do you think?"

"Look," Kate said, sitting up in her chair. "I know plea bargains are often no worse than a jury might decide. But manslaughter doesn't fit anywhere here. By every definition this is first degree murder."

Foster put the other foot up on her desk, laced her long fingers together. "So. Tell me."

Kate took a deep breath. Everything rode on convincing this blunt-talking young woman —

everything. "You read the reports, heard the interview tape —"

"It'll make for drafting a good complaint. You should see the horseshit I get from the bozos in narcotics. I wish more detectives gave us so few procedural problems."

"I appreciate that." And she did. "This is what I think about Kyle Jensen. He's a drug user who rolled gay men from bars like Malone's because that kind of gay man can't afford to report that kind of crime. He's —"

"Can you give me that?" Foster said. "Substantiate it?"

"I'm working on it." She was not ready to admit that she had made unsuccessful trips to Malone's, and to several other bars, asking patrons and bartenders if they recognized the booking shot of Kyle Jensen. She had left a stack of her business cards, inviting any sort of information, even anonymous. But eliciting cooperation from the gay male community would be a serious problem when LAPD was viewed as homophobic, and for ample reason. Police chief Daryl Gates had fought recruitment of openly gay officers, with the dismissing comment, "Who'd want to work with one?" The department was being sued by a former police sergeant whose sexual identity had been discovered and who had been harassed into resigning for fear of his life. Gay and lesbian cops within LAPD were known only to one another — and she herself needed to be very careful what she revealed to this woman.

Kate said, "I'm certain Jensen knew Teddie

Crawford was gay. This was a man so far out of the closet — everyone I've talked to so far says Teddie Crawford was proud he was gay."

"Okay," Linda Foster said, making a note on her pad.

At least she had not reacted as Taylor had — but Kate could not tell if "okay" meant anything more than simple acknowledgment of the fact. She continued, "Everyone I've talked to so far says Teddie Crawford didn't have any sort of drug habit — which doesn't mean anything, of course, and toxicology will tell us the truth — but the people in his life are indicative of the person he was. And he seems very much . . ." She searched for a word. "Cherished. His aunt and uncle are de facto parents, really nice people. Teddie was the center — the bright center — of their lives." She ached with the memory of her interview with Joe and Margaret Crawford, their stunned faces, their numb pain and bewilderment.

The coffee pot chuffing behind her, Linda Foster crossed her arms and contemplated Kate. "So. You think Jensen is homosexual?"

Kate said carefully, "A lot of us in the homicide business think multiple stabbing involves sexual pathology."

Foster shrugged impatiently. "Yeah, well, so Jensen could be repressed. Or this could be a pure and simple skinhead-type hate crime. Or maybe he actually didn't know Teddie Crawford was gay and maybe two men skulled out on cocaine testosteroned it out with each other."

Irked by Foster's habit of making conclusory

judgments about her statements, Kate at the same time knew she was playing devil's advocate. But it was still difficult to control her rising agitation.

"Your last theory doesn't mesh with this crime. Teddie Crawford is far from being any sort of fighter. Jensen told us he fought like, and I quote, a fucking cat. Why would he take on somebody as big and muscled as Jensen? According to Jensen, Teddie Crawford was wasted on cocaine. Yet this wasted man, scant minutes before he died, was showing Jensen around his restaurant, explaining how he and his partner put the place together, where he bought the napkins, how many he bought, how much he paid."

Foster looked at her with a thin smile. "Yes, not exactly the cokehead type I've come to know and love. So, that leaves us with Jensen killing a homosexual — either the one in Teddie Crawford, or the one in himself."

Kate was struck by the wording of this last assessment. She said reflectively, "Somebody once said that the hater actually longs for the object of his hatred."

The coffee pot stopped chuffing. Foster got up and yanked out the plug, pulled out the strainer holding the coffee grounds, dumped the grounds into her waste basket. "So, figure this guy's repressed. Okay, I'll buy that — but I don't know if a jury will. If he's been rolling gay men, what made him kill for the first time, and why this man?"

"How do we know Teddie Crawford was the first time?"

"Good point." Foster poured coffee into two mugs of dubious cleanliness and handed one to Kate, sat down again. "You don't take cream or sugar," she said in a tone that meant no right-thinking person would. Amused, shaking her head, Kate accepted the coffee mug.

Foster sipped her coffee. "So. We still have to sell intent, premeditation, malice aforethought and beyond-a-reasonable-doubt-and-to-a-moral-certainty to Mr. and Mrs. America on the jury, Kate."

"You listened to the tape," Kate said. "He talked about sand niggers, slope heads —"

"An equal opportunity bigot," Foster said.

"Right," Kate said, chuckling. "Like most bigots." She was warming to this woman. Who served an excellent cup of coffee. "He goes to great lengths to claim heterosexuality. When he talked about the first time he saw Teddie Crawford —"

"I need us to call him Teddie," Foster interrupted. "It makes him a person to me."

Now she liked this woman. "When Jensen talked about the first time he saw Teddie, he took pains to point out he was looking at Gloria Gomez, not Teddie. He claimed Shirley Johnson was his live-in girlfriend, claimed she helped him take off his bloody clothes when it was actually Burt Dayton — he wanted no insinuations about a man helping him undress. When he met Teddie at Malone's, Jensen said they introduced themselves by first name. But men interested only in conversation with each other introduce themselves by full name. Men cruising each other use first names."

Foster was making rapid notes on a legal pad. "You're very good at your job, Kate."

Please be good at yours. "I've been doing it a long time," she said. "There's more. You heard his regret that his father wasn't around to see how brave he'd been about the cuts to his hands. Kyle Jensen is a man with a war hero father he could never measure up to, a mother he's estranged from."

"Three more cheers for the traditional American family," Linda Foster muttered.

Kate said, "For me, one of the telling moments in that entire interview was how upset he got when I asked whether he'd been in any other gay bars. I think Jensen took one look at Teddie and knew he was gay. And when Teddie told him he was a partner in a restaurant, that cinched him as a robbery victim."

"But a murder victim?"

"Jensen never had these circumstances before," Kate argued. "This was different from rolling a guy in a parking lot or in a car. Teddie had no car, and that put Jensen in control. He had a smaller man than himself as a victim, private surroundings to do whatever he wanted."

"So Teddie managed to get his hands on a knife to defend himself, Jensen got it away from him and killed him."

That scenario felt somehow wrong, but she could not argue against it. Not effectively. Not yet. She said, temporizing, "Charlotte Mead at the lab will be giving us a lot more information about the crime scene evidence."

Again she took a deep breath. "Look, Linda, I don't want this case dumped on a cheap plea bargain. Manslaughter? No way. This murder was no accident, it was not spur-of-the-moment. This killer stabbed a man thirty-nine times. I don't want him back on the street after a few years of easy time. Do you?"

Tapping her pen on her legal pad, her eyes unreadable behind the reflections on her glasses, Foster did not respond.

Kate had to convince this woman who had shown more understanding of the ramifications of this homicide than anyone else. "Let me tell you about this case," she said, feeling her control slipping into heedlessness. "Nobody cares about this case. My male partner hates this case because Teddie Crawford was gay. Male officers in my department hate this case because the witnesses are gay — they did toss-off interviews and toss-off reports to prove it. The male pathologist hates this case because Teddie Crawford was gay, and you saw his autopsy report."

"The men in this office hate this case too," Linda Foster said quietly. She pulled off her glasses, tossed them on her desk, looked at Kate with intense gray-green eyes. "I have no illusions why it was assigned to me."

Kate said, "There won't be any press coverage at the prelim or the trial — who cares about a dead gay man? Teddie Crawford is a throwaway human being, this is a throwaway case. Nobody gives a good goddamn."

"Nobody but you and me," Linda Foster said. "Let me refill your cup and let's talk about our witnesses at the prelim."

— 8 —

"Kenneth Pritchard," Kate said, flabbergasted.

"Kate Delafield," the tall, dark-haired man returned as he stood outside the 13th floor courtroom of the Criminal Courts Building. Smiling, he reached for her hand and shook it vigorously.

"I saw the name on the arraignment report," Kate said, trying to recover her composure. "I didn't think it could possibly be the same Kenneth Pritchard."

He chuckled. "I saw your name as investigating

officer and knew damn well it was the same Kate Delafield. I'm surprised you remember me."

"Of course I remember you." With effort she summoned a smile for this handsome, well-tailored man who had so suddenly — and painfully — reconnected her to her past. "When did you leave Guardian?"

"Three years ago November. Criminal law was an old dream — I have to tell you Anne's death was one of the factors that got me off my duff. The reality's a lot different from the dream, Kate . . ." He shrugged. "But the deep end of the pool is still more interesting. I'm glad to say Butler, Steele and Simon want their attorneys to take some public defender cases."

He put his briefcase down on the plastic bench molded into the wall and looked at her with candid dark eyes. "You look well. Much better than the last time I saw you. I hope you know Anne's death was a terrible shock for me, too. There aren't that many people you call friends in the business world. It's been what, five years?"

"Six." Six years and five months, to be exact, since the day of Anne's funeral — the last time she had seen Kenneth Pritchard, corporate attorney at the insurance company for which Anne had worked. Of all people, for him to be the defense attorney for Kyle Jensen . . . Shocked by this new ingredient in the Teddie Crawford homicide, she looked blindly past him, down the wide corridor to the clusters of people waiting in resigned patience outside other courtrooms.

Pritchard said, "Anne was so very proud of you, Kate. She talked about you constantly."

"Yes. Thank you. I guess we'd better get in there." She reached to the closed double doors of the courtroom, but he moved around her and pulled a door open.

She preceded him awkwardly, galled by her feeling of defenselessness, that she should be so unprepared for an incursion into her professional world by someone who knew intimate details of her life. Her lesbian life.

She was immediately soothed by the courtroom, affected as always by its aura. The high bench and the jury box, bereft of their judges, seemed no less symbolic or majestic. The simple dark shapes of the wooden paneling and furnishings seemed to brood over the handful of people within the chamber's confines.

Inside the railing separating the court's inner sanctum from the spectator benches, Linda Foster sat hunched over her notes at the right-hand end of the counsel table, looking like a somber, perched bird in her dark jacket and skirt. A portly bailiff, who Kate vaguely recognized, sat at his desk looking through a notebook; a bald male clerk, head down, worked in his cubicle to the right of the judge's bench; a Latino court reporter waited in alert readiness at his machine.

In the aisle separating the two rows of spectator benches, three witnesses for the prosecution stood exchanging low-toned pleasantries: pathologist Brian Whitson, and Patrol Officers Jim Foley and Nancy Simmons. Ignoring them, Kenneth Pritchard pushed his way through the gate to the inner court and placed his briefcase on the left-hand end of the counsel table.

Kate nodded to the group, then took a seat at the rear of the courtroom beside two other prosecution witnesses. She smiled reassuringly. "Francisco, Gloria, how are you?"

"Doing okay," Gloria answered for both of them, turning grave dark eyes on Kate.

Wearing a navy blue dress with a square neck, her shoulder-length dark hair brushed to a sheen, she sat erect, her small hands clenched in her lap. Francisco Caldera, in an oversize gray jacket that looked as if it could slide off his frame, managed a smile for Kate. They looked like children frightened into formal behavior. Kate said soothingly, "It'll be all right, this is routine and will be over with very quickly."

Gloria Gomez said, "I'll finally get to see . . . him."

"Best to get it over with now," Kate offered.

The bailiff's phone buzzed. He spoke softly, briefly, and then said to Kenneth Pritchard, "Bringing in the prisoner." He unlocked the door next to his cubicle, and a few moments later emerged with Kyle Jensen.

There was a sigh from Francisco Caldera; no sound at all from Gloria Gomez. Kate noted that even in the absence of an empaneled jury, Jensen, in his prison blues, had been cleaned up for court. He was shaven, his moustache substantially trimmed, his hair neatly shortened to the nape of his neck. The hands were unbandaged — but then ten days had passed since he had been booked. He quickly sat down next to Pritchard, stuffed both hands into his jumpsuit pockets.

"Come to order," intoned the bailiff, "court is now in session."

Judge Michael Torgeson strode into the room through a door beside the clerk's cubicle, several folders under an arm. He took his place on the bench, opened his top folder. "*The People versus Jensen*," he intoned. He looked up, his glance raking the courtroom. "Case number A9471341."

Kate watched as Michael Torgeson ascertained which attorneys were present, and the other opening particulars necessary for the court reporter's record. She knew this thin, ascetic-faced judge, knew he would be sharp and attentive in a rote performance, like an expert mechanic working on a routine brake job. This preliminary hearing was for the sole purpose of showing probable cause for binding the case over for trial; the trial itself would be assigned to another judge.

The prelim was very useful to the defense for viewing prosecution witnesses and to learn the prosecution's major evidence and general approach to the trial. For this reason, Linda Foster would present the minimum witnesses necessary. And the defense would present none at all.

"The People call Francisco Caldera," Linda Foster said in a clear, confident voice.

Francisco sighed again, a sound that was close to a sob. "It'll be okay," Kate said softly as he made his way past her.

He answered Linda Foster's opening question tremulously, seeming to shrink back from the microphone and into his chair as he identified himself and stated his address. But the impersonality of her questions about his actions the morning of February 4th gradually calmed him — until Foster led him up to his discovery of the body of Teddie Crawford. She handed him a black and white photograph taken at the murder scene. "Is this the person you found?"

He crumpled in his chair. His Adam's apple bobbing, he nodded.

Foster said softly, "Please identify this person for the record, Mr. Caldera."

"It's Teddie," he whispered. "Teddie Crawford."

"Let the record reflect that the witness has identified Edward Ashwell Crawford, also known as Teddie Crawford, the victim." Foster handed the photograph to the judge. "People's Exhibit One," she said. "I have no further questions."

"Mr. Pritchard?" the judge said.

"No questions," Kenneth Pritchard said.

Pale, trembling, Francisco Caldera left the stand. He had not, Kate observed, looked even once at Kyle Jensen.

"The People call Dr. Brian Whitson," Linda Foster said.

Kate stared contemptuously as Whitson, a husky young man wearing slacks and a sport jacket over a red sweater vest, walked through the swinging doors held open by the bailiff and took the stand.

Three days ago she had confronted Taylor with the autopsy report, waving it at him: "Who *is* this Whitson?"

"A new guy, he seems okay."

"*Okay?* He didn't probe the wounds!"

"So?"

"He *has* to probe the wounds, he's *required* to give measurements of stab wounds." Had she herself attended the autopsy instead of Taylor, she thought in fury, she would have challenged Whitson on the spot to perform the work mandated for him.

"Jesus, Kate. Who gives a crap? There was plenty enough organ damage to establish cause of death. Why poke around in the body of a guy who might have AIDS?"

Turning her back on him, she had immediately called Geoff Mitchell at USC Medical Center to determine the proper channels for reporting Whitson's professional misconduct.

"I don't blame anyone for being afraid," she had raged at Mitchell. "But you have safeguards, all the proper tools, it's his *job* —"

"I agree, Kate," Mitchell had told her. "Sorry it's too late for your case, but aside from your making a formal complaint, he's shot himself in the foot. A good defense attorney reads a pathologist's previous autopsy reports. The incomplete autopsy he did on your man will cripple him as a future expert witness in forensic medicine."

". . . a total of thirty-nine homicidal stab wounds," Whitson was laconically replying to Linda Foster's questions. "Inflicted to the upper extremities, twenty-three to the back, twelve to the chest and arms, as well as cuts to both hands and fingers, and fresh abrasions and contusions on the face and scalp."

Kate glanced at Kyle Jensen. He sat slumped in his chair, feet straight out, staring at the floor.

"Cause of death was three stab wounds in the

back, penetrating the right lung, and two stab wounds in the chest penetrating the left lung, causing massive internal and external hemorrhage, with almost total collapse of both lungs."

"Would you elaborate on the cuts to the hands," Linda Foster said.

"There's a deep cut and severing of tendons at the base of the fourth digit of the right hand, accompanied by dislocation. The palmar aspect of both hands shows slash wounds from the junction of the wrist and palm. The cuts on both hands probably represent so-called defense wounds."

"Thank you," Linda Foster said. "No further questions."

"Mr. Pritchard," Judge Torgeson said.

Kate watched Kenneth Pritchard get to his feet with the grace and confidence one might expect from a man who, she recalled Anne telling her, had been in the top ten of his class at Georgetown. Kyle Jensen, his eyes on the silk-suited attorney assigned to him, had to be pleased by his good fortune. Still, Kate reflected, it was a common misperception to believe that a private attorney was automatically superior to a public defender. PDs were cruelly overburdened, but in her experience they were canny, work-toughened, highly committed trial attorneys with invaluable courtroom and case law expertise simply because they handled so much work. Pritchard, in this case, was an unknown factor. It was impossible to gauge how capable he might be.

"Thank you, your honor," Pritchard said. "Doctor, the drug and alcohol readings?"

"Alcohol level was point oh three. Toxicology is still pending — another week, probably."

"About the wounds to the decedent's hands. You described them as representing so-called defense wounds. So-called, because there could be another explanation?"

"No, so-called because it's layman's terminology. The wounds are classic by any terminology, but yes, there can always be another explanation."

"No further questions."

Kate was not surprised that Pritchard had ignored the incomplete autopsy report. Teddie Crawford had indisputably died at the hands of Kyle Jensen, and from the defense's point of view, the extensive detail that Linda Foster would draw out at trial regarding the victim's death throes would include fewer specifics about the depth and dimension of the fatal wounds.

She watched Kenneth Pritchard as Patrol Officer Jim Foley tonelessly described his discovery of the crime scene and that he had found no evidence of forcible entry and no sign of a weapon. Patrol Officer Nancy Simmons, a wiry young woman in a crisply pressed uniform, testified to the execution of the search warrant, and the property which had been discovered in the seat compartment of Kyle Jensen's motor bike, including a bloodstained knife. Pritchard, busily taking notes, had no questions for either of these witnesses.

"The People call Gloria Gomez."

The young woman rose stiffly from beside Kate and marched to the stand as if she were wearing boots instead of high heels.

As Foster led Gomez through the standard opening questions, then asked her to identify and confirm the objects found in Jensen's motor bike had belonged to Teddie Crawford, Gomez never took her eyes from Jensen. Jensen never took his eyes from either his shoes or his attorney.

"Do you recognize this wrist watch, Ms. Gomez?"

"Yeah, it's Teddie's Seiko," she said fiercely. "Teddie's blood-soaked Seiko."

"Objection. Move to strike," Pritchard said, not looking up from his note-taking.

"Strike that," the judge said to the court reporter. "Ms. Gomez, answer the question and only the question."

Kate watched in profound sympathy as Gloria Gomez stared at Kyle Jensen in baffled, frustrated, furious hatred. The suffering from a crime of homicide never ended with the criminal act.

The questioning of Gloria Gomez ended with three more People's Exhibits — Teddie Crawford's watch, ring, and wallet — and Gomez was dismissed as a witness. As she passed the counsel table she hissed clearly and distinctly to Kyle Jensen, "You motherfucking slimeshit."

Kyle Jensen jerked upward. Pritchard gripped his shoulder and pushed him down, the bailiff rose from his desk. The judge rapped his gavel. "Ms. Gomez, any more out of you and you're in contempt. One more word of profanity and you're in jail. Do you understand me?"

"Yes, sir," she said, her tone on the bare edge of defiance. "I got nothing more to say."

Linda Foster spoke up quickly: "The People call Detective Kate Delafield."

Kate felt the familiar thrill of tension as she approached the witness stand and took her place in the chair behind the microphone. But she relaxed

into confidence as Linda Foster skillfully confined
her questions to when Kyle Jensen had been advised
of his constitutional rights, the contents of the typed
statement signed by him, and the facts in the
criminal complaint. Since every word she said here
would be evaluated and used to undermine her
credibility, any extraneous questions about the crime
scene, or any fact not in the complaint, would open
a Pandora's box of cross-examination from Pritchard
that would be used to challenge her statements at
trial.

"Detective Delafield, the man named Kyle Jensen
who you questioned and arrested — do you see that
man in this courtroom?"

"Yes." Kate pointed at Kyle Jensen. "Seated to
the left of the defense attorney at the counsel table."
Jensen looked up, but his diamond-shaped blue eyes
did not register her, as if the witness stand were
empty.

"Let the record show that the witness has
identified the defendant," Linda Foster said. "No
further questions."

Tensing as Kenneth Pritchard approached the
stand, Kate sat back in her chair to convey the
opposite.

Kenneth Pritchard looked at her as impassively
as if he had never seen her before. Kate understood
that any pleasantries between them existed in the
past. She was now the enemy. "Detective Delafield,
who besides the defendant did you talk to at
Hollywood Presbyterian Hospital?"

"I spoke with the admissions clerk, Doctor Henry
Mercer, and Patrol Officer Dale Morissey."

"Were you aware that the defendant was under medication?"

She concentrated on narrowing the focus of her replies only to what he asked. "Yes, I was."

"Who told you?"

"Doctor Henry Mercer."

"What did he tell you?"

"Objection, hearsay," said Linda Foster.

"Overruled. Ms. Foster, this is a preliminary hearing. Detective, answer the question."

Kate said, "He enumerated the medications and stated there was no medical objection to talking with the defendant."

"At the hospital, did the defendant complain of being in pain?"

"Yes. At that point I terminated the questioning."

"When you questioned the defendant in his hospital room, did you advise him of his Miranda rights?"

She said carefully, "There was no reason to."

Pritchard smiled. "When did you place him under arrest?"

"At ten twenty-seven p.m. that evening."

"Where did you arrest him?"

"In an interview room at Wilshire Division."

"How did Mr. Jensen come to be in that interview room?"

"He came in voluntarily."

"He walked in off the street, Detective?"

"He agreed to be given escort from Hollywood Presbyterian Hospital by a patrol car."

"Did he indeed. Did he complain of pain while you were questioning him?"

"Yes."

"Was he given medication?"

"Yes."

"At what point was he given medication?"

"When he asked for it, which was after relating the details of the homicide and learning that he would need to repeat them."

"Thank you, Detective." His smile contained confidence.

Foster had been right, Kate thought as she returned to her seat. Pritchard's questions had been designed to set up a motion to suppress Jensen's confession. And also to intimidate her.

"Your honor," Linda Foster said. "The People have no further witnesses. We move for bind over of the defendant for trial."

"Your honor," Kenneth Pritchard said, "the defense moves for dismissal on the grounds that the State has failed to prove the material allegations contained in its complaint."

"Your motion is noted and denied, Mr. Pritchard," Judge Torgeson said. "Based on the allegations contained in the complaint, I find probable cause that a crime was committed, and that the crime was committed by the defendant. The defendant is ordered bound over to Superior Court, for trial date —"

"Your honor," Kenneth Pritchard said, "in view of my client's inability to make bail, and a preponderance of evidence in his favor, the defense requests a speedy trial."

"A speedy trial," murmured the judge. "What a concept." To chuckles from the courtroom, he consulted a calendar. "Judge Alicia Hawkins just had three weeks open up, beginning May eighth. Do I hear any objections?"

A few minutes later, the trial date was agreed upon. Court was adjourned.

"It went well," Linda Foster told Kate in the hallway outside the courtroom.

Kate nodded. A courtroom was a battleground, a setting for brutal warfare structured like a highly civilized chess game. Some moves were automatic, like the prelim, to set up the real contest.

"There were no surprises," Foster said. "I don't like surprises."

"There was one surprise," Kate said. "Kenneth Pritchard is the same one I knew from years ago, he's moved into criminal law."

Linda Foster shrugged. "Yeah, well, so what?"

— 9 —

On the Saturday two weeks before the trial of
Kyle Jensen would begin, Kate sat in her Nova in
front of Tradition at one-forty-five in the morning.
Wearing jeans and sneakers and a gray LAPD
sweatshirt, sipping from a carton of coffee she had
bought at the 7-Eleven on the corner, she
contemplated the shuttered restaurant alongside its
companion businesses, their dark windows guarded
by retractable iron grates. No other cars were parked
on the lifeless street; sparse traffic traveled
past her.

The last time she had been here was six days after the murder of Teddie Crawford. In a follow-up interview with Francisco Caldera, he had confessed that he could not enter the restaurant because the kitchen was filled with Teddie's blood; he could not bring himself to clean it up, nor could he ask anyone else to do so. "Do you have a wet mop in the restaurant?" she had asked. She had gone into the place that evening, swabbed the blackened floor, wiped down the spattered cabinets and walls, made the kitchen spotlessly white once more. This homicide was not the first time she had performed such an act.

On Monday she would meet with Linda Foster for pre-trial planning. Toxicological reports were in place; and Charlotte Mead had completed her blood spatter analysis of the crime scene. Linda Foster possessed all of these reports, as did Kenneth Pritchard, as part of the discovery process which required the prosecution and the defense to submit all written material to one another. The defense, as customary, claimed they had no written material to furnish.

This homicide investigation was the same as any other in terms of putting together the tightest possible case — except that Kate herself had done work she would have either performed with Taylor or delegated. She was still conducting background interviews, following up on a few details. And there was one other element differentiating this case. She needed to be here at this hour, on this day of the week — the hour and day when Teddie Crawford had died.

Since she was the investigating officer of his

death, he was exposed to her in an eerie intimacy
that did not allow him protection or privacy. The
nakedness of his body was open to her scrutiny, the
contents of his home and his life hers to probe.
From his family, his friends, his lovers, his
possessions, she now understood that he was not a
man of silences and restraint. She understood the
voluble, chaotic energy of his personality, the
extravagance of his style, the flash of his dress, the
bite of his wit. She understood his romanticism, his
generosity, his sweet optimism.

To speak with total authority to Linda Foster,
and beyond her, to a jury, she needed to add one
final piece. She needed to see — to understand —
what had happened in the kitchen at Tradition. To
understand it in her bones.

She drove down the dark alley behind Tradition,
got out of the car. Restaurant keys in hand, she
closed her eyes briefly. "I am Teddie Crawford," she
whispered.

Then she was climbing off the motor bike she
had been riding behind Kyle Jensen. Preceding Kyle
Jensen to the back door of her restaurant, unlocking
the door. Walking in and pridefully throwing the
light switch to illuminate the immaculate kitchen.
Eager to show Kyle the rest of this place she and
Francisco had so lovingly built.

Kyle wants to do cocaine first. Okay. Then I'll
enjoy watching this good-looking man slide that
leather jacket off that broad chest. Watch his body
as he lays out some lines. Okay, I'll do just a little
of it, to keep him company, be sociable.

Now I get to show him my restaurant. It's so
pretty from the light from the kitchen, all shadows,

quiet and romantic — but let me turn the room lights on so he can see everything. Kyle, I told you how Francisco and I found this place . . . Putting it together was such great fun, we searched out the tables, the chairs, the linens . . . I picked up a hundred napkins at a bankruptcy sale, only a dime apiece, feel the fabric, isn't it fine? The customers love the impressionist paintings, they add a lot of charm to the place, don't you think?

Let me turn out the lights again. Kyle, sit at a table with me, feel the comfort, the romance in here . . . See the windows, how the street light filters in through the gauzy window coverings. Take my hand, Kyle . . .

Come on, man, don't pull this hetero-butch number, it's a bore, I don't go along with the pretense any more. Get real, why don't you? Who do you think you're kidding? You came here to do coke and do me, so don't say you're not gay. You're gay, man, you're gay as I am.

Wait a minute, where the hell you going? What do you want in my kitchen? Get out of here. Just get the hell out of my restaurant.

A terrible mistake. I've got to get him out of here, oh Jesus, he's twice my size . . .

Let go of me! Oh God this tiny kitchen . . . I'm trapped, trapped. *Wait, no . . . Take anything you want, just don't . . . Don't . . .*

She slumped down onto the cold tile of the claustrophobic kitchen, her back against the wall, seeing him frantically thrash on the floor, slamming his head into the wall as he rolled in the small room trying to protect his face and chest from the slashing knife, Kyle Jensen leaping on him,

straddling him, pinning him face down as he thrust
the knife again and again into the frenzied body
beneath him until . . .

Jensen finished, getting up, his jeans crimson.
His jeans wet and warm with blood. Moans, the man
rolling over onto his back, his arms feebly clutching
at himself to staunch his wounds . . .

She stared at the ceiling. Its white brightness the
last image in the dimming eyes of Teddie Crawford.

She rose to her feet, turned the lights out, again
lowered herself to the floor and sat with her back
against the wall in utter blackness.

She felt his fear. His terror at the ebbing of his
life. With her own sense of sight blanked out she
listened to the building as Teddie Crawford had last
known it, its creaks, the hum of the refrigerator, the
constant drone of the city, all the sounds so ordinary
to the man who had belonged here in this place
where he had felt safe, where he had found
validation, where he had been confident and proud.
Until the blood-lust of a stranger.

She got up and turned on the lights. Pulling
photographs out of an envelope in her shoulderbag,
she arranged them over the table. Photographs of
Teddie Crawford's corpse lying amid pools of blood.
Autopsy photographs of Teddie's naked body, its pale
torso studded with dark red gashes. Crime lab
photographs of the knife, bloodstained from blade-tip
to handle, recovered from Kyle Jensen's motor bike.
Another lab photograph, of Jensen's jeans, so
blood-saturated that Jensen's white shorts, the
subject of another, separate photograph, were also
soaked scarlet.

She now knew with gut-deep, settled certainty

that Teddie Crawford had never held the knife. Had never picked it up to either threaten Jensen or defend himself. It was not in his nature. It was Kyle Jensen who had come at Teddie Crawford, and with explicit intent. Kyle Jensen who had sat astride a male body and used a knife to thrust into that body until his pent-up lust was spent.

"Teddie," she murmured, picking up a closeup photo of the handsome face, "when Kyle *first* came at you with that knife, exactly what in the world happened? How did Kyle get cut?" But the knowledge was forever hidden behind the staring dark eyes fixed lifelessly on the ceiling.

She stacked the photos, tucked them back in their envelope. She was prepared to see Linda Foster — except for this one final, crucial point. Since Jensen had had the knife first and not Teddie, the defense wounds on Teddie's hands were clearly explainable. But how had Jensen come to have such severe wounds to his own hands?

"Nobody's coming in today but you, I skipped wearing the monkey suit," said Linda Foster. She finished priming her coffee pot and plugged it in.

Kate tossed a folder onto a corner of the desk, thinking that even in powder blue pants and the soft cling of a white cashmere V-neck sweater, Linda Foster looked sharp and tough. Shrugging out of her corduroy jacket, Kate said, "I'll get comfortable too."

"Do that," Foster said absently, her eyes on the thick, three-ring murder book splayed open on the desk in front of her, her long fingers running over

its index tabs. "So. I've pored over every word. I
think as a general approach we need to have Mr.
and Mrs. America on the jury see Teddie as a
regular citizen, don't you?"

Kate, settling herself in the chair across from
Linda Foster, sat up straight. "You mean play down
the fact that he was gay."

At her tone, Foster looked up. "Kate, the bottom
line is, we need to figure a way to reach the jury. It
doesn't take much brainwork to figure the scenario
Pritchard'll work up. The heterosexual defendant's
the good guy, the homosexual got what he asked
for."

"The homosexual panic defense," Kate said
evenly, commanding herself to be calm.

"Well . . . not exactly. Pure homosexual panic
needs clinical proof. Proof of psychosis, of a
breakdown into violent psychological panic — very
hard to prove. You need a certifiably loony tunes
client."

Shifting her holster, Kate sat back in her chair,
eased by the knowledge that this woman had done
some research, and could be talked to. "There was a
case last year," she said. "The killer got
manslaughter, but the judge said the gay man he
killed was responsible for his own death because of
his reprehensible act in making a sexual advance."
She had read about the case in the *Advocate*. She
decided not to mention the dismal fact that the
comments had been made by a judge in San
Francisco.

"I know the case," Foster said. "And another
really gross one in Kalamazoo where the jury came
in with not guilty even though the defendant first

beat the crap out of the victim, then came back and finished him off with a sledgehammer." She pointed to a stack of photocopies on the side of her desk. "Lots of cases, Kate, and let me tell you, the claim of homosexual advance comes up even with no evidence. The creeps think of it after they've killed. And defense attorneys take it and slip it in, figuring some dipshit on the jury will buy it and they'll get a lesser verdict and a lighter sentence."

Kate asked in a casual tone, "Would you use it?"

"Me?" Foster grinned. "Only with gay men prettier than I am. I have enough trouble competing with women. Let me tell you, I have real trouble with that defense, and I usually don't have ethical problems if an attorney isn't actually manufacturing evidence. But killing somebody is an *outrageous* response to a proposal of sex. I mean, come on. Be upset, even be revolted. But kill? I couldn't buy that from a client, they'd have to find somebody else who would."

Kate leaned forward. "Linda, what you just said — why do you think we can't communicate exactly that to a jury?"

"Because I'm no Gregory Peck."

Kate looked at her.

"*To Kill a Mockingbird,* Gregory Peck trying to reach a white jury about a black man — remember? To Mr. and Mrs. America, gay people are a different species. And let's not even talk about AIDS. If Pritchard gets his way, the jury'll think Jensen's rubbed out one of *those,* not one of *us,* and he didn't do that much of a bad thing."

"You make very good points, Linda," Kate said quietly. "But I have to tell you I think it's a mistake to try and rehabilitate Teddie into someone acceptable to a heterosexual jury."

Foster got up, poured coffee. "I'm listening."

"Do you know what the term queen means among gay men?"

"Men in drag, right?"

"Sometimes, not always. Mostly it's men who parade their feminine qualities, men who are overtly gay. Linda — Teddie Crawford was a queen."

"This is good news?" Foster handed Kate a mug of steaming coffee.

Kate smiled. "Actually, yes. If Teddie was that obvious, why was Jensen so shocked when Teddie made an advance — assuming he did? I think we *need* to state from the outset that Teddie was gay. Unashamedly gay, ostentatiously gay. And that way we set up proving that Jensen knew exactly what Teddie was, and chose to victimize him."

"Granting you that, Kate, we still have a jury that may think when it came down to really having a sex act with a man, he freaked. A jury that may think that under those circumstances they would, too."

"You want to make Teddie a regular citizen?" Kate challenged her. "Then make him exactly that. As a regular citizen he met an adult at a bar, like a lot of regular citizens do. He was led to believe that the adult he met shared the same interest he did. He left with that adult expecting to have a nice evening. When Kyle Jensen agreed to come to Tradition, Teddie had a right to believe that Jensen's expectations were the same as his own. Because Teddie Crawford was a regular citizen. A regular gay citizen."

"Sounds pretty shaky to me." Foster grinned at her. "Certainly Pritchard won't be expecting it. We still have the problem of Jensen's defense wounds."

Satisfied by Foster's response so far, knowing the strategy-discussion had not ended, Kate accepted the change of direction. She took the folder from the corner of the desk and opened it.

"There's something strange about those wounds, Linda. I had Doctor Mercer make drawings of the cuts in Jensen's hands. They aren't the kind of glancing wounds you'd expect in this kind of fight for possession of a knife. Some of those lacerations are deep and *severe*."

Kate handed the drawings to Foster. "I've thought and thought about those wounds. They just don't make sense as defense wounds. Why the cut between the thumb and forefinger and not to the palm of the right hand? Why wouldn't a man as powerful as Jensen get the knife away from Teddie before he got a wound that almost took his thumb off? Not to mention the other damage?"

"All kinds of wounds can happen during a knife fight," Foster said. "And maybe Teddie's fear gave him more strength than you'd guess from his size. It often does, you know."

Kate said doggedly, "How did he get that wound on the outside edge of his palm? How did he get —"

"Look, I think this could be important, too. My, uh —" She looked at Kate. "What do *you* call somebody you live with? I hate the word lover, it's too personal. I barf over significant other."

"Companion or partner," Kate said, grinning.

"Companions are for old ladies. My partner's a woodworker by hobby. Why don't I get him to duplicate the murder knife out of plywood or something? Maybe we can come up with a demonstration, a plausible scenario of how Jensen got those wounds to explain it to the jury."

"I did something like that for another stabbing case I had," Kate said, remembering a death investigation a few years ago in a Wilshire District highrise.

"Did it help?"

"Nope."

"Terrific."

Kate said, grinning, "But I did get the killer."

"I'm sure you did," Linda Foster murmured, and sipped from her coffee, scrutinizing Kate over the rim.

— 10 —

The Nightwood Bar held perhaps twenty patrons at this 9:00 p.m. hour, most of them familiar faces to Kate. Four women at the back of the bar were playing Scrabble; three others lounged at tables beside the bookcase reading books; two more were immersed in a table-top video game. The others sat at tables talking or in attitudes of quiet relaxation. On the jukebox Patsy Cline was singing "I Fall to Pieces."

Kate made her unobtrusive way through the room, returning a few smiles and waves, and hoisted herself onto a barstool. She grinned at Maggie Schaeffer who stood behind the bar, Nike-shod feet spread, arms crossed, her deep-set, hooded dark eyes scrutinizing Kate, the silvery lettering of DYKE POWER on her lavender sweatshirt picking up the silver of her close-cropped hair. Smoke rose in lazy curls from the cigarette in an ashtray behind her.

"The usual?" Maggie inquired in a soft voice incongruous to the burly, assertive-looking woman from which it emerged.

Unbuttoning her jacket, Kate flexed her aching shoulders. "Make it a double."

A young woman wearing a yachting cap and, despite the chill of this May evening, a sleeveless T-shirt tucked into cutoff jeans, swung herself up onto the barstool beside Kate. "A double *is* your usual," she said.

Kate gave a deliberate, audible, exaggerated sigh, then said, "Hello, Patton." She said to Maggie, "Under the circumstances, double my usual double."

Maggie was already pouring Cutty Sark freely over a glass of ice cubes. "Bug off, Patton. Obviously our favorite cop's had a bad day."

A husky Latina wearing a vest and leather pants took the stool to Kate's left. "Cop? This woman's a cop? What the fuck you letting into our bar, Maggie?"

"I even let in queers, Tora," Maggie said, sliding a napkin over in front of Kate and placing the drink on it.

Grinning, Kate turned to Tora, her palm meeting the palm raised in greeting.

"This place has gone totally to hell," said Raney,

one of two black women who had come up behind Kate. "Maggie even lets *us* in." Audie, the other black woman, slid a plump arm around Kate in a brief warm hug.

Sitting angled to the bar, Kate smiled gladly at the five women surrounding her. She had impulsively stopped by here after a lengthy evening meeting with Linda Foster, the need to be in this place more compelling than her desire to go home to the singular comforts of Aimee. These lesbian faces, this warmth, this companionship, were exactly what she had come here looking for.

"Why the double dose of poison?" Patton asked Kate. "The murder business slowing down?"

"Never." The scotch was familiar welcome hotness in her throat, a faithful spreading warmth throughout her body, its action even swifter tonight: she had scarcely eaten all day. "The Teddie Crawford case," she said.

The five women waited in sudden stillness. They were following every phase of the case, as was the entire gay community. The *Los Angeles Times,* surprisingly, had carried an article about the forthcoming trial, and several out-of-state gay press reporters had called Kate, seeking information or commentary. She could offer nothing beyond the statement that the case was being vigorously prosecuted.

Kate said heavily, "We finished jury selection today."

"Ah," Maggie said.

"Jury selection," Patton scoffed. "You mean picking kangaroos for the kangaroo court?"

Swirling the scotch around her ice cubes, Kate closed her eyes for a moment to inhale the smell of coffee brewing on the bar behind Maggie, and a faint aroma of Aramis from Raney, recognizing the scent from a certain patrol cop who doused himself in it. On the jukebox Whitney Houston began "All At Once."

Patton rubbed her hands over her bare thighs. "Have I got this scoped out right? The kangaroos can't figure out why we need a trial over a dead fag."

"Patton, for once give it a rest," Maggie said, looking at Kate. "The woman's dead tired. The woman's told us before she can't comment on the case."

"Jury selection's a matter of public record, Maggie." She would not take the offered out. "I can talk about this."

Kate fixed her eyes on the amber liquid in her glass. "The deputy district attorney asked each person in the jury pool one basic question: Do you think a homosexual is as good as anyone else?"

"Dumb question," Tora said, hands on her hips. "Everybody knows we're scum."

Kate did not smile. Her mind filled with images of faces, faces containing not hate but earnest expressions of discomfort and a straining for tolerance. "Four people said we were mentally ill. Four more said we wouldn't have problems if we'd stop pretending we're normal and just keep quiet." Kate took a deep swallow of her scotch, seeing again Linda Foster's tense, impassive face as the young woman questioned and dismissed-for-cause one potential juror after another.

"Well, sure," Patton said. "Jeez, that nice pope says it's okay for us to love each other, so long as we just don't *touch.*"

Audie ran a fluid hand over Raney's Grace Jones haircut. "That's reasonable enough, don't you think so honey? Let's never touch, what do you say?"

Raney's histrionic groan drew a smile from Kate. She continued, "One woman couldn't get it through her head why we made life so tough on ourselves when we could just go out and get ourselves cured."

Audie nodded sagely. "Just say no. You hear that, Raney honey?"

Raney groaned again. "Audie," Kate said, grinning at her, "what about this business one guy mentioned, about homos in the schools teaching kids to be queer?"

"Well sure," said Audie, a kindergarten teacher. "We call the course Queer 101."

"Listen," Patton said amid the laughter. "Let's pick a kangaroo court for Kate and get this stupid trial over with." As Diana Ross began "Where Did Our Love Go?" Patton leaped from her barstool and began dancing. "Okay, all together now, name the slimebag who's got to be the judge."

"Jesse Helms," came the chorus.

"Yeah yeah yeah," Patton crooned. "On the jury we for sure got Danne-meyer, Dor-nan, An-i-ta Br-y-ant —" She snapped her fingers as she sang and danced.

"William F. Buckley," Kate said, laughing, her

body swaying to the infectious beat of the song. "For the guy who said Buckley was right about us needing to be tattooed."

"Four, we got four," Patton said, ticking him off on her fingers as she spun.

"Patrick J. Buchanan," said Tora, dancing opposite Patton.

"Yeah, yeah, that's five." Patton dipped and swayed. "And that Cardinal back East, what's his name? Six. Hey, we got to have Phyllis Schlafly and her righteous hair spray. Seven!" she shouted. "Do I hear eight?"

"Eddie Murphy and Andrew Dice Clay," said Raney, bopping and spinning to the music.

"Nine. We need three more —"

"And two alternates," Kate said, beating both hands on the bar.

"Easy," Maggie said, who was doing her own stiff-legged boogie behind the bar. "The supremes."

"Our Diana Ross?" Raney exclaimed, stopping to gesture at the jukebox. "The fuck you say."

"No, knothead," Tora said, energetically tapping the heels of her cowboy boots as the song reached its final chords. "Those five fools on the Supreme Court that said we don't count."

"Yeah, right. There you are, Kate," Patton said, collapsing back on her barstool and dusting her hands. "A judge and jury who know all about our lives. Perfect."

As the song ended, the other patrons in the bar burst into applause for the impromptu dance, adding a few cheers and whistles.

Applauding along with them, Kate said, "Thank you all very much, that takes care of it."

Audie slid an arm around Raney. "So . . . what kind of jury did we actually end up with?" Her dark eyes added, *And what do you think about it?*

"Six women, six men," Kate said, quickly sobering, calling into her mind the faces in the jury box that she had scrutinized for every possible clue. "Two women alternates."

"More women on the jury itself would be better, I think," Maggie said softly.

Kate nodded. "The defense figured that, too." And Kenneth Pritchard had maneuvered as deftly as Linda Foster. "Of our twelve, two men and two women are black, one's a Latina, one's a male Chinese." She added, "Big city juries tend to have older citizens, they're more likely to have the time to serve. But our jury has three men and one woman under forty, two males in their twenties."

"That seems good," Raney said. "Don't you think?"

"Bigots come in thirty-one flavors," Patton said.

"Patton's right about that," Kate said.

But she did think that the jury's age composition was an area where clearly Linda Foster had out-thought Kenneth Pritchard. Foster had selected older women and younger men, subscribing to Gloria Steinem's dictum that men tended to become more conservative as they aged, while women, with their children grown and off on their own, looked around at the world and turned into radicals. Also, younger males on the jury might add balance to the jury's view of cocaine at the murder scene.

"The mix of people on the jury seems representative," Maggie commented.

"Representative of *what?*" Patton's voice echoed in

the bar; every woman in the place looked over at
them. She jabbed a finger toward Kate. "Ask this
woman — *ask* this woman how many gay people are
on this jury!"

"Patton, I have no idea," Kate said calmly. "The
question was never asked."

However, Kenneth Pritchard had used his
allotment of peremptory strikes — the dismissals
used by each side to disqualify potential jurors
without citing a reason — very carefully. Toward the
end of the lengthy selection process, two jurors
accepted by Linda Foster had been dismissed by
Kenneth Pritchard because, Kate was certain, they
fit gay stereotypes: the woman had short hair and
wore mannish pants and the male spoke in a
high-pitched voice.

A slender Latina in a maroon sweatsuit came up
and circled Tora with an arm. "Hi, Kate. You've all
been having a great time over here."

Tora winked at Kate, then said to her partner, "I
got a question for you, Ash. Do you think a
homosexual is as good as anyone else?"

"Well . . ." Ash rubbed her chin. "I wouldn't
want my daughter to marry one."

Laughing, the group began to move off into the
bar. Patton said to Kate, "I know you need your
beauty sleep for tomorrow or I'd whip your ass at
pool."

"Next time, Patton," Kate said. "And we'll see
whose ass gets whipped."

As Patton wandered away, Patsy Cline sang the
piercing opening notes of "Sweet Dreams." Maggie

said, "Speaking of sweet dreams, how's Candice Taylor?"

Kate grinned at Maggie's name for Aimee, a cross between Candice Bergen and Elizabeth Taylor, Maggie's opinion of Aimee's beauty. "For the duration of the trial you can call Candice Taylor the widow Taylor. She's still adjusting to life with a homicide cop."

Maggie caught someone's eye across the bar, nodded, took two pilsner glasses from a plastic tub. Filling them with draft beer, she said, "Kate, she'll keep on trying to adjust till you share your work with her."

Kate sighed and swallowed more scotch. "Look, she's beautiful because she's young, fresh, naive. I tell her some things, but I'm not going to come home and dump ugly all over her. Case closed."

Maggie's warm, calloused hand covered Kate's. "Katie, it's good to see you loving somebody. But the way you are with this young woman — holding back — you're still lonely."

Kate sighed again and did not respond. They had had this conversation before. "I need to get home to her, Maggie. Tomorrow's a very big day."

Maggie placed the draft beers on a tray and then leaned across the bar. She said softly, "Kate, about this jury. Tell me what you honestly think. Do we have a chance in hell?"

Finishing her drink, Kate rattled the ice cubes, reflecting over the question. "I honestly don't know, there's no way anyone can ever figure a jury. But . . ." In her mind was the level, gray-eyed gaze of the strong-faced grandmother she hoped would be the jury foreperson. "Maybe we've got reason to hope . . . maybe this jury will be fair."

"Fair," Maggie repeated, picking up her tray. "Isn't that all we've ever asked on this earth?"

PART TWO

— 11 —

"Come to order, court is now in session."

At the command from the Bailiff, the murmuring conversations broke off in the fifteenth floor courtroom, Division 113 of Superior Court, in the downtown Criminal Courts Building in the city of Los Angeles.

Kate, seated in the first row outside the railing behind the counsel table, watched as Judge Alicia Hawkins, a stack of documents in one arm, entered and moved to the bench. Without a glance at her respectfully quiet audience she took her place

beneath the large gold medallion of the Great Seal
of California, sitting precisely between the flags of
the United States and California, the high back of
her modular chair extending several inches above her
dark hair. Picking up a pair of half glasses attached
to a chain around the neck of her judicial robes, she
perched them on her nose and frowned at the
contents of her folder.

Kate had been a witness in cases before Judge
Hawkins and knew she was a woman of quick if
impatient intelligence who held her courtroom under
strict control. Kate liked the formality. The casual-
ness, the laxity of other courtrooms seemed to
degrade the majesty of the laws of a society
enforcing its code of civilized behavior.

She remembered with gratitude the Judge's
handling of the pre-trial motion to quash Kyle
Jensen's confession, a suppression hearing at which
Kate had testified for three hours. The hearing had
been important to the defense because the stakes
were high: the possibility of having Kyle Jensen's
confession ruled inadmissible as evidence.

With gentility and every courtesy, Kenneth
Pritchard had gone for the jugular, deluging Kate
with insistent pin-point challenges to her every
contact with Jensen, an exhaustive process designed
to break her concentration and elicit a response
different from a previous answer. At the first
objection from Linda Foster that Pritchard was
repeating his questions, Judge Hawkins had
sustained the objection. And from then on, she had
displayed her own gift for pin-point detail,
remembering what he had asked from even an hour
before, and how he had asked it, forbidding

repetition. And she had ended the hearing by throwing out the motion to quash.

"*The People versus Jensen,*" Judge Hawkins said crisply. "Case number A9471341. Is the defense ready?"

Kate watched in a gathering of tension as the immaculately tailored Pritchard rose to his feet. "Yes, your honor." His deep voice resonated in the quiet room.

"Are the People ready?"

Linda Foster did not rise; she hastily finished a note on a yellow legal tablet, looked up and answered quietly, "Yes, your honor."

The judge focused on the court reporter seated at the desk below her, his face blank, his hands poised over his machine. His fingers danced to her words: "Yesterday we finished empaneling and instructing the jury." Her gaze encompassed the jury box. "Good morning, ladies and gentlemen." The brief smile was luminous on her thin dark face. Over their hesitantly murmured responses she continued, "Today we begin with opening statements. Are the People ready?"

"Yes, your honor."

Foster pulled the yellow sheet of paper from the legal tablet, slid it under a sheaf of notes, gathered up the notes in a black leather binder and moved to the small podium facing the jury box.

Kate assessed the conservative lapel-less navy blue jacket fitting down over the hips, the white silk blouse with a tie, the knee-length skirt, the navy blue pumps with modest heels. Foster's severely conventional clothing and lightly made-up face seemed adequate enough compensation for her

stylishly frizzy hair and oversize rose-tinted glasses.
And the jury would not know that she was a rookie
deputy district attorney about to make the opening
statement of her first homicide case.

Foster placed her notes on the podium, her long
fingers straightening the pages with unstudied grace.
Unhurriedly, she contemplated the six women and
six men, who stared solemnly back at her. Finally,
she placed both hands over her notes and leaned
toward the jury. Kate too leaned forward, her pulse
accelerating.

"Good morning, ladies and gentlemen." Foster
smiled, and held the smile as the jury chorused its
response. "For the next several days you will learn
about a young man named Teddie Crawford. A
bright, talented, beloved young man. A young man
on the threshold of his life. You will learn exactly
how this young man died. And you will learn why
this man —" She broke off. Without turning her
head she pointed behind her.

Kate's gaze, along with that of the jury, flashed
to Kyle Jensen. Wearing black chinos and a blue
shirt under a dark blue crewneck sweater, he
slouched beside Kenneth Pritchard in easy athletic
grace, arms crossed, legs straight out in front of him
and balanced on the heels of his shoes; he stared at
a spot on the floor in front of the jury box. Linda
Foster continued quietly, "You will learn why this
man, Kyle Jensen, killed him."

Foster looked down at her notes. "We will
present convincing evidence of an act of first degree
murder. But first . . ." She closed her notebook,
concealing her notes under its black cover. "Before
that, I want to speak directly and candidly."

She leaned forward, her hands extended over the
podium and loosely clasped. "Teddie Crawford was a
gay man." Her eyes rested on one juror after
another. "Whatever you think about that, he would
not want the fact minimized in this courtroom.
Because Teddie Crawford had accepted his life as a
gay man. He never pretended to be anything else.
He lived his life — his brief life — openly as a gay
man. The defense will tell you the defendant did not
know Teddie Crawford was gay until moments before
the defendant killed him. We will prove to you the
impossibility of such a claim. We will prove to you
that in the early morning hours of February fourth,
this defendant —" Again she pointed behind her,
"— committed first degree murder. This defendant
knew Teddie Crawford was gay. This defendant knew
exactly who he was killing and why."

Linda Foster leaned back and opened her
notebook. "Now I'll tell you exactly what happened
that night."

There was a collective sigh in the courtroom, a
release of tension. Kate herself remembered to
breathe. She was heady, almost dizzy with the sheer
theater of what she had just witnessed. In her
estimation, rookie Linda Foster had conducted
herself, and the opening of her first homicide trial,
perfectly.

Kate had known that Foster would take her
advice about confronting the issue of Teddie
Crawford's sexual identity — but she had not known
how unflinchingly Foster would strip it open. And
now that it was out there . . .

". . . met Teddie Crawford at Malone's Bar,"
Foster was saying, "a place frequented by the

defendant. Teddie Crawford invited him to his restaurant. And the defendant, with every evidence — every evidence, ladies and gentlemen — that Teddie Crawford was a gay man, took him there on his motorcycle . . ."

The jury sat unmoving. The youngest of the six women, a straight-haired blonde wearing glasses, drew Kate's notice; she was slumped in her seat, her head so ˙ low that she appeared to be gazing into letters on her blue sweater that spelled PARIS.

As Linda Foster stepped over to the large sketch of the murder scene stipulated for use in the opening statements, Kate consulted her jury chart. Number four was Judy Harrow. Thirty-eight years old, a telephone operator, married to a telephone repairman, no children. As Kate watched her, juror number four raised her head, flicked a glance over the crime scene sketch, then resumed her contemplation of her sweater. Kate decided that maybe number four would be all right, she simply had her own way of listening and absorbing information.

". . . and here in the tiny kitchen of Tradition, the defendant, five-feet eleven inches tall to Teddie Crawford's five feet-eight, outweighing Teddie Crawford by forty-three pounds, overpowered him and repeatedly stabbed him, stabbed him to death. And afterward, with Teddie Crawford bleeding and dying on the floor, amid the indescribable horror and gore of this murder, he attempted to clean himself off at the sink of Teddie Crawford's restaurant. He took the watch, ring and wallet from the dying man's mutilated body. Soaked in blood from head to foot, he went home . . ."

Juror number eight, the older woman Kate thought might end up as jury foreperson, unbuttoned the gray blazer she wore over a navy blue skirt and blouse, and settled in to rapidly copy the crime scene sketch into a spiral notebook.

". . . the defendant's own admission of his crime. This defendant is guilty of murder in the first degree and we will prove that guilt to you. And we will prove it beyond a reasonable doubt."

Foster stepped away from the sketch clipped to the courtroom blackboard, moved confidently back to the podium and gathered her notes. "Thank you, ladies and gentlemen, for your attention."

Win or lose, Kate exulted, Linda Foster had come out of her corner battling for Teddie Crawford.

Judge Hawkins finished making a notation. "Mr. Pritchard," she said.

"Thank you, your honor." Pritchard closed his leather binder, picked it up, then tossed the binder back onto the counsel table. Empty-handed, he strode to the podium.

Tall and slim in his dark gray suit and gray-blue striped tie, he stood with his hands at his sides, gazing somberly at the jury as if measuring and absorbing each face. And each juror's face acquired tense self-consciousness under his gaze, Kate noted, including number four, who had raised her attention from her PARIS sweater.

"Ladies and gentlemen," Pritchard began, so softly that the jury leaned toward him. "So far this morning we've had lots of drama in this room from the district attorney." His voice strengthened. "So much drama that I'm reminded of one of those old time movies set on a Scottish moor, one of those

scenes where the special effects man —" Pritchard's
hands began motions of constructing clouds around
him, "— pumps in fog around the feet of the actors
to add lots of damp misty gray atmosphere. The
State is pumping in the same kind of special effects.
Adding billows of fog to what is, when all is finally
said and done in this courtroom, a very sad and
very simple story."

Pritchard's fine, supple hands clasped the sides of
the podium. "The State has declared this case to be
first degree murder. The State has concocted a
fog-filled scenario to dramatize its claim." He paused.
Then his voice rang in the quiet courtroom. "Amid
all the billows of fog the one *fact* is that a young
man is tragically dead." He continued, snapping off
his words, "*Why* he died is the issue before us. *Why*
he died is what the twelve of you must decide."

His voice softened. "As you listen to the State's
witnesses and the State's version of events, do not
for one moment let anything deter you from that one
central question: *why* did this young man die?
Remember that in the State's thirst for a first-degree
murder conviction, they bear the burden of proof.
They must *prove* that the young man seated at the
counsel table is guilty — beyond a reasonable doubt
and to a moral certainty — of premeditated murder."

He fell silent, his gaze again moving from juror
to juror. "We all bear responsibility for our acts," he
said, so quietly that again the jury leaned forward to
hear. "As does my client, Kyle Jensen. And, ladies
and gentlemen, as does the dead man himself, the
young man whose tragic death has brought us here
today."

Again he paused. "When the State has finished

with all of its dramatic posturing, when it has finished filling this courtroom with all of its layers of fog —" Again his hands created billowing clouds, "— you will learn the truth of what happened on February fourth. In the meantime, I ask you for an open mind. Ladies and gentlemen, I thank you for your attention."

Kate looked dismally at the sober faces of the jury. If Pritchard had been surprised by Linda Foster's decision not to minimize Teddie Crawford's sexuality, by her aggressive attack on Kyle Jensen, he had recovered quickly.

Judge Hawkins finished making a note and looked up. "Ms. Foster, do you have anything further?"

"No, your honor," Linda Foster said evenly.

"Are the People ready to proceed?"

"Ready, your honor."

"Call your first witness."

— 12 —

As a somber-faced Francisco Caldera left the stand, Judge Hawkins became involved in a low-toned conference with her court clerk. Kate glanced at her watch. Gloria Gomez, next to be called, would probably conclude her testimony before the judge recessed for lunch.

Caldera, clad in flowing black trousers and the same oversize gray jacket he had worn at the preliminary hearing, seated himself beside Gloria Gomez who took his hand and patted it, then resumed her staring at Kyle Jensen. Gomez had

declared that she would not miss a moment of the
trial, but had also pledged to conduct herself with
restraint. Pritchard had not insisted on sequestering
trial witnesses from the courtroom; Kate suspected
that he wanted to portray his client as an underdog
to the jury, he wanted a courtroom of supporters for
Teddie Crawford in contrast to virtually none for
Kyle Jensen.

Caldera had given the same testimony as before
but with a calmer demeanor. In the four-month
interval since Teddie's death he had become even
thinner, his eyes shadowed and remote as if he had
learned stoic endurance of his pain. From what Kate
had heard, Tradition was failing; neighborhood
customers shunned the restaurant, and gay patrons
were also avoiding a scene of nightmare.

Behind Kate, Burt Dayton squirmed on the
uncomfortable wooden bench, his shiny electric-blue
shirt straining over his body-builder torso. Dayton,
Kate had learned, made daily jail visits to Jensen;
had brought Jensen the clothes he now wore in the
courtroom.

Joe and Margaret Crawford were not present;
Kate was relieved that they had chosen not to
witness a proceeding that would flay them with
repeated grisly depictions of Teddie's death. But Carl
Jacoby, Teddie's ex-lover, was here, a dark, scowling,
bristling presence in the row behind Burt Dayton.
Jacoby had refused to cooperate with Linda Foster,
refused to speak to Kate other than to characterize
Officer Mark Parks, who had initially interviewed
him, as "a Nazi gay-hater." Kate had urged him to
file a complaint, but he had disdained both her and
her advice.

No one, Kate reflected, could ever fully realize the agonies inflicted on a homicide victim's survivors. Friends and acquaintances who immediately flocked around with protestations of shock, with fervent offers of support, soon resumed their own lives, while the bereaved were left to endure an endless gauntlet — the loved one's death agonies dissected in callous detail as the case dragged its way through a labyrinthine court system that seemed more cruelly capricious than just.

Kenneth Pritchard had had no questions for Caldera, and Kate doubted that he would cross-examine any of these first witnesses. The facts of Teddie Crawford's death were not in dispute, and Pritchard's line of defense had been made clear, not only from his opening statement but also from his take-it-or-leave-it plea bargain offer of involuntary manslaughter. His estimation, obviously, was that a jury would decide no worse — perhaps even acquit his client.

If the trial went as mapped out in Linda Foster's strategy session, the patrol officers at the crime scene would take the stand, then Brian Whitson, the autopsy surgeon who had resigned from the coroner's office, so the story went, to enter private practice in Palm Desert.

Over the next few days Burt Dayton would testify, and Napoleon Carter and his lab technicians, and Charlotte Mead. And then Stacey Conlin, a prosecution witness who, Kate was certain, would come as an unpleasant surprise to Kenneth Pritchard. The strongest witness would conclude the prosecution's case — Kate herself.

Then it would be Pritchard's turn. From the

subpoenas he had issued, he would offer an "expert" on the effects of cocaine; then Kyle Jensen's mother, who was planning to fly in from Pittsburgh, undoubtedly to protest that her Kyle was really a good boy. All of this as a lead up to Pritchard's star witness: Kyle Jensen, testifying in his own defense.

And then there was Kate herself. That Pritchard would attack her objectivity as primary investigating officer she had no doubt. His unfailing courtesy and cordiality to her contained smugness, a coiled assurance. When and how would he attack?

Deliberately, she had not discussed with Linda Foster Pritchard's knowledge of her personal life, and her instinctive certainty that he would attempt to reveal it on the stand. She would tell Linda, of course, but at this point it would only distract the young district attorney from the framework of her case. And Kate herself was still mulling over the ramifications.

Over the past four months, apprehensiveness had built within her. Aimee had sensed she was troubled, but Kate had avoided all discussion. I don't want to alarm her, she had told herself.

But she knew that she simply did not want to hear Aimee's opinion no matter how much she was growing to love Aimee, no matter how intelligent and logical Aimee's opinion would be — because it would come from the perspective of a twenty-six-year-old without the life experience to truly know what was at stake. She would tell Aimee after the fact.

Close confidante Maggie Schaeffer had more than sufficient life experience, but Maggie's advice would not deviate an iota from what she had said all along: *There has to be an end to it. All of you staying in the closet will never put an end to it. You have to come out, Kate. How long can you live like this? How long can you tolerate LAPD behaving as if there's something wrong with you?*

The situation was hers to deal with. No one she knew could help her. Anyone else's awareness of the situation would serve only to distract her, just as the knowledge of Pritchard's impending ambush would distract Linda Foster.

But as Kate looked around the courtroom, the knowledge of what she could lose flooded in on her.

She loved this majestic room. She loved being a police officer. She loved that reach into herself to find the fortitude, the sheer guts it took to protect and to serve. She loved the intensity of touching life in the raw. She loved knowing she was good at her work, she loved this one area in her life where she could operate with sureness and competence, where she could sometimes help, sometimes make a difference.

She held no illusions that her sexual orientation was not a subject of conjecture at LAPD. But conjecture was one thing, confirmation another. The discrimination lawsuit against LAPD by former Sergeant Mitch Grobeson was prime evidence of what could happen to even an exceptional cop and an exceptional career.

She could lose what she knew best, loved best. If being a police officer was taken from her, what in the world would she do with her life?

Looking at Kenneth Pritchard out of an immeasurable darkness, she felt anger at Anne. How could Anne ever have had this man for a friend?

—13—

"The People call Charlotte Mead."

Kate sat straighter in her seat in the first row behind the counsel table. She had read the crime reports, had heard detailed testimony from Napoleon Carter and his technicians, but now she would finally hear the impartial analysis that would strengthen — or critically weaken — the prosecution's case against Kyle Jensen. Jensen, in his daily attire of pants and shirt and crew neck sweater, sat in his usual posture beside Kenneth

Pritchard, arms folded across his chest, feet outstretched.

Mead, a neat sheaf of papers under one arm, wearing a navy blue V-neck dress unadorned by scarf or jewelry, entered the inner court through the railing gate held open by the bailiff, clumping her way to the stand on loose-fitting square-heeled pumps.

Linda Foster, unobtrusive in a simple gray suit and wine-colored scarf, completed her standard questions eliciting Charlotte Mead's academic and professional credentials as an expert witness, then said, "Ms. Mead, would you explain to the jury your approach to this particular crime scene."

"Certainly." Swinging around in her chair, Charlotte Mead adjusted her microphone with practiced ease, fixed her pale blue eyes on the jury and addressed them directly. "My job is evidence collection and analysis, to extract information for the court. As customary, I went through this scene with a photographer and an assistant."

Kate smiled. Mead's voice contained not a trace of her on-the-job testiness; her tone was vibrant, her gaze so sharp that even juror number four was constrained to raise her face from her contemplation of the PARIS sweater she had worn since the trial began.

"This crime scene was relatively intact because police presence had been minimal and the decedent's body hadn't been moved. The first thing I did was look at where things were in relation to the body, at whatever looked odd, and then I had the area critically photographed."

Linda Foster, having been briefed by Kate about

how Charlotte Mead preferred to conduct herself in a courtroom, downplayed her own assertive presence by standing well to the side and away from the witness stand, notebook in hand, allowing her witness unimpeded communication with the jury. She asked, "Would you explain what looked odd, and why?"

"Well, the scene was unusually bloody," Mead said, settling comfortably into her chair. "The floor was a massive pool. Scuff marks and footprint impressions everywhere in the blood, a distinct castoff pattern of blood on the wall."

"We'll get into each of those things in a moment," Foster said easily. "What does critically photographing a scene mean?"

Her head cocked to hear the question, Charlotte Mead did not take her eyes from the jury. She said conversationally, "We work only from the scene, but we take reference photographs so we can lay the scene back together. We photograph the entire floor in sequence, the footwear impressions on the floor, the blood spatter pattern on the wall. Then we begin our sketching, measuring, documenting." She gestured with large, blunt-fingered hands. "We measure blood drops to figure the angles of where the blood had to start from to get onto the wall. And of course we take samples, critical stains, cross-sections from the floor and walls."

"What did your samples tell you about the origin of the blood?"

"The first step is called species identification," Mead told the attentive jury — three jurors were taking notes. "We confirmed all the samples were blood, and blood of human origin. We unsealed blood samples taken from the decedent and the defendant

and determined that two ABO types were present,
type O Positive from the defendant and type AB
from the decedent. The preponderance of blood shed
at the scene was type AB from the decedent, but all
blood samples taken from the scene matched blood
samples from either the suspect or the decedent."

Foster made a note on her legal pad. Kate knew
she had paused to allow these facts to sink into the
jury's consciousness. Foster asked, "What determi-
nation did you make about the footwear impressions
in blood?"

"In every case they matched the footwear
collected in evidence from the suspect."

"There were no other footwear prints present?"

"None."

Foster turned to Judge Hawkins and made
reference and confirmation for the record to exhibits
of Kyle Jensen's Puma jogging shoes. She said to
Charlotte Mead, "You immediately informed the
investigating officers at the scene that the suspect
had to have been cut. On what basis did you make
that judgment?"

"There was a single red globule on the counter
near the sink. Here's this massive pool of blood on
the floor —" Mead gestured for the jury as she
continued, "— but this one drop's all by itself. It
could hardly have come from the deceased. And
blood on one of the faucet handles and on a bar of
soap — the usual indications of an assailant trying
to clean himself up. Plus, we had blood spatter
evidence . . . a castoff pattern."

"Before we discuss this castoff pattern, what did
your tests of samples taken from the sink area
show?"

"All the blood from the sink area is O Positive, from the defendant, including blood we isolated in the drain. None of the blood in this area matched that of the decedent."

"Ms. Mead, would you now explain what you mean by a castoff pattern?"

"A castoff pattern occurs when an individual holds an object that's bloody and swings it back." She demonstrated, flinging her hand back. "It'll throw blood off. In this case, we determined that all the blood in the castoff pattern was O Positive from the defendant, and he was throwing blood off his own profusely bleeding hand."

"Objection," Pritchard said. "Outside this witness's area of expertise — she is not an MD."

Foster countered in an incredulous tone, "Your honor, she is a blood spatter expert."

"Overruled," said Judge Hawkins impassively.

Foster said to Mead, "How did you know he was bleeding profusely?"

"The size of the castoff drops in ratio to their height — and the position of the decedent's body."

Mead consulted the notes in her lap, and as she proceeded to give precise dimensions to the jury to demonstrate her findings, Foster looked on with a satisfaction that Kate shared. This was effective testimony, and going very well. Foster said, "There was other blood on the wall not in a castoff pattern, is that correct?"

"Yes."

"What can you tell us about that?"

"Well, we measured various key drops. The lowest drop that has an upward direction tells you everything had to take place underneath that drop."

"Ms. Mead, could you clarify that a bit more?"

"This is how it works." Again Charlotte Mead demonstrated with her large square hands. "The direction of blood flung onto a wall has to either be on its way up or on its way down. If the blood is flung up, then the assault had to happen below where the blood was flung up." Focusing on juror number seven, a young man in a gray bomber jacket, Mead said, "Let me go through that again," and nodded afterward as if satisfied that he too understood her.

"Thank you," Foster said. "Previous testimony has established that the victim's hands had wounds — the palms slashed, the little finger of the right hand almost severed. Was there any evidence of a castoff pattern from the victim?"

"No."

"Was there any evidence that the victim ever had the knife?"

"Objection," Pritchard said quietly. "Speculation."

"Sustained," Judge Hawkins said.

Foster said, "Ms. Mead, excluding the castoff pattern, which we've established as belonging to the defendant, to whom did the blood on the wall belong?"

"Entirely to the decedent."

"And how high was the highest drop on the wall?"

"Thirty-seven inches above the floor."

"So," Foster said, "this blood spatter pattern. What conclusions can you draw about it to a reasonable scientific certainty?"

"That these two people had to be down on the floor during the entire altercation."

Pritchard started to rise in objection, then subsided.

"Ms. Mead," Foster said. "We direct your attention to two People's exhibits, numbers twenty-three and twenty-nine."

Again, Kate saw Pritchard tense. He had lost his pre-trial claim that the photos, part of a photographic exhibit of the clothing recovered from the plastic bag taken from Kyle Jensen's apartment, were too inflammatory to be admissible. Number twenty-three was of Jensen's gory jeans. Twenty-nine was of Teddie Crawford's perforated and even gorier shirt.

Foster handed Mead the photo of the vividly blood-soaked jeans. "You examined these jeans as part of clothing the defendant wore the night Teddie Crawford died. What conclusions can you draw to a reasonable scientific certainty?"

"We took cross sections from all over the jeans. The blood is of human origin, and entirely that of the decedent." Charlotte Mead pointed. "Heavy staining in the crotch area is consistent with the defendant straddling the victim."

Foster took the photo to the jury box where it was hastily passed from hand to hand. Foster displayed the second photo. "You examined the victim's shirt. What conclusions can you draw to a reasonable scientific certainty?"

"We took cross sections from all over. All the blood was of human origin, and also that of the decedent."

Taking this photo to the jury box, Foster asked, "What were your findings regarding the vertical marks at the base of the wall?"

"Marks from the decedent's bloody hair. He was slipping around in his own blood as he struggled, got his head soaked, banged it up against the wall."

"Thank you, Ms. Mead," Linda Foster said with satisfaction. "No further questions."

Kenneth Pritchard unhurriedly finished making a note, turned back the page, rose and walked slowly to the witness stand and stood directly in front of Charlotte Mead.

"Ms. Mead, how much of the crime scene did you examine?"

Charlotte Mead did not look at him; she continued her direct discourse to the jury. "My sole area of expertise is blood and blood spatter. I took critical stains from where anyone bled. Off the floor, the walls, the sink area, and of course, the decedent."

"Did you examine the restaurant outside the kitchen area?"

"No, I did not," Mead told the jury.

Pritchard, obviously assessing that Mead would look at him only if he stood directly in front of her with his back to the jury, walked to the left of the witness box and leaned on it in a relaxed manner. "The only place you took critical stains from was the kitchen, you took no critical stains from anywhere else, is that correct?"

"Correct."

"You have alluded several times to the massive pool of blood on the floor. And that identifiable footwear impressions belonged entirely to Mr. Jensen. How would you explain the absence of footwear prints from Francisco Caldera, who discovered the body?"

"Could be a number of factors. The nature of his footwear — they may have been smooth-soled. The possibility that he slid in the blood, leaving only a scuff mark pattern. Or that he took more care than the defendant in how he conducted himself around the body."

"Move to strike that last remark," Pritchard said to Judge Hawkins. "Speculation."

"Overruled, Mr. Pritchard. You asked for her speculation."

Pritchard's relaxed expression did not change. "In reference to the wounds on Mr. Crawford's hands, you testified that there had been no castoff pattern from Mr. Crawford, is that correct?"

"Correct."

"But the castoff pattern you claim comes from my client — would that not have originated from my client's own wounds?"

"That's correct."

Kate mentally groaned. Charlotte Mead, neutrality personified, would answer Pritchard's questions exactly and without any regard to any shadings, however truthful those shadings might be.

"You stated that the castoff pattern indicated profuse bleeding. Is that not because the wounds were quite severe?"

Charlotte Mead nodded. "Blood like that, the defendant really tore up his hands."

Tore up his hands, Kate thought. The same phrase the emergency room surgeon had used . . .

There had to be — had to be — an explanation for Jensen's hands, an event in the crime scene that analysis had not yet accounted for . . .

"Ms. Mead, where exactly did you find blood that matched that of my client?"

She consulted her notes. "On the counter. The taps. In the drain. On the murder weapon. On the defendant's clothing. The castoff pattern on the wall."

"Nowhere else?"

"Nowhere else."

"Ms. Mead, in a scene which you yourself describe as a massive pool, isn't it possible that the copious amount of blood from Mr. Crawford could have simply masked the presence of other blood?"

She nodded. "Yes, but . . ." She hesitated, as if she would add more, then merely said, "Yes, it's possible."

Pritchard, Kate thought gloomily, was thoroughly undermining Foster.

"Ms. Mead," Pritchard said, "would you repeat your contention about the meaning of the highest drop of blood spatter being thirty-seven inches from the floor?"

"My conclusion, from the height of the spatter and the bloodiness of the scene, is that these two people had to be on the floor during the entire altercation."

"Isn't it possible that there could have been a fight above the floor that did not involve blood being spattered on the wall?"

"Not much of a fight," Mead said.

"Just answer the question please. Was it possible, yes or no?"

"Yes."

"You found hair marks on the wall. Did you find actual hair you could identify as that of Mr. Crawford?"

"No sir, we found no individual hairs. But the decedent's —"

"Isn't it true that the hair marks could also have been those of Mr. Jensen?"

"Well, only if —"

"Yes or no."

"Mr. Pritchard," said Judge Hawkins, "allow this expert witness to answer your questions."

"Yes," Charlotte Mead answered simply. Judge Hawkins smiled.

Kenneth Pritchard also smiled. "No further questions."

Kate stared at Linda Foster, anxious to see how she would reconstruct what Pritchard had damaged.

Foster, seated at the counsel table, rose but did not approach the witness stand. "Ms. Mead, was there blood in any other area of the crime scene other than what you've testified to?"

"No, there was not."

"The victim's shirt, was it uniformly soaked in the victim's blood?"

"No. Not uniformly. There was much less blood on the front. There wasn't a trace of white left, but some of the upper body areas were pink instead of crimson."

"Did you test the front as well as the back of the shirt?"

"I tested all areas on the shirt."

"Did you find any blood from the defendant?"

"Of all places I sampled on the shirt, I found no blood from the defendant."

"There was no blood on the front of the shirt from the defendant, is that correct?"

"Correct."

"About the hair marks on the wall — can you draw the conclusion to a scientific certainty that they are solely those of the victim?"

"Yes."

"On what basis?"

"Three. reasons. The decedent's hair was soaked in blood. The marks extended no more than four inches above the floor. And the defendant's T-shirt had only traces of blood on the back, meaning that if the defendant put those hair marks on the wall, he'd have had to do it bending over while he was on his knees."

Linda Foster smiled, as did Kate. "Ms. Mead," Foster said. "In your expert opinion, where was the victim during the fatal assault on him?"

"On the floor. From all those marks on the floor and on the wall, and all that blood, he fought for his life on the floor, he never got off the floor."

"No further questions," Linda Foster said.

"Mr. Pritchard?" Judge Hawkins said.

"I have nothing further, your honor."

Linda Foster said, "The People call Stacey Conlin."

The courtroom stirred with interest. Judge Hawkins picked up her half-glasses to scrutinize a thin young blonde in black tights and black mini-skirt, pink tank top and black leather Eisenhower jacket, who teetered to the stand on spike heels that were, Kate estimated, at least five inches high.

Kenneth Pritchard rose to his feet. "Objection, your honor. This individual is not on the witness list."

"Your honor," Linda Foster said, "the importance of this witness did not come to light until after the trial began."

Judge Hawkins nodded. "Very well. You may proceed."

Pritchard sat back down and folded his arms, confident, Kate supposed, that this witness's appearance would by itself damage her credibility.

Stacey Conlin had been mentioned — although not by name — by Kyle Jensen in his recounting of how he had arrived at Tradition on the night of Teddie Crawford's death. But Kate, hard-pressed to complete work on the case without Taylor's involvement, had assigned low priority to interviewing her, never dreaming that Conlin's recollection of that night would result in incriminating evidence.

Conlin took the oath and stated her name. Linda Foster asked, "What is your occupation, Ms. Conlin?"

Conlin pulled a lock of hair back from her face and leaned toward the microphone, gazing uncertainly, shyly, at the jury box. "I'm . . . like, a clerk."

Foster nodded encouragement. "And where do you do this work?"

The voice was soft, but clear. "At the 7-Eleven on the corner of Third and Sweetzer."

"On February fourth of this year, what shift were you working?"

"Graveyard."

Judge Hawkins chose to ignore a few titters in the courtroom. Linda Foster asked, "Is that eleven to seven?"

"Yeah."

"Do you see anyone in this courtroom who came into the store during your shift?"

"Yeah. Him." She pointed a pink, inch-long fingernail at Kyle Jensen. "He came in with Teddie. Teddie Crawford."

"Let the record show that the witness has pointed out the defendant," Foster said. "What time was this, Ms. Conlin?"

"Five after two."

"How do you know the time?"

"Teddie said my watch was really neat. So, like, I looked at it. How you do when somebody says that."

Kate grinned as Conlin pushed up the sleeve of her leather jacket to reveal a red plastic wrist watch with a face only slightly smaller than a saucer.

Foster was also smiling. "Did you know Teddie Crawford well?"

"Yeah, he came in all the time."

"On the night in question, did Teddie say anything else to you?"

"Yeah. He was buying cigarettes for this dude —"

"You mean the defendant?"

"Yeah."

"Teddie bought the cigarettes?"

"Yeah."

"You're positive of this?"

"Yeah, he gave me a fifty-dollar bill and I kidded

him about it." Again the pink fingernail pointed. "He was showing off for this dude."

"Objection!" Pritchard said vehemently. "Speculation, move to strike."

"Sustained. Strike that last remark," Judge Hawkins instructed the court reporter. "The jury will disregard."

Foster said, "Tell us what happened — what was said between you and Teddie, as best you remember it."

"Okay. Like, he came in with the dude —"

"Objection," Pritchard complained. "Objection to the witness's characterization of my client."

"Ms. Conlin," Judge Hawkins said softly, "you might refer to Mr. Jensen by name or as the defendant."

Stacey Conlin held up both pink-fingernailed hands. "Like, I call all the guys dude, no offense. Anyway, they came in and Jensen says he wants Kent Lights and Teddie plunks down a fifty. So I wink at Teddie and say somebody musta died and left you this big bill. He winks back and says no, he's givin me a test how good I make change. And so I give him the change and he just stuffs it in his wallet without even lookin at it and then he says he likes my watch. So I look at my watch and say that's a real compliment comin from a queen like you. So he laughs and the two of them leave, that's it."

"A queen," Linda Foster said slowly, deliberately. "You called Teddie a queen?"

"Yeah."

"What did you mean by that?"

She fidgeted in the chair. "Like, you know, a queeny gay guy. A gay guy with . . . attitude. You walk the walk, you talk the talk. You know, a *queen.*"

Amid titters in the courtroom Foster said, "And he laughed, you said."

"Yeah."

"You felt okay calling Teddie a queen?"

"Well sure," she said. "He called his own self a queen, he was fine about being gay."

"And the defendant," Foster said. "Where was the defendant while this conversation was taking place with Teddie?"

"Right there. Right beside him."

"The entire time?"

"Yeah. The whole time."

"Thank you, Ms. Conlin. No further questions."

Kenneth Pritchard did not rise from the counsel table. "Ms. . . . Conlin," he said as if skeptical that it was her real name. "You said Mr. Jensen asked for cigarettes and Mr. Crawford plunked down a fifty. Did Mr. Jensen have an opportunity to pay for the cigarettes?"

"He didn't even try."

"Your honor," Pritchard said sharply. "Please direct the witness to answer the question."

"Answer the question yes or no to the best of your ability, Ms. Conlin."

"Uh, no."

Pritchard asked, "Did you exchange any conversation with Mr. Jensen?"

"He asked for the Kents, that's all."

"While you were exchanging witty conversation with Mr. Crawford, what was my client doing?"

Stacey Conlin drew back her shoulders, her tiny breasts outlined in the tank top. "What do you mean, what was he doing? He was standing there."

"Was he looking around at the store, looking at you, what was he doing?"

"I told you, he was standing there the whole time I was talking to Teddie."

"He added nothing to your conversation?"

"Didn't say diddley."

"Then how do you know he was listening to what you said?"

"Cause he was *standing* there."

"Can you say with absolute *certainty* that he was paying attention?" His voice rose. "That he was even *listening?*"

"I told you what went down," she said with dignity. "And that's all I got to say."

"No further questions," Pritchard said.

"I have nothing further," Linda Foster said.

"The witness may step down," Judge Hawkins said, and favored Stacey Conlin with a smile. The jury, Kate saw, had also liked this witness.

Judge Hawkins adjourned for the day.

— 14 —

"Kate, come on in." Lieutenant Mike Bodwin beckoned energetic welcome from behind his desk, gesturing her to a chair.

Closing his door, Kate took a seat across from him amid the comfortable clutter of a room pleasantly redolent of pipe tobacco. Windowless to the outside world as were all the cubicles in the Detectives Squad Room, the lieutenant's office was paneled in dark wood, but well-lighted, the walls brightened by LAPD award plaques and commendations. Papers, file folders and notebooks lay

in haphazard stacks on his desk and credenza, along
with family photos and an array of golfing trophies.

Bodwin leaned toward her, his broad shoulders
hunched inside his suit jacket. "You look tired,
Kate."

"I am," she admitted.

On this late afternoon of day four of the trial her
gray jacket and pants felt as grimy as their color.
And she still had a meeting with Linda Foster
before this day would end. Shifting her hips on the
hard plastic chair, resenting more than usual the
polite small talk necessary before she could state her
business, she said, "Every time I take a homicide
case to court, I wish I knew a better way to prepare
and stay on top of the mountain of detail."

Rubbing two fingers across a jaw lightly pitted
with acne scars, he looked at her with narrowed
dark eyes. "Yeah, and this is a rough case, Kate."

"No problems in being ready, though," she
assured him, uncomfortable under his scrutiny. How
much did he suspect of the conflict between her and
Taylor? She didn't know Mike Bodwin very well, but
she did not mind this craggy-faced, slightly
portentous officer, one of many officers she had
worked under in her police career. In his first year
at Wilshire Division he had dispensed a minimum of
supervision; whether this was due to his own
uncertainties as a supervisor or a reasoned decision
to allow her performance to speak for itself, she did
not know, and had not cared about knowing, until
now.

She said, "We're well prepared for court,
Lieutenant. But my work on this case wasn't as
timely as it should have been." She sat up in her

chair, anger again rising with the memory of Stacey Conlin's testimony. That a key witness had to be inserted into a trial at virtually the last minute might make for good television drama, but it was damned poor police work.

Bodwin said drily, "Carrying this case by yourself might have something to do with it."

She looked at him. "Ed's talked to you, then."

He shook his head. "The case file talked — all those reports with just your signature. And I'm not quite as dumb as I look." He took his cold pipe from the ashtray, knocked out the ash, set it back down. "You run your own show, no problem, you and Ed are pros." He picked up a gold Cross pen. "Then you work a major case by yourself, you formally request an appointment for the first time since I've been in the department, you come in and close my door." He grinned. "Looks like serious shit to me."

Disarmed by his grin, she smiled back. "I've always appreciated your confidence in me, Lieutenant. And you're right — the reason I'm here is the Teddie Crawford case." She continued soberly, "Going solo on a major death investigation is something I don't want to do again, there's too much risk of error. But any death investigation Ed Taylor and I handle could turn out to be another Teddie Crawford case."

"Listen Kate, it's tough." He continued carefully, "These are changing times, it's tough as hell keeping up with all the shit we have to do to please everybody. But I damn well expect anybody who wears a badge to do their job the best way they know how. If somebody has trouble with that, I need

to know it. But I can't solve any problem unless I'm
clear on what it is. What are you telling me about
you and Ed?"

She released a breath. "Only that I request
another partner."

Bodwin's face did not change. He tapped his pen
on his blotter. "Want to tell me about it?"

"No, sir."

Lacing his pen through his fingers, he was silent.
It occurred to Kate that Bodwin had chosen not to
smoke his pipe in her presence. She was irritated by
the absurdity of it, and that she could not very well
tell him to go ahead and smoke in his own office.

He said, "You and Ed, seven good years. What
would it take to patch this up?"

"At this point," Kate ventured, "a new partner
would probably be good for us both."

He grinned faintly. "A new partner for Ed would
mean he'd have to work."

She did not respond, unsure whether he was
joking or probing.

"Like I said, Kate, I'm not as dumb as I look. I
know how much water he rows. We both know Ed's
got his twenty years in, he can pull the pin any
time. We put him with another partner . . ."

He sighed. "He's a fixture in this office. And
you're the best homicide cop I've got. I've often been
tempted — but, well, you and Ed have worked so
well together, nobody really wants to disturb a good
thing."

He put the pen down and steepled his fingers.
"You really want to do this, Kate?"

She said firmly, "I have to."

He sighed again. "Well, right now I want you to focus on this case, finish it up. When do you testify?"

"Tomorrow morning."

He consulted his calendar. "I'll sit in." Looking at her, he frowned. "Some problem with that?"

"No sir," she said.

"How's the case look?"

She managed a smile. "You know how these things are — the homicide could be on film and still be touch and go with a jury. But we've got an excellent prosecutor." She got to her feet. She had to see that prosecutor now — one final difficulty on this difficult day.

Bodwin said, "I'll get back to you, Kate. But I want you to think on this some more."

"Yes, sir," she said.

Leaving his office, looking around the familiar, crowded confines of the Detectives Squad Room, she felt a sense of disorientation, of displacement. Her police career had moved into uncharted waters.

Linda Foster, her suit jacket tossed over a file cabinet, sat at her desk immersed in a legal brief, the sleeves of her white silk blouse pushed up above the elbows. Casting a glance at Kate, she jerked her head at the Farberware coffee pot. "Be useful, get us some coffee." Focused again on her reading, she groped for her coffee mug and handed it to Kate.

Kate did as she was instructed and then sat

across from Foster. Foster finally put down the brief, took off her glasses and tossed them on top of it, massaged her temples. "God, am I pooped."

"Tell me about it," Kate said.

Foster grinned, animation lighting the gray-green eyes. "But it's going okay. Considering the meat of the case is still to come."

"Yes. We'll know a lot more when we see Jensen on the stand."

"Him, yeah." Foster waved a hand. "I was thinking about your testimony."

Kate took a deep breath. "I need to talk to you about that. Beyond just going over the questions you'll ask on the stand."

"Sure." Cradling her coffee mug in both hands, Foster looked at her inquiringly.

"You don't want any surprises. So there's something I need to tell you."

Foster started to say something. Looking into Kate's face, she nodded instead, holding her mug very still.

Kate said, "Remember I told you I knew Kenneth Pritchard from before? I never did know him all that well. But a woman I . . . lived with knew him very well. She died six years ago." Her gaze fixed on Linda Foster, she said evenly, "Pritchard knows the personal circumstances of my life with her."

Foster looked down, turning her mug in her hands, looking into its contents. "Okay. Am I stupid? I don't get how that's connected with your testimony tomorrow."

Kate said quietly, "I believe he'll try to bring out

my private life when I'm on the stand. To make the
point to the jury that I'm prejudiced in my
investigation of the death of a gay man."

Foster closed her eyes. "Fuck." Again she looked
into her coffee mug. "Yeah. He seems enough of a
slime to do that. And it shouldn't fly a foot.
But . . ."

"But it might," Kate finished for her.

"No, I really don't think it'll fly. It shouldn't get
past the objection stage. But the jury will hear the
question. And that's all Pritchard really wants."

"My lieutenant will be in court tomorrow."

"Double fuck." Foster put down her mug. "Kate, I
can't prevent Pritchard from asking the question."

"I know that. You're certain Judge Hawkins will
disallow it?"

"Reasonably certain. She *should* disallow it. But I
can't guarantee it."

"If she does allow it —"

"Say no more." Foster held up a hand. "I
appreciate your telling me. If lightning strikes a part
of Hawkins' brain, and she overrules my objection, I
don't need to know how you'll answer Pritchard."

Kate nodded.

"I have to tell you this, Kate. The way I read it,
the way I read him, he may hold off, not ask the
question on cross-examination. He may really set it
up — not cross-examine you at all, but reserve his
right to question you later, and then call you as a
defense witness."

Kate sat perfectly still. "Triple fuck," she said.

Linda Foster chuckled. After a moment, Kate
joined her. Their laughter filled the office, reaching
frenzied heights.

"This case," Foster gasped, wiping her eyes. "This case is a wonder. I'll tell you one crazy thing, Kate. I found out I can really get into doing what I do."

"I'll tell you one thing, Linda — you're very good at it."

Foster's eyes, still wet from laughter, met Kate's. "Thanks. That means a lot to me."

There was a sudden, awkward silence. Acutely mindful that what she had revealed lay between them, Kate felt excruciatingly self-conscious. She had never before admitted her sexual identity to a heterosexual person.

"I . . ." Foster cleared her throat, tapped a finger on her desk calendar. "This time of year's always been tough for me. April thirtieth, my daughter would have been ten."

"I'm so sorry," Kate said, taken aback. "What . . ."

"Angie was the brightest two-year-old you can imagine. She managed to get into the garage, found some turpentine."

"Oh my God, Linda," Kate uttered.

"Jack and I were real careful about the blame. But they say most marriages don't survive the death of a child. Ours sure didn't. I won't ever get married again, I know I can't replace Angie. But I'm glad to have the partner I'm with, I'm glad to have my seven-year-old — David's real special to me."

"I'm sure he is." Numbly, Kate searched for something else to say, piercingly aware of what had occurred between herself and this woman she had just come out to, this woman who had in turn disclosed the most painful moment in her life as payment in kind.

"Okay, enough of this having fun," Foster said briskly. "Let me get you some more coffee, let's get to work." Reaching for Kate's mug, she said, "I'll tell you something, my friend. There's one fact Pritchard can't do a thing about. His son of a bitch client is *guilty*. And I'm gonna put him in jail if it kills me. I'm gonna put him in jail till his ass mildews."

— 15—

"The People call Detective Kate Delafield."

Kate took the oath from the court clerk, and settled herself in the witness chair behind the microphone. She had chosen carefully her gray and white houndstooth jacket, gray pants, white turtleneck blouse — conservative clothes, not too sober but appropriate to the gravity of the proceedings, quality clothing that looked good on her and was so simply styled that she would not have to think about adjusting it.

Turning slightly toward the jury, she

concentrated on keeping her posture erect but not stiff. In the arena that was this courtroom, every aspect of her would be magnified and scrutinized, tallied and judged irrevocably. Her competence, and most of all, her credibility, would be assessed each time she spoke: what she said, how she said it, how she looked when she said it. All her months of work on this homicide case would be distilled into the next few intense hours of testimony as she recounted all her actions in the process that had led to the arrest and prosecution of Kyle Jensen.

Lieutenant Bodwin was not as yet present; Kate expected him perhaps mid-morning after she had finished the more routine phase of her testimony. From an angle of vision she could see Kyle Jensen, arms crossed, staring at her; Kenneth Pritchard, neatly attired in a dark blue suit, was doodling with the pen he would use to take notes for his cross-examination.

His cross-examination. She would not think about Kenneth Pritchard and what he would ask. There was no point. From the moment she had walked into that scene of murder at Tradition, events had been set into motion that seemed, at this moment, inexorable.

Do the best you can for Teddie Crawford, she told herself. You're all he has.

You're all he has. She would use it as a mantra.

Linda Foster, smartly turned out in a long maroon jacket over a black skirt, approached Kate with barely subdued eagerness. She loves this, Kate thought. The clash, the contest, the risk. This woman was born to be a high stakes player.

Foster addressed Kate firmly: "Would you please

state your name and rank, where you work and how long you have worked there."

And so it began.

As Linda Foster paused to leaf back in her pages of notes, juror number four put her face down into her PARIS sweater. Her face had been in her chest during Kate's first two hours on the stand, while Kate had testified to each item of evidence she had collected and why, where she had collected it, when she had conveyed it to the crime lab, its property tag number and item number, and the corresponding crime lab number. But juror number four had focused on Kate during the recounting of Jensen's statements, her eyes squinting in concentration behind her glasses, a forefinger absently combing the ends of her straight blonde hair. And the three note-taking jurors had been constantly busy, especially juror number eight, the older woman who remained Kate's choice as probable jury foreperson.

"Detective Delafield," Foster said, finding the note she sought. "In his statement at the hospital and at Wilshire Division about how he cut his hands, the defendant said that he cut them on a ham can in the rear of his apartment building, is that correct?"

"Yes, that's what he told me," Kate said.

"We have offered in evidence the photographs of the search area for that ham can. A can which was never found, is that correct?"

"That's right."

"Nor did you find any blood whatsoever at the rear of the defendant's residence."

"No I did not."

"So the defendant was lying. In his statement about what he stole from the victim's body, the defendant said that he had, and I quote, 'Tossed it. An alley. Don't ask me where. I just tossed it.' Is that correct?"

"That's correct." Foster, Kate thought, was bringing to a skillful and effective conclusion all these hours of testimony . . .

"So the defendant was lying. When you asked the defendant whether he had ever been in a bar named Malone's, or knew the bartender, he denied it — is that correct?"

"Yes, that's correct."

"So the defendant was lying. In the defendant's statement about his whereabouts on the night of the murder, he stated he was with Shirley Johnson. Is that correct?"

"That's correct."

"So the defendant was lying. In the defendant's statement about who helped him remove his blood-soaked clothing, he claimed it was Shirley Johnson when it was actually Burt Dayton. Is that correct?"

"That's correct."

"So the defendant was lying. This defendant lied again and again. All this defendant did was lie —"

"Objection!" Kenneth Pritchard barked.

"Sustained," Judge Hawkins said.

Foster looked into Kate's face. She gave Kate an almost imperceptible grin. A thumbs-up sign of encouragement, Kate knew.

"I have no further questions. Thank you, Detective." Foster strode back to the counsel table.

Kenneth Pritchard rose in leisurely fashion, left his note pad on the counsel table, and approached the witness stand, hands in his pockets. Kate tensed, remembered her body language, and leaned back.

"Detective Delafield." Her name, spoken softly, seemed almost musical in the courtroom.

Kate held his gaze with difficulty, chilled by his easy assurance. She kept her own face expressionless.

"Detective Delafield, when you entered the crime scene on the morning of February fourth, did you see signs of disturbance anywhere except in the kitchen?"

"No, I did not," she said, extending her answer beyond a simple "no" to show her firmness of tone to Pritchard and to the jury.

"Did you see blood anywhere except in the kitchen?"

"No."

"Now, you have enumerated objects collected in evidence which you contend my client took from the defendant — a watch, a ring, and a wallet, is that correct?"

"Correct."

"There was money in Mr. Crawford's wallet when you collected it in evidence, in the amount of sixty-seven dollars. Is that correct?"

"That's correct."

"Money which had not been taken out of the wallet by my client. Correct?"

"Yes."

"Is there a cash register in the dining room of Tradition?"

"Yes."

"Was that cash register disturbed in any way?"

"No, it was not."

"Was the cash drawer open?"

"No."

"Was there blood anywhere on the cash register?"

"No."

"Detective, isn't it true that there was, in fact, money in that cash register?"

"Yes, there was."

"Thank you, Detective," he said softly. Again he smiled at her. "No further questions."

Sagging in relief, the tension emptying out of her, she flashed a glance at Linda Foster. Foster, her lips thinned, her nostrils flared, was glaring at Pritchard as he walked back to the counsel table.

What was Pritchard doing? Why had he not asked her the question she knew he would ask? Why had he not even reserved his right to recall her as a witness? And beyond that, how to explain the sum total of his cross-examination, after her four hours of testimony?

"Redirect?" Judge Hawkins inquired of Linda Foster. If the judge was surprised by Pritchard's conduct, her smooth dark face did not reveal it.

"Yes, your honor." Her face composed, Foster rose to her feet at the counsel table. "Detective, you have just testified that no money was taken from the victim's wallet or from the cash register."

"That's correct," Kate said obediently.

"Wouldn't the condition of the defendant's hands make it imposs —"

"Objection!" shouted Kenneth Pritchard. "Speculation."

"Sustained," Judge Hawkins said impassively. "The jury will disregard the question."

"No further questions," Linda Foster said.

"Do you have anything further of this witness, Mr. Pritchard?" Judge Hawkins asked.

"No, your honor."

"The witness may step down." She looked inquiringly at Linda Foster.

"Your honor," Foster said, "the State rests."

Judge Hawkins nodded, then glanced at the courtroom clock. "Court is in recess until two o'clock."

Only then did Kate think to look out beyond the courtroom railing. To meet the warm, smiling gaze of Aimee. Surprised, nonplussed, Kate managed a grin.

Seated in the back row of the courtroom, Aimee touched her index finger to her lips and blew a surreptitious kiss, then got to her feet and made her unobtrusive way from the courtroom. Kate mentally shook herself, realizing that her tension had been so great, her focus on her testimony so intense, that she had not seen Aimee come in, nor Lieutenant Bodwin, who sat in the front row staring in bafflement at Kenneth Pritchard.

Kate pulled herself to her feet and left the witness stand, passing the counsel table without looking at Kenneth Pritchard or Kyle Jensen.

"Fine job," Bodwin greeted her in the outer court. He jerked his head at Pritchard, who was taking a document from his briefcase. "The look on your face when he said no more questions —" He chuckled. "That's the strangest, most piss-poor cross-examination I've ever seen."

She shrugged. "I have to believe he's got something else up his sleeve."

"Maybe so," Bodwin said indifferently. "Kate, if you haven't changed your mind, I'll be talking to Ed. About our conversation yesterday," he added as Linda Foster came through the railing gate and over to them.

"Go ahead," she told him. "Lieutenant, may I present Linda Foster. Linda, Lieutenant Bodwin."

"Fine job, counselor," he said, nodding to her. "You've got this one in the bag."

"Not hardly, Lieutenant," she answered, her face closed and hard. "But your detective here did an outstanding job."

"We both agree on that." He shook Foster's hand and took his leave.

Kate said in a low tone, "What the hell's Pritchard doing?"

"Fucking theatrics," Foster hissed. "He'll —" She broke off as Pritchard opened the railing gate and came up to them.

"Kate," he said, "I thought I'd serve this on you personally." Smiling, he handed her the document he had taken from his briefcase, and sauntered off.

She looked down at a formal subpoena to appear as a witness for the defense.

"Playing it to the max," Linda Foster snorted. "The slimy little prick."

— 16 —

Ferris Sweeney had been relaxed in the witness box ever since Linda Foster had risen to state courteously that the People would not challenge Kenneth Pritchard's qualification of him as an expert witness in the area of drug and alcohol abuse.

A fiftyish man with thin gray hair combed straight back and a sparse gray moustache, he wore a tweed sport jacket with patches at the elbows. He had been answering Kenneth Pritchard's questions with calm authority.

"So, Mr. Sweeney," Pritchard said, leaning on the

witness stand, "what you've told us here today is that in your years of work with victims of drug abuse, you have determined definite behavior patterns common to users of cocaine."

"Yes, that's right."

"And that cocaine intoxication can result in impairment of judgment."

"Very definitely."

"In *severe* impairment of judgment."

"Indeed," Sweeny said regretfully. "Depending on the amount ingested and the pattern of abuse."

"Can cocaine ingestion result in loss of emotional control?"

"Yes."

"Can it result in uncontrollable behavior?"

"Yes."

"In violent behavior?"

"Yes."

"In homicidal behavior?"

"Yes."

"Thank you," Pritchard said. "No further questions."

Linda Foster rose and moved to the witness stand. "Mr. Sweeney," she said politely, "about cocaine, amounts of cocaine, impairment from cocaine, and all the statements you've made today about this substance. On what controlled scientific laboratory tests do you base your statements?"

He looked disappointed in her. "My observations are empirical of course," he replied. "Based on years of experience in working with alcohol and drug abusers."

Foster looked astonished. "You have no laboratory

source material on which to base any of your claims?"

Sweeney bristled. "In the current political climate in this country, the lack of funded laboratory studies of drugs and drug users is a fact. And a disgrace."

"Mr. Sweeney," Foster said, "have you yourself ever taken or experimented with a controlled substance?"

"No. No, I never have."

"Then your statements are based entirely on your experience in drug abuse programs with chronic drug abusers, is that correct?"

"Yes, that's right."

Foster pointed to the jury and said in an incredulous tone, "So you have come here today to appear before this jury and claim knowledge based not on scientific evidence, but on statements made to you by dope addicts."

Ferris looked even more disappointed in her. "That is a gross —"

She turned to Judge Hawkins and said disdainfully, "I have no further questions of this witness."

Kate, grinning in delight, watched juror number four cross her arms over her PARIS sweater and look scornfully at Ferris Sweeney.

Judge Hawkins impassively asked, "Redirect, Mr. Pritchard?"

Pritchard looked unperturbed. "I have nothing further."

"The witness may step down."

"Your honor, let's get right down to it," Pritchard said. "The defense calls Kyle Jensen."

* * * * *

Kate remembered Taylor's summation of Kyle Jensen's chances at trial: "He could even get off. A jury's looking at this red-blooded normal guy, they'll figure he freaked out and just lost it, that's all."

Jensen's moustache had been freshly trimmed, his blond hair barbered; for his appearance on the stand he had donned a maroon V-neck sweater, navy blue pants and a white shirt with a blue tie. Red, white and blue, American as apple pie, Kate reflected sardonically, watching the faces of the jury and their agreeable evaluation of him. Just your normal blue-eyed, clean-cut, good-looking American boy.

Pritchard, one hand clasping a notebook, the other in his jacket pocket, approached the witness stand, casually elegant in his dark blue suit. He asked without ceremony, "How old are you, Kyle?"

"Twenty-seven."

"What do you do for a living?"

"Before all this went down," he said steadily, "I worked for Green Haven Landscapers."

"And where are you from?"

"Pittsburgh. Been out here about a year."

Jensen's high-pitched huskiness seemed to be playing well in the courtroom, Kate estimated. Masculinity was so often a matter of packaging . . . She remembered one night when she had awakened out of a doze to a high-pitched male voice emanating from the TV, to discover that the voice belonged to Clark Gable.

Pritchard said, "Your father is deceased, is that correct?"

"Yeah, that's right," Jensen said, his face immediately clouding.

An effective opening, Kate conceded. Exploiting the soft spot in Jensen about his father opened Jensen to the jury, won him immediate sympathy.

"He was a veteran of the Korean War, wasn't he?"

"A decorated vet," Jensen corrected him.

"Quite badly wounded, was he not?"

"Yeah, he got shot up pretty bad."

"Your mother is living?"

"Yeah, she can't be here, she's real sick."

Sure, Kate thought, remembering Jensen's contempt for his mother. Pritchard was doing a good job manufacturing all-American credentials for Jensen.

"Do you have brothers or sisters?"

"Objection, your honor," Linda Foster said curtly. "This episode of *The Waltons* is irrelevant."

Kenneth Pritchard spoke angrily into the laughter in the courtroom. "Your honor, this testimony is directly relevant to my client's background and character."

"Objection overruled," Judge Hawkins said disapprovingly to Foster. Kate was delighted by the grins on the faces of the jurors, by Foster's puncturing of the mood in the courtroom.

"Do you have brothers and sisters?" Pritchard repeated.

"No, sir."

"Kyle, I want to move now to the events of February fourth. You were at Malone's Bar on that Friday night." Pritchard waited.

"Yes, sir."

"What were you doing there?"

"Drinking beer. I just stopped in."

"Describe for us your meeting with Mr. Crawford."

Jensen shifted in the witness chair. He already needs a cigarette, Kate thought.

"I'm at the bar drinking my beer. He comes in with this woman and another guy —"

"Why did you notice him?"

"I'm sitting with my back turned to the bar, kind of eyeballing the place and whoever came in the door. Next thing I know he's at the bar getting some beers . . ."

Seated in her usual place in the courtroom, notebook in her lap, Kate listened acutely to the recounting of Jensen's meeting and conversation with Teddie Crawford. She would add her own nuances to Linda's notes of discrepancies between what Jensen had said in Kate's interviews with him and what he was saying now with quiet earnestness to the jury. She remembered how convincing he had been in his hospital room, until she had begun dissecting the truth.

"How many beers did you have at Malone's?"

"Four."

"Who paid for your drinks?"

"Me. I did."

"All right. Now, did you go anywhere in the bar itself with Mr. Crawford?"

"Yeah, the john. The restroom."

"For what purpose?"

"To do some coke."

"Who supplied the coke?"

"We both had some."

Kate made a note and circled it. Jensen had previously claimed that all the cocaine had been supplied by Teddie Crawford.

"How many lines of cocaine did you ingest?"

"Two."

"When you went to the restaurant, how many lines of cocaine did you ingest at the restaurant?"

"Four."

"Whose cocaine?"

"Some his, some mine."

"Kyle, why did you tell the police it was all Mr. Crawford's cocaine?"

"Because I was in deep sh . . . I was in deep enough without getting busted for possession or dealing or God knows what."

"All right. So you're at Tradition. Describe what happened."

"I did the coke, I'm really sailing. He shows me around his restaurant. Then . . ."

Jensen clasped his hands together on the railing of the witness box. He really wants a cigarette bad, Kate speculated.

"Then what happened, Kyle?"

He flicked a quick glance at the jury. "He groped me."

Pritchard moved to stand directly in front of Jensen. "Describe what he did, Kyle," Pritchard said gently, persuasively, like a priest in a confessional eliciting details of a sin.

"Ran his hand across my chest. I stepped away. "Then —"

"How did you feel about that?" Pritchard interrupted. "When he did that?"

"Like I was shot in the back. No damn way did I
expect that."

"Up to this point, Kyle, did you have any inkling
that Mr. Crawford was a homosexual?"

"Not a clue."

At a high-pitched comment of "Oh Mary, please,"
and several other snorts of derision in the courtroom
— Kate recognized Gloria Gomez's voice — Judge
Hawkins rapped her gavel sharply.

Unruffled, Pritchard said, "There was testimony
from a 7-Eleven clerk about conversation between
her and Mr. Crawford. What do you remember about
that?"

Jensen said forcefully, "I went in the place to get
cigarettes. He went in with me, paid before I could
get my money out." He said more heatedly, "I
remember he talked to this brassy-looking clerk, I
didn't pay attention, what did I care what he had to
say to some clerk?"

"All right. At the restaurant, he showed you
around the place. Then what did he do?"

Jensen fixed his gaze on Pritchard. He cleared
his throat. "Skimmed his hand down over my crotch.
Said I . . . said he liked the look of my basket."

"Meaning what?"

"Meaning . . . he liked . . . what he saw between
my legs."

"How did you feel about this comment about your
genitals?"

Jensen's voice rose. "Freaked, totally freaked. I
told him right away I'm not gay. I mean, I was
freaked."

"When you told him you weren't gay, what did
he say to that?"

"He just laughed. He says maybe I need to do more coke."

Kate listened in chilled triumph to this new information, a scenario similar to what she had envisioned the night she had gone alone to Tradition to reconstruct the murder.

Pritchard said, "How did you feel about his remarks?"

Jensen shifted his shoulders, adjusted the tie in the V of his sweater. "Freaked. Totally freaked he said that." The diamond-shaped eyes narrowed, glittered. "Totally freaked he thought coke could make me into somebody like him. Like for even a *second* I could be *anything* like *him*."

"Okay, Kyle. What did you do?"

He clasped the railing of the witness box. "I'm cool. I tell him again I'm not gay. So he laughs and says okay, have it any way I want, come on in the kitchen. So I go in there with him."

"Why? Why did you do what he said?"

"The front door's locked, the kitchen's the way outta there. Besides, my leather jacket's in there."

"Okay, take this one step at a time. So you go into the kitchen. Did you try to leave?"

"Yeah. Yeah, and he gropes me again, he says . . ." He hesitated, flicked his eyes toward the jury, back to Pritchard. "He says I don't have to do anything to him, just let him suck my cock."

Pritchard took several moments to look into his notebook, allowing the words to hang in the courtroom. Kate scanned the solemn faces of the jury, then made a note that Jensen had omitted the coke he had previously mentioned ingesting in the kitchen.

Pritchard asked quietly, "How did you feel when he suggested that sex act, Kyle?"

"I could of vomited on him."

Kate noted that in the interview Jensen had made the identical comment, but in relation to seeing Teddie Crawford with the knife, not in reaction to anything Teddie had said.

"What did you say to him, Kyle?"

"I pick up my jacket, tell him I'm getting the hell out of there."

"Then what?"

"He yanks a big knife out of a rack, holds it up. I say 'Easy, easy.' I figure he's doing it because I'm bigger than he is, it's the only way this fai — this guy's got of making me stay."

A very key ad lib onto his confession, Kate thought, circling her note.

"What did he say to you then, Kyle?" Pritchard asked.

"He says he wants to do me, that's all, and I'll really like it."

Kate flashed a glance over the jury, the twelve as immobile as statues, the six men especially stone-faced. Even one vote for acquittal could result in a hung jury . . .

Pritchard asked Jensen, "What did you say?"

"Nothing. I turn to lay down my jacket, figuring I can get him to relax a little so I can take the knife away. Then I make a quick grab for his wrist." Jensen snaked out his right hand in demonstration for the jury. "But he jerks the knife so I catch it in my hand. So then I go after the knife, I see I got to get it away from him right now or he'll really cut me. So I grab at it with my other hand —" Again he demonstrated. "I knee him and we both go down on the floor. He's still got the knife and he's fighting like an animal, all of a sudden we're fighting like crazy . . ."

Pritchard let silence accumulate. "Then what, Kyle?"

Staring out over the courtroom, he shook his head. "I dunno. I don't remember after that. I just lost it, man. I just fu . . . I just plain lost it. I don't remember after that."

"All right, Kyle. The *last* thing you remember is you're fighting with him like crazy. What's the very *next* thing you remember?"

"Him stopping. He finally stopped fighting me. I see the blood all over the place, all over me, my hands bleeding."

"Then what?"

"I freaked out. All I knew was I had to get the hell out of there. I grabbed paper towels, they soaked right through, I tried to wash up, saw how bad I was cut. So I got some dish towels . . ." He trailed off, looking uncertainly at Pritchard.

Pritchard repeated, "You freaked out."

"Yeah. Yeah, the coke, you know, I was smashed as hell on the coke."

"Kyle." Pritchard lowered his voice. "Kyle, why did you take Mr. Crawford's wallet and jewelry?"

"I was scared spitless, I knew I was in real bad trouble, I figured nobody'd believe what happened, I'd be in the gas chamber for sure. I thought about my fingerprints, I started throwing everything I'd put my hands on into a plastic bag. I took his stuff thinking I could make it look like a robbery."

Kate thought: I may gag.

Pritchard asked, "If you were trying to make it look like robbery, why didn't you go through the cash register?"

"Never thought about it, I couldn't think straight —"

Pritchard repeated, "You couldn't think straight."

"Yeah. Yeah, the coke, I was smashed as hell on the coke."

The second time Pritchard had prompted him on the smashed-on-coke business, Kate thought.

"Then what, Kyle?"

"I got outta there. Wrapped my hands good as I could in towels and climbed on my bike and split."

"Why did you tell the detectives that Shirley Johnson had helped you out of your clothes?"

"Who wouldn't? The guy I got messed up with was a fa — was gay, I didn't want anybody on the cops getting the idea I was gay too. Especially when I share a place with a guy."

Pritchard nodded. "But Shirley Johnson did take you to the hospital."

"Yeah. I didn't want to go, she said all this stuff about infection, said my hands were cut too bad not to go."

"Why did you agree to go to Wilshire Division to be questioned?"

Jensen said angrily, "The woman cop lied to me. Said they had to do some kind of report because my cuts were so bad."

Kate barely smothered a grin.

"I believed her," Jensen said aggrievedly. "I didn't know shit about my rights. I figured I'd really get into hot sh— uh, water if I said no, they'd suspect something funny for sure. I really believed her, I figured I'd just go and get it over with. I was scared, I wasn't thinking too good."

"Were you taking medication for your hands?"

"Yeah."

"At the hospital when they first questioned you?"

"Yeah."

"At Wilshire Division?"

"Yeah. My head wasn't any too clear."

"Kyle, the fact is that on February fourth a man died. How do you feel about that?"

"Terrible. I wish to God I could change what happened." His face, his voice, were earnest. "I never had a clue what happened that night could ever happen." He focused his blue eyes on the jury. "I just hope you believe me, I didn't mean for it to happen."

You didn't mean to get caught, Kate thought, looking at him in cold vituperation.

"No further questions," Kenneth Pritchard said.

Linda Foster rose.

Judge Hawkins glanced at the courtroom clock. "In view of the hour, shall we commence cross-examination tomorrow?"

Foster nodded. "That's quite acceptable, your honor."

— 17 —

"So, Jensen's story — discrepancies up the kazoo." Linda Foster tapped her notebook as if it were a fat bank account. "Pritchard already knows cross-examination will be hell. And Jensen — when I'm through with that bastard he's gonna think he's a McDonald's hamburger."

Kate grinned. She sat relaxed, drinking coffee, in Linda's office upstairs in the Criminal Courts Building.

Foster looked intently at her. "But Kate, I keep thinking about those cuts on Jensen's hands, about

you going to Tradition that night to feel what
happened, to know in your bones how it went down
with Teddie. So, I think it would help if I did what
you did."

She's talking confident, Kate thought, but she's
worried. She said, "Why don't we both go."

"Good," Foster said with alacrity. "Can we meet
around eleven? Is that okay?"

Kate said, "If you get there first, stay in your car
and wait."

Foster grinned at her. "Yes, Officer."

Kate let herself into her apartment.

Aimee came out of the kitchen and embraced her.
Stepping quickly back, she stuffed her hands in the
back pockets of her shorts and said with a touch of
diffidence, "I made spaghetti, I didn't know when
you'd be here."

"Smells wonderful." Shrugging out of her jacket,
Kate savored both the aroma in the apartment and
the sight of Aimee in white shorts and a tank top.
She took off her gun belt, laid it and the jacket
across a chair. "I need to meet Linda in a couple of
hours." She turned back to Aimee and said warmly,
"It was such a surprise to see you there today. It
was good."

"I'm glad." Then Aimee said in a rush, "I decided
this morning to call in sick and go see you but I
wanted to do that since this trial began, I wanted to
ask if it would be okay, you've been so preoccupied I
thought you might be upset if I said anything —"

"I can see that," Kate said contritely, pierced by

the defenselessness in Aimee's face. She had come to
understand that Aimee's assertive ways camouflaged
a precarious confidence. "I get completely involved in
a homicide trial." Much less this one, she thought.
She remembered Anne's good-humored exasperation
at her absences, physical and mental, when a case
was in trial.

Aimee said, "Today I thought I'd just look in the
courtroom and see this Linda Foster, see you on the
stand . . . But there was something about how you
looked — I just had to stay there, be there with
you."

Kate said simply, "I'm very glad you were."

"I was proud of you." Aimee placed her hands for
a moment on Kate's shoulders. "You're so good at
your work, the jury believed every word you said."

Kate captured her hands. "I hope you're right. I
don't know if I could've concentrated as much if I'd
known you were in the room. All I know is how
good it was to see you afterward."

"I'd like to think . . . you need me for
something."

"I do," Kate said in surprise. "I feel so very lucky
about you —"

"I want to be more than that to you. Mostly I
feel like . . . just some kid who sort of stumbled
into your life."

"You're much, much more." She spoke this truth
in wonder. Maggie had said, *The way you are with
this young woman — holding back — you're still
lonely.* Until now she had not been able to see how
desolate her lonely life raft of self-sufficiency had
been.

She squeezed Aimee's hands. "Tomorrow will be

. . . a very hard day for me." For now she could not tell her more. "Could you . . . maybe call in sick again?"

Aimee grinned. "I feel a relapse coming on." She moved toward the kitchen. "Come have dinner before you have to go see this other woman in your life."

Tradition was closed, its front door padlocked. Francisco Caldera had closed the restaurant permanently the day the trial began. Kate led Linda Foster from the alley into the kitchen and flipped the lights on to a room unchanged from her memory; yet she felt an indefinable, terminal alteration in its atmosphere. Like Teddie Crawford, Tradition, also, was gone. Tradition, also, had bled to death. She looked around with poignant regret, with mourning.

Foster placed her briefcase on the counter. Gesturing Kate to silence, she paced the kitchen, arms crossed over her cotton knit sweater, grimly looking at the pristine floor and walls. She walked into the restaurant; Kate knew not to follow. Instead she emptied her own briefcase, spreading photos and drawings across the table.

Several minutes later Foster came back into the kitchen, head down, hands shoved into the pockets of her black denim pants. Again she paced back and forth, the only sound an occasional squeak from her tennis shoes on the tile floor.

She finally muttered, "I'm goosebumps from this place, fucking goosebumps."

Kate picked up the photograph given to her by Gloria Gomez, an image of a dark-haired young man in three-quarter profile, smiling, his brown eyes lighted with eagerness. She had looked at this photo many times, but now she said thickly, through a throat filling with tears, "Teddie had so much life in him, he had so much guts . . ."

"Especially compared to the shit who killed him." Foster yanked open her briefcase and dumped out its contents — documents, a notebook, a plywood model of a knife — and said with fierce impatience, "So, you're convinced Teddie never had the knife. Jensen's cuts say different, his cuts are the defense's big weapon. Let's brainstorm a scenario I can attack with."

Kate pointed to a set of drawings, the emergency room surgeon's sketches of the wounds in Jensen's hands. "We'll start with Jensen's claim of how Teddie was holding the knife, see if there's any possible way his cuts could have happened that way." She picked up the plywood knife. "Okay, I'll be Teddie . . ."

Half an hour later, having traded roles, having tried every variation on a knife fight she could think of, Foster said in frustration, "Jensen's cuts make no damn sense at all, Kate. Okay, granting there's some way he could slice his thumb and the palm of each hand — how could he get all those cuts on his fingers at the same time from a single-edge blade? How did he even *get* those little cuts? You grab a knife that's coming at you with your hand, not your fingers. And how in hell did he manage to get cut on the *outside* edge of his right palm? Strong as he is, how could he get so *many* cuts — and get his thumb cut through to the bone before he kneed Teddie and got him down and took the knife away?"

"I've been asking myself all those things for months," Kate said.

"Kate, this is a serious question. Do you think the wounds could be self-inflicted?"

"I've considered that. It would explain the cuts on the fingers. But why would he almost amputate his thumb? Why would he cut the outside edge of his palm?"

"Maybe he was too wiped out on cocaine to know how he cut himself."

"Do you believe that?"

"Not for a fucking minute." Foster tossed down the plywood knife and with a grimace picked up the crime lab photograph of the murder weapon. "Of all the photos," she said, "this is the hardest one to look at. For me."

"Me too," Kate said. "It's the dried blood from top to bottom. It . . ." She trailed off.

"Yeah," Foster said. "You can't help but see the slick, gory mess it was when Jensen was finished."

"Linda." Kate reached to Foster. "Give me that photo."

After a single confirming glance, Kate put the photo down, picked up the plywood knife, balanced it in both hands. "Now it all makes sense," she whispered, staring at the knife. "How he was cut. And why. The blood spatter on the wall. Oh God, Linda, I know what he did."

— 18 —

"Mr. Jensen," Linda Foster opened her cross-examination, "why were you in a place like Malone's?" Her tone was polite, curious.

He looked at her without expression. "I was having some beers."

"Yes, that we understand. But why were you drinking at a bar frequented by gay men?"

"Objection," Kenneth Pritchard said. "No foundation for such an assertion."

"Objection sustained," Judge Hawkins said.

Foster said, "Mr. Jensen, there must be dozens and dozens of bars between where you live and Malone's. What was the attraction of this particular bar?"

Kate, delighted by Foster's immediate aggressiveness, observed the slight rise of Jensen's chest as he bolstered himself to answer. He was well-turned out again today, in navy blue pants, a white shirt and gray tie under a gray vest sweater. "I found the place, that's all," he declared. "I made a delivery near there. I liked it. If fags — if gays hang out there I didn't know it."

"The bar is in West Hollywood, Mr. Jensen. That never gave you a clue about its possible clientele?"

Judge Hawkins gaveled down a ripple of amusement in the courtroom. Jensen answered with irritation, "I didn't know where it was. I could of cared less where it was."

"Mr. Jensen, would you say you had a good memory?" Foster's tone had become polite again.

"Well . . . yeah." He seemed disconcerted by this new direction of questioning. "Yeah I do," he added emphatically.

"Given that good memory, is it fair to say that you'd tend to remember things less well today than you did right after they happened?"

Jensen hesitated, searching for Foster's angle, inspecting the question for some moments. Kate looked at the jury. No one was taking notes; all twelve, including PARIS, were keenly watching the everything-at-stake battle forming into shape before them.

"Yeah," Jensen finally concluded, "I'd have to say that's fair."

"Is it fair to say there are even things you would remember right after they happened that you would no longer remember today?"

Again he reflected. "Maybe. Well, yeah, anybody'd have to forget a few things."

"So it is then fair to say that your memory is more clouded today than it was the day after Mr. Crawford's death?"

He looked at her with grim suspicion. "I dunno, maybe a little bit."

"But you do agree that you remembered things better immediately after his death than you would remember them today."

"Okay, I'd have to say that's fair."

"All right. I want to ask you some questions about the statement you gave to the police the very evening of the day Mr. Crawford died."

Gotcha, Kate thought. Foster had set him up.

"You testified yesterday that you did two lines of cocaine at Malone's. How much cocaine did Teddie Crawford do?"

He shrugged. "I didn't pay that much attention. I was doing my own thing."

"You testified yesterday that you had four lines of cocaine at Tradition. How much did Teddie Crawford do?"

"I didn't notice."

"How very odd, Mr. Jensen," Foster said. She moved unhurriedly to the counsel table and consulted a sheaf of papers, its individual pages tagged with colored paper clips. She picked up a page marked with an orange clip. "In the statement you gave to the police, you said Mr. Crawford had done two lines at Malone's and three lines at Tradition. You said he was really wasted."

"I don't know what I said. I was scared of the cops," he declared.

"And you're not scared right now?" Foster asked with only a trace of sarcasm.

He pointed to the jury. "I figure I got twelve people who'll be fair."

"I'm certain they will be. Mr. Jensen, you've been sitting in this courtroom listening to scientific testimony from the crime lab and the pathologist that blood and tissue samples from the victim's body showed only traces of alcohol and ingestion of no more than a line of cocaine. Could that have had something to do with the change in your testimony?"

He said combatively, "No, it's just like I said."

"Yesterday you twice testified that you were, quote, smashed as hell on coke, unquote." Adjusting her glasses, she picked up a page marked with a green clip. "In your statement to the police, you volunteered about Mr. Crawford's state of intoxication, quote, Yeah, he was really wasted, unquote. In reply to their question, quote, And you? Were you wasted? you replied, quote, Nah, I was high, that's all, unquote. What about that, Mr. Jensen?"

"Anything I said to the cops I said because I was scared."

"And you're not scared right now?"

Jensen fixed a wide, blue-eyed gaze on the jury. "I feel okay here."

Enlisting their aid, Kate thought. It might work on one of them — and all he needs is one.

Foster said, "Refresh my memory on a point, Mr.
Jensen. When was it during your association with
Mr. Crawford that you wanted to vomit all over
him?"

Again Judge Hawkins gaveled down laughter in
the courtroom. Kate grinned. Jensen answered
testily, "When he groped me."

"I see." She selected a page with a yellow clip.
"In your statement to the police you said it was
when the victim picked up the knife. Yesterday you
said it was when the victim proposed an act of
fellatio. Today it's something else altogether."

"What difference does it make?" he snapped. "The
whole thing made me want to vomit."

She picked up a page with a white clip.
"According to your statement to the police, after the
victim expressed sexual interest in you, you went
back into the kitchen with the victim and did
another line of cocaine. Did you, or did you not do
that?"

Jensen cast a glance at his lawyer. But
Pritchard's gaze, Kate noted, was fixated on Foster's
sheaf of paper-clipped pages. "Yeah," Jensen said.
"Okay, I did a line in the kitchen."

"So, appalled though you were by what Mr.
Crawford had just proposed, you chose to do more
cocaine rather than leave."

"Hey, it wasn't like that, there was a line left on
the glass, that's all, it was my coke —" He broke
off.

"Yes, it wouldn't do to waste cocaine, would it?"

"Objection," Pritchard complained. "The State is
badgering the witness."

"Sustained," Judge Hawkins said. "Careful, Ms. Foster."

"Yes, your honor." Foster picked up a page with a blue clip. "In your statement to the police, you said that when Mr. Crawford was holding the knife you leaned over to pick up your jacket to distract him. Is that what you did?"

"No, it was like I said yesterday, I was putting *down* the jacket."

"I see. And yesterday when you described Mr. Crawford picking up the knife, you informed us, quote, I figure he's doing it because I'm bigger than he is, it's the only way he's got of making me stay. Unquote. It's the first time you've mentioned this assessment, Mr. Jensen. Why is that?"

"I finally added it up, that's all."

"Or did you realize how ludicrous it was to claim that a man as attractive as the victim would need to threaten someone at knife-point for sex?"

"Objection," Pritchard barked.

"Objection sustained."

Jensen said belligerently, "He'd need to stick the damn knife in me for sex."

"Would he indeed," Foster said. She asked almost casually, "When you finished stabbing the victim, was he dead?"

Casting his gaze downward, Jensen said softly, "He wasn't moving."

She picked up a page with a red clip. "That's not what I asked you. In the statement you gave the police the day Mr. Crawford died you said you could hear some sound from him."

"I wasn't sure if I heard anything."

"But maybe you did."

"I can't say."

"Did it occur to you to get help for this dying man now that he was no longer a threat to you?"

"I just wanted out of there."

"I'm sure. Where were you when you finished stabbing the victim?"

"What do you mean? I just remember kneeling there, holding the knife."

"With him between your legs?"

Jensen's body jerked toward her. "What the hell do you mean?"

"Weren't you straddling his body, Mr. Jensen?"

He said vehemently, "I'm telling you I don't remember."

"You said you thought about your fingerprints, you started throwing everything you'd put your hands on into a plastic bag. Is that right?"

"Yeah, right."

"You've testified that you were smashed as hell on cocaine, yet you had the presence of mind to try and make it look like a robbery — isn't that right?"

"I was confused. Messed up as hell."

"In point of fact, no fingerprint of yours was found at the murder scene. You've testified that you were smashed as hell on cocaine, yet you had the presence of mind to remove every source of your fingerprints from the scene — isn't that right?"

"Hey, I wasn't there very long, I didn't touch all that much stuff."

"You've testified that you were smashed as hell on cocaine, yet you managed to ride your motorcycle —" Foster consulted her notebook — "four miles through the city with your hands bundled in makeshift bandages — isn't that right?"

He gripped the railing with both hands. "Hey, what happened at that restaurant would sober anybody up."

"Yesterday you complained about being questioned by the police after the surgery on your hands, that your head wasn't any too clear." She asked sarcastically, "Were you smashed as hell on pain pills, Mr. Jensen?"

"Nothing like the coke, but my head was fuzzy."

"Is your head fuzzy right now?"

He looked at her warily. "No."

"Then let me test your memory." She picked up a page with a violet clip. "When you were questioned at Wilshire Division, didn't the detectives ask what your situation was with pain medication, whether you felt well enough to talk to them?"

"Well, yeah, but I didn't think I could say no."

"Do you remember telling the police that the medical treatment to your hands was not exactly brain surgery?"

"Yeah. But I was trying to get it over with and get outta there."

"Mr. Jensen, let me again test your memory." She picked up a page with a pink paper clip. "Do you remember being informed of your rights when you were at Wilshire Division?"

"I didn't understand what it all meant."

"You were informed of your rights, Mr. Jensen. You said, and I quote, what bullshit, unquote. Remember that?"

"I was just trying for . . . an attitude."

"The officers who questioned you tried again to carefully explain your rights to you and you made your bullshit remark again, Mr. Jensen. Do you remember that?"

"Hey." He shook his head. "It was all like TV stuff to me."

"In this courtroom yesterday you accused the police of misleading you, you said that you quote, didn't know shit about your rights, unquote. Don't you think you bear some responsibility for that?"

"Objection your honor," Pritchard complained. "The State is again badgering the witness."

"It hardly seems so, Mr. Pritchard," Judge Hawkins said. "Overruled."

But Foster did not give Jensen a chance to answer the question. "Shirley Johnson," she said. "Who is she to you?"

"A girl I like a lot."

"Is she your girlfriend?"

"No." He managed a slight grin. "Not yet."

Foster picked up a page with a brown clip. "Why did you tell the police that she was?"

"No big deal. I didn't want them thinking I was a fag — I mean, gay."

"It seems very important that people not think you're gay."

He said belligerently, "Wouldn't it be to you?"

She smiled. "I'm not the one who's here to answer questions, Mr. Jensen, but it would be no big deal to me. Let's talk about you and the victim and the knife. Would you take us through the scenario again of what happened in the kitchen when you claim he picked up the knife?"

"I turned to lay down my jacket, to distract him so I can take the knife away. I grab at his wrist —" He demonstrated as he spoke, "— but he jerks the knife and I get it in my hand, he cuts me. I grab at it with my other hand, I knee him and we both go down on the floor. That's it."

Kate admired Foster's self-control. She had to be elated as Kate that Jensen had again physically demonstrated Teddie Crawford's so-called act just as he had on direct examination. But Foster's face had not changed.

Foster said, "When he held the knife toward you, was the cutting edge up or down?"

"Up."

"Are you sure?"

"Yeah." He held up hands criss-crossed with red scars. "He cut me. What more do you need?"

You'll see, Kate thought. You're set up but good, you lying bastard.

Foster said, "You've got real problems with your powers of observation, Mr. Jensen. Correct me if I'm wrong on any of these points. You did not observe that Malone's Bar was in West Hollywood. Even though you were standing next to the victim, you did not hear any of his conversation with Stacey Conlin, the clerk at the 7-Eleven store. You did not observe how much coke the victim ingested. After you finished stabbing him, you did not observe whether you were straddling him. You did not observe whether the dying man was alive after you finished stabbing him. And you did not observe what is patently clear to everyone else in the universe: that the man you killed was a gay man."

"Objection, last statement draws a conclusion."

"Sustained, the jury will disregard the last statement."

Foster scarcely waited until the judge finished speaking. Standing in front of Kyle Jensen she demanded, "Why were you in Malone's Bar?"

He squared his shoulders to confront her. "I told you, to have some beer."

"You claim you did not know Mr. Crawford was gay."

"I didn't."

"Then what attracted him to you?"

"I wasn't attracted to him, goddammit. He was just a guy."

"If you were not attracted to Mr. Crawford's attributes as a gay man, then were you attracted to the jewelry he wore, the jewelry you took from his mutilated body?"

"Objection!"

"Your honor, I am trying to determine a reason why the defendant accompanied a gay man to a private place at two o'clock in the morning."

"Objection overruled. The witness will answer."

"I just wanted to have a good time. I took the dude back to his restaurant, that's all there was to it."

"Except after you took him there you killed him."

"I never meant to. I never meant for any of it to happen."

Linda Foster marched back to the counsel table and picked up the sheaf of papers with their bright paper clips. "A lie, Mr. Jensen, like the rest of your testimony. Lies which will soon —"

"Objection!"

"Sustained. Strike that from the record, the jury will disregard." Judge Hawkins added reprovingly, "Ms. Foster —"

"My apologies, your honor. I have no further questions for this witness. At this time."

Kate sat on her hands to keep from applauding.

Kenneth Pritchard stood beside Kyle Jensen for redirect examination, facing the jury. "Kyle," he asked his client, "how long have you been in Los Angeles?"

"About a year."

"Are you familiar with the geographic divisions in Los Angeles, its various communities?"

"No, sir."

"Would you know, for example, where West Hollywood left off and where Hollywood began?"

"No, sir."

"On any occasion when you were in Malone's Bar, were there women in the bar?"

"Yes, sir. All the time."

"Would you say that it's unusual to run into a gay man in a straight bar in Los Angeles?"

"No, sir. Why would it be? Everybody knows the town's full of bars and gays."

"Kyle," Pritchard said gently, "have you ever been arrested?"

"No, sir."

"Ever had to give a statement to the police?"

"No sir."

"Ever been in police custody for any reason?"

"No sir."

"How did you feel when you were being questioned at Wilshire Division?"

"Scared. Scared spitless. I didn't know what they could do to me. The whole thing was a nightmare." He added, "And it's like it's never ended."

"Kyle," Pritchard said intensely, "I want you to tell this jury exactly why you went to Tradition that night with Mr. Crawford."

"Because he was a nice guy, I liked him, his place seemed a good quiet spot to do coke in and have a good time. That's all. I swear it."

"No further questions," Pritchard said.

"I have nothing further at this time," Linda Foster said.

"The witness may step down," Judge Hawkins said.

"Your honor," Kenneth Pritchard said, standing erect beside the counsel table, "the defense calls Detective Kate Delafield."

— 19 —

Glancing at the twelve faces turned to her, the familiar yet enigmatic faces she had so exactingly scrutinized over the past days, Kate wondered what these twelve must think about her taking the stand as a witness for the defense. Did they imagine her a Janus-like creature who would offer contradiction to her previous testimony? Kate met Aimee's puzzled eyes and gave the slightest of nods to reassure her.

Now that she had reached this day, this moment, she felt calm. The answer to the question Kenneth Pritchard would ask was within her, and what mattered was understanding how she would answer and why, not whether or not Judge Hawkins would allow the question.

Pritchard walked to the witness box and stood gracefully balanced on the balls of his feet, hands in the pockets of his trousers. "Detective Delafield, are you familiar with the West Hollywood area?"

So this was his lead-in. "Somewhat," she answered. She would not give him an excess word. Nor would she take her eyes off him.

"What can you tell us about it?"

"Objection," Linda Foster said mildly, "irrelevant."

"Your honor." Kenneth Pritchard's tone managed to convey both surprise and disappointment. "The State itself has brought the West Hollywood area under discussion."

"Your honor," Linda Foster countered, "the People focused on a narrow and relevant field of inquiry."

"By all means let me rephrase the question to suit the State's specifications," Pritchard said, adding an ironic little bow toward Linda Foster. "Detective Delafield, do you have a professional connection with the city of West Hollywood?"

To blunt Pritchard's game-playing, Kate answered soberly, drily, "West Hollywood is policed by the Sheriff's Department. All police departments interface with each other."

"Detective, can you give us an explanation of why West Hollywood is known as a gay city?"

"Objection, irrelevant."

Pritchard turned indignantly to the bench. "The People have repeatedly emphasized Mr. Crawford's sexual preference. I fail to understand an objection to questions relevant to that issue."

"Objection overruled, the witness may answer."

"Let me repeat the question, Detective," Pritchard said. "Can you explain why West Hollywood is known as a gay city?"

He's enjoying this, Kate thought. "I don't know that it's considered a gay city by everyone," she replied. "It has a significant gay population, its city council has several openly gay and lesbian members."

"Are you familiar with gay bars in West Hollywood?"

"Some are known to me, yes."

"Any particular reason why they're known to you?"

"Yes," she said quickly, before Linda Foster could object. "Most police professionals are familiar with major features of their own Division or an adjacent territory — and West Hollywood is an adjacent territory."

"Is Malone's Bar known as a gay bar?"

"I wouldn't know how it's known."

Pritchard's smile was tolerant; she was quarry he would inevitably corner. "Detective, do *you* know it as a gay bar?"

"Not by the definition of a gay bar as a bar that's exclusively gay."

"But is Malone's a bar that gays frequent?"

"Its owner has described it as such a bar."

"Well then," Pritchard asked with a resigned air, "is it known as a gay bar within the gay community?"

"Objection, calls for hearsay."

"Objection sustained."

Pritchard indicated with a good-humored shrug that he would abandon this unavailing trail.

"Detective, from your knowledge of West Hollywood, is it true that it has a Gay Pride march each year?"

"Yes."

"Are you familiar with the West Hollywood march?"

"Objection, your honor. Irrelevant."

Judge Hawkins contemplated Kenneth Pritchard, then said to Kate, "You may answer this question, Detective."

Pritchard repeated, "Are you familiar with the West Hollywood march?"

"Yes."

"Have you been to that march?"

"Objection," Linda Foster insisted. "The People object to this entire line of questioning."

"Objection sustained. The jury will disregard the last question. Counsel, get yourself off this patch of ice right now."

"Yes, your honor. Detective, would it be fair to say you worked very hard on this case?"

Pritchard's dark eyes picked up sheen as Kate did not answer immediately. But she had paused only to formulate an answer. "I don't think anybody should receive more, or less, justice than anyone else," she said. "I work hard on every case I'm involved in."

She was pleased by the dispassionate mask that replaced the confidence on Kenneth Pritchard's face.

"A noble ideal," he said. "Like so many of the so-called ideals of police work. But isn't the truth of the matter that you put inordinate effort into this particular case?"

"Objection —"

"Your honor," Pritchard interrupted Foster, his voice rising, "this line of questioning goes directly to the propriety of the investigation of this —"

Judge Hawkins' voice rose over his: "The objection is sustained, the question is to be stricken from the record, the jury will disregard it. Counsel, you will desist, the foundation for such a line of questioning is totally improper."

Even knowing that Pritchard was accomplishing his objective, Kate was gratified by Judge Alicia Hawkins. That she was clearly provoked by Pritchard's tactic, that her ire was visible, would have an ameliorating effect on the jury.

"Your honor," Pritchard persisted, "it seems only proper that I be allowed to pursue whether a police officer took an inordinate personal —"

"Objection!"

"— and lacked professional objectivity —"

Judge Hawkins gaveled down all further interchange. "Not another word, either of you. Members of the jury, you will disregard. Mr. Pritchard, your remarks will be stricken from the record, you are displaying contempt for this court. Approach the bench, both of you."

Kate watched the jury; they were rapt, held by the electricity of the drama. Juror number four stared in open-mouthed fascination, hands clutched over the PARIS letters on her sweater, as Hawkins, Pritchard, Foster, and the court reporter assembled into a tight knot at the far end of the bench.

Out of an angry buzz of discourse Pritchard's voice rose. Kate clearly heard, ". . . if she's a *lesbian* . . ." countered by Foster's furious,

". . . Latino officer? Black officer?" and Judge
Hawkins' order, "*Lower* your voices, Mr. Pritchard
not *another* word . . ."

A minute later, the conference broke up. Foster
and Pritchard looked flushed — Foster with outrage,
and Pritchard, Kate surmised, with victory.

Judge Hawkins resumed her seat on the bench
and said coldly to Pritchard, "You may proceed."

"I have no further questions," Pritchard said.

Kate thought: Of course not, you turd.

"I have no questions, your honor," Linda Foster
said, looking at Kenneth Pritchard with loathing.

"The witness may step down," Judge Hawkins
said.

Kate walked through the inner court, her gaze
fixed on Aimee's stunned face, trying to soothe her
with her eyes. As she passed the jury box she put
thumb and forefinger together in a surreptitious *it's
okay* sign to Aimee. She took her usual place in the
first row of benches behind the counsel table.

The answer she had been prepared to give she
would explain to Aimee, she would share with Aimee
this entire case. But her answer, so crucial to her,
had never even mattered to Kenneth Pritchard. He
had achieved his end — that the jury clearly hear
him try to ask the question. Now the next question
was, how would it all play with this jury?

Kate glanced up to meet the stare of juror
number eight. The woman's gray-eyed gaze immediately slid away.

"Your honor," Kenneth Pritchard said, "the
defense rests."

With effort, Kate resisted any further analysis of

what had just transpired. She needed her full
concentration for what would now occur.

Linda Foster rose. "Your honor, the People have
a rebuttal witness." Her voice contained echoes of
her anger. "The People submit as evidence sketches
of the surgically repaired wounds to the defendant's
hands, to be marked as People's exhibits fifty-nine
and sixty."

"Objection —" Pritchard began.

"Your honor," Linda Foster snapped, "the
defendant raised his hands while he was on the
stand, the defendant has already shown his own
scarred hands to this jury."

"Objection overruled," Judge Hawkins said crisply.
"The sketches will be designated People's exhibits
fifty-nine and sixty."

Foster handed the two sketches to Kenneth
Pritchard who glanced at them and assented, "As
stipulated."

Linda Foster announced, "The People call Dr.
Henry Mercer."

— 20 —

Henry Mercer, Kate thought, looked scarcely less rumpled in his baggy gray suit than he had in his hospital greens. And his air of bristling impatience was as ill-concealed here as it had been in the emergency room at Hollywood Presbyterian Hospital. Yet in this courtroom, like an ER, the impatience seemed to confer on him a mantle of authority.

Mercer sat in the witness chair rubbing the long slender fingers of his left hand back and forth over his close-trimmed beard, casting restless glances over the jury and courtroom as Linda Foster organized several pages of notes. He fastened his intense gaze on her as she moved toward the witness stand, sketches in hand.

"Dr. Mercer, I draw your attention to People's exhibits fifty-nine and sixty. Are these sketches of the wounds you treated in the hands of defendant Kyle Jensen?"

He leaned forward to examine them. "Yes, February fourth." The answer was swift, the tone abrupt.

Foster took the sketches over to the jury box. At the counsel table she removed the plywood model of the murder knife from her briefcase and displayed it to Kenneth Pritchard, then addressed Judge Hawkins. "Your honor, this is a model of People's exhibit thirteen. We will be using this duplicate of the recovered knife in demonstration."

Foster again approached the witness stand. "Dr. Mercer, the wounds you treated in the defendant's hands consisted, in general, of severe lacerations, is that correct?"

"Correct."

"Would you describe in layman's terms the wounds to the defendant's right hand."

He traced a fingertip on his own right hand. "In layman's terms, the major wound was to the web between the thumb and forefinger. Incised to the bone, with some evidence of tearing. Also a minor cut to the outside of the palm. Minor cuts to all the fingers."

"And to the left hand?"

"A simple cut across the palm, another inside the thumb. Minor cuts to all the fingers."

"Thank you. Now, using this knife in

demonstration, I'm going to set up a hypothetical situation."

"Objection," Pritchard protested. "Objection to this entire fishing expedition."

"Your honor," Foster said, "the People have called this witness to support their charge of first degree murder."

Kate smiled. Pritchard had to regret an objection that had harvested so dramatic a response.

Judge Hawkins picked up her half-glasses and peered through them at Foster. "Proceed," she said. "Preferably with a minimum of theatrics."

"Dr. Mercer," Foster said, standing beside the witness box and facing the jury, "assume a man is holding a knife in both hands." She gripped the handle of the demonstration knife in both hands. "Assume this man has been stabbing another man repeatedly." She lifted the knife over her head and brought it down.

"Objection, this is deliberately inflammatory, this is pure speculation."

"Your honor," Foster repeated, "the People have called this witness to support their charge of first degree murder. I am laying the foundation."

"Proceed," Judge Hawkins ordered.

Foster handed the plywood knife to Mercer. He turned it gracefully in his fingers as if evaluating it as a surgical tool. She walked over to the evidence table. "Let the record show that People's exhibit number thirteen, the actual recovered knife, is being shown to the jury." Foster displayed an open-top box containing a bloodstained knife held down by wires.

"Objection. Your honor, this is entirely inflammatory."

"Overruled, the recovered knife is in evidence."

"Dr. Mercer, assume that the knife you hold, identical in size and shape to the one shown here in People's exhibit thirteen, has become covered, coated, slick with the stabbed man's blood."

Kate's gaze swung to Kyle Jensen, who sat immobile, staring at Mercer, and then to the engrossed jury, then to Kenneth Pritchard, who was scribbling rapidly on his legal pad.

"Dr. Mercer, assume that the knife has become so slick that the attacking man's hands slip and slide on the knife as he stabs his victim."

Pritchard's pen froze over his pad, his head jerked up. "Objection! Objection to this entire blue-sky speculation."

"Your honor," Foster said implacably, "the People have called this witness to support their charge of first degree murder."

"Objection overruled," Judge Hawkins said curtly. "Proceed."

Kate watched with savage enjoyment. Pritchard had to object, she exulted — Foster was attacking his only real defense — but every time he objected, Foster could repeat her phrase, and emphasize the importance of this witness and his evidence.

"Dr. Mercer, this is my question. Given this scenario, could the wounds on the hands of such an attacker correspond with the wounds you treated on the defendant's hands?"

"Your scenario could account exactly for the wounds I treated."

Judge Hawkins gaveled insistently against the wave of sound in the courtroom. Kyle Jensen, staring down at the counsel table, was shaking his head.

Foster waited for quiet, and a few moments beyond
that. Then she said, "Would you explain for the
jury."

Mercer gripped the knife handle, placing his left
hand on top of his right. "First of all, blood's very
slippery stuff, like oil. So as the knife picks up gore,
the hands begin to slide, the bottom or right hand
would slide over the haft. That would open the
minor cut to the outside edge of the palm."

His intense dark eyes had narrowed, as if he
were unravelling an interesting but not too
complicated problem. "Then the bottom hand slips
over the haft, onto the blade."

Kate watched the jury carefully. All the faces
were alert with comprehension.

"As the stabbing continues —" Mercer
demonstrated with the knife, "— with each stab
there's an up and down sawing action on the web of
flesh between the thumb and the index finger, and
the haft would help tear open the wound. A heavy
sharp knife like this one, it wouldn't take much to
saw and tear the web open to the bone."

"Objection, your honor." Pritchard's voice was
quietly emphatic. "This is inflammatory speculation."

"Your honor," Foster countered, "the witness is
speaking entirely in his area of expertise."

"Overruled. You may proceed," Judge Hawkins
said to Mercer.

Mercer had been looking at Pritchard with
annoyance. "Now for the left hand," he continued,
and again demonstrated with the knife. "The left
hand would slide down as well but would receive far
less trauma, it would be cut across the palm and up

inside the thumb. And the fingers of both hands would acquire cuts from the twisting and shimmying of the blade."

Ostensibly checking a note in her notebook, Foster finally said into utter silence in the courtroom, "Doctor, wounds such as these would produce copious bleeding, would they not?"

"Indeed they would."

"Previous testimony has established that two arcs of the defendant's blood on the wall were cast off in the act of stabbing."

"Only two? With hands this badly cut, if they'd been cut *before* the stabbing began, there'd have been lots of arcs on the wall, blood would have been thrown with every act of stabbing. So those two arcs had to land at the end of the stabbing, not the beginning. Further proof of the scenario."

Pritchard had not objected, and Kate looked at him in astonishment, as did Judge Hawkins. He had to be completely stunned, Kate thought. He had allowed Mercer to answer Foster's last question, to testify in an area clearly outside his expertise.

"Thank you, Doctor," Linda Foster said, her voice brimming with satisfaction. She took the knife from him, returned to the counsel table. "No further questions."

Pritchard got to his feet, moved slowly, thoughtfully to the witness box. Kate was amused to see both Pritchard and Mercer rubbing their chins as they contemplated each other.

"Dr. Mercer," Pritchard said in a respectful tone, "would you answer me a question about the wounds to the hands of my client?" He moved back to the

counsel table, picked up the demonstration knife.
Gripping the knife, he returned to the stand. "With
the kind of wounds you describe in my client's right
hand, wouldn't those wounds be compressed by the
act of holding a knife?"

"Yes," Mercer said. "So?"

Poor Pritchard, Kate thought in amusement. To
add to his difficulties, Mercer obviously felt that he
had said his piece clearly and definitively, and he
now would be churlish over being challenged or
having to retill the same ground.

"Wouldn't compression on the wounds affect
them? Staunch and control the amount of blood
flowing from them?"

"So? It's why you've got only two arcs on the
wall instead of more."

"Or perhaps there's another explanation
altogether, Doctor," Pritchard snapped. "You and the
district attorney have constructed a scenario to fit
her convenient theory of Mr. Crawford's —"

"Objection!"

"Sustained. Mr. Pritchard —"

"I'll rephrase, your honor."

"I haven't constructed any scenario," Mercer
barked.

"Move to strike," Pritchard said quietly.

"Motion granted, the jury will disregard. Dr.
Mercer, please wait until you're asked a question."

Mercer's bony shoulders moved in a disdainful
shrug.

Pritchard said, "The district attorney has
reviewed with you a scenario surrounding Mr.
Crawford's death. But isn't it entirely possible, isn't
it just as likely, Dr. Mercer, that the wounds to Mr.

Jensen's hands could result from some other scenario?"

"Give me the knife." Mercer peremptorily held out his hand.

"I beg your pardon?"

"You want me to answer your question, give me the knife."

Dubious, then suddenly eager, Pritchard handed it over. Foster looked worried, and Kate watched with concern. Mercer could demolish his own testimony.

"Okay. Your man could maybe ward off a blow and get a slash on the outside of his palm. He could maybe twist his hand some weird way and get the web cut, get his palm cut, whatever. Same with the other hand. Or . . ." Mercer held the knife in both hands and began a stabbing motion. "Or he could very simply stab somebody using both hands on a very bloody knife and get the exact wounds that he's got. Now what makes more sense?"

Linda Foster was beaming at Henry Mercer. What a wonderful witness, Kate thought joyfully.

Pritchard said sternly, "Dr. Mercer, please. Just answer this question. *Is* another explanation possible?" His voice rose. "*Is* it possible, Dr. Mercer?"

"Of course it's possible," Mercer said contemptuously. "Anything is possible."

Pritchard deliberately turned his back on Mercer. "No further questions."

"I have nothing further," Foster said in triumph.

"The witness may step down."

Linda Foster rose. "Your honor, the People have no further witnesses."

Pritchard nodded acknowledgment.

Kate watched Pritchard sit down at the counsel table and confer with Kyle Jensen. The defense had been dealt a body blow, but she knew with every instinct in her that Kenneth Pritchard was not nearly finished.

— 21 —

"Ladies and gentlemen," Linda Foster began her closing address to the jury, "certain facts in this case are not in dispute."

Kate sat quietly watching the jury, thinking that their faces seemed more unreadable to her than any jury she had ever observed — probably, she conceded, because never had she felt so enmeshed in a case.

On this, the last day of the trial, Foster would make her closing address; Pritchard would follow. Kate was certain that Pritchard had saved a major weapon for his summation, and she could guess the nature of the weapon. But since the prosecution bore the burden of proof, Foster would be allowed a rebuttal to Pritchard's closing statement. Then the case would go to this enigma of a jury.

The courtroom benches were nearly filled. Of the people in the room known to Kate, Gloria Gomez and Francisco Caldera sat behind her, along with Jimmy Malone, who had closed his bar until the verdict came in. At the back of the room were Aimee, and Carl Jacoby, Teddie Crawford's ex-lover — who did not know that he was sitting next to Kate's own lover. The press was also present — correspondents from the *Advocate,* the *Lesbian News* and *Frontiers,* a reporter and photographer from the *Los Angeles Times.* Burt Dayton sat with the blonde, gum-chewing Shirley Johnson. Stacey Conlin from the 7-Eleven, wearing jeans, high heels and a white fake-fur jacket, had edged in shyly, taking the seat nearest the door. Margaret and Joe Crawford had called Linda Foster or Kate each day of the trial, but they had not been able to bring themselves to come to court.

Foster's simple, dark gray suit and high-collared white blouse were perfect attire, Kate thought, for this final proceeding on this final day. Foster stood slim and straight at the podium, a sheaf of notes in front of her as she continued her address to the jury.

"We know for a fact that twenty-three-year-old Teddie Crawford met defendant Kyle Jensen at a bar frequented by gay men. We know for a fact that Teddie Crawford invited the defendant to his restaurant, that they went there on the defendant's motorbike, stopping on the way at a 7-Eleven store. And we know that at the restaurant, defendant Kyle Jensen killed Teddie Crawford."

Without looking, Foster pointed behind her, toward Kyle Jensen. "From here on, we have this defendant's fuzzy, inconsistent, contradictory story as to how and why he killed his victim. In his statement to the police, the defendant claimed that Teddie Crawford was quote, really wasted on coke, unquote, while stating that he himself was merely high. Then, hearing in this courtroom test results on the victim's body that clearly refuted his claim, he changed his story to tell us that he hadn't noticed how much cocaine the victim had taken. And the defendant decided that he himself had been quote, smashed as hell, unquote. His hope, ladies and gentlemen, is that you will accept his claim of drug intoxication as an explanation for his despicable crime."

Kate looked at Jensen. He sat immobile, staring into his hands which were loosely clasped on the counsel table. Pritchard appeared relaxed beside him, making notes with a thick black fountain pen.

"Next we have the defendant's story of the so-called sexual advance." Foster's tone became more sarcastic. "The defendant says about the victim, quote, I wanted to vomit all over him, unquote. First he tells us this impulse swept over him when the victim picked up a knife. Then he tells us no, it was when the victim proposed an act of fellatio. Then he says no, it's when the victim groped him. This defendant claims to be so appalled by the victim's

behavior that he wanted to vomit all over him —
yet it was more important to him to snort cocaine in
the kitchen than to leave the victim's restaurant."

Foster picked up a note marked with a yellow
paper clip. Smart to use the paper clips again, Kate
thought. Remind the jury of all Jensen's lies.

"In his testimony this defendant said that Teddie
Crawford picked up a knife because, quote, I'm
bigger than he is, it's the only way he's got of
making me stay, unquote." Foster tossed the
paper-clipped note onto the podium. "Ladies and
gentlemen, examine this statement. This defendant
claims that Teddie Crawford wanted to perform an
act of fellatio on him. Aside from the ludicrous idea
that Teddie Crawford, a vital and handsome young
man, would need to demand sex at knife-point —
how is it that Teddie Crawford would manage to
perform such an act at knife-point?"

Judge Hawkins gaveled against the wave of
laughter that gathered strength in the courtroom.
Linda Foster seemed startled by the sound. Kate
well understood. Foster was focused on the jury,
nothing existed for her except the jury.

As the courtroom noise subsided Foster continued,
"You have listened to testimony from people who
knew Teddie Crawford. You now know that Teddie
Crawford did not, for a moment, hide his sexuality
in a closet. Stacey Conlin, the clerk at the 7-Eleven
store, openly teased him about being a queen — the
most flamboyant sort of gay man — right in front of
the defendant. This defendant tells you he wasn't
listening. This defendant tells you he didn't notice
that his victim was gay. This defendant actually

thinks you're going to believe he didn't know that this conspicuously gay man was gay."

Kyle Jensen, still staring down at his hands, was slowly shaking his head.

"And then we have the defendant's account of the murder itself," Foster said derisively. "Teddie Crawford came at him with a knife, the defendant tells us. As we now know, ladies and gentlemen, this is hogwash. We know the victim never had that knife. We have expert testimony from the surgeon who repaired the defendant's hands as to the actual source of those wounds. This testimony only brings into focus other facts about the gory scene of murder at Tradition."

Foster picked up a page flagged by a red paper clip. "Blood from the defendant was found *only* in these places: On the murder weapon. In the cast-off pattern on the wall. On the counter top and the taps and in the drain of the sink where the defendant attempted to clean himself up after the murder."

She placed the page on top of her notes, leaned over the podium. "Equally significant, ladies and gentlemen, is where *no* blood from the defendant was found. Blood spatter expert Charlotte Mead testified that she had tested all areas of the victim's shirt, and found no trace of any blood from the defendant — not even on the front of the shirt. Consider what this means. If the cuts to the defendant's hands were defense wounds as he claims, how would he not get his own blood on the victim's shirt while he was stabbing him? He never got any blood on the victim because he was not cut until he

cut *himself* in his final thrusts into Teddie
Crawford's body."

Foster's hand gestured in an arc. "We have the
cast-off blood on the wall. Two patterns, belonging
solely to the defendant. If the defendant had cut his
hands defending himself as he claims, how could he
slash and stab the victim thirty-nine times and have
only two arcs of blood on that wall? The truth is
that the defendant cut his own hands in the act of
murdering Teddie Crawford, and he threw those arcs
as he came to the end of his murderous rampage."

Foster took the demonstration knife from the
shelf of the podium. "The defendant has convicted
himself with his own demonstration of what
happened at Tradition, and, ladies and gentlemen,
you saw it. You saw him sit right there in the
witness chair and demonstrate how Teddie Crawford
came at him with a knife. In both his interview with
the police and here in this courtroom he was asked
if the cutting edge of the knife was up or down.
Both times he said it was up. You heard me ask if
he was sure. He said that he was."

Foster pointed the knife toward the jury. "But if
the victim was holding the knife like this, with the
cutting edge facing *up,* and if the defendant reached
up for the knife as he demonstrated with his own
hand, then how could he have been cut between the
thumb and index finger?"

Foster held the knife in position for a long
moment, waiting, Kate knew, for this dramatic
disclosure to sink in.

"The wounds to the *victim's* hands are the true
defense wounds, ladies and gentlemen. The victim,
five feet-eight to the defendant's five-eleven, one

hundred and forty-two pounds to the defendant's one
hundred and eighty-five — had his own hands
slashed and a finger almost severed in his desperate
and futile attempt to defend himself from this
pitiless killer."

Foster put the knife away and selected a page
with a yellow paper clip. "The defendant says he left
Malone's Bar with the victim quote, Because he was
a nice guy, I liked him, his place seemed a good
quiet spot to do coke in and have a good time,
unquote." She laid the paper down. "But the fact is,
Teddie Crawford had only a minor amount of cocaine
in his body. And the truth is, the defendant came to
Tradition knowing exactly what he would do when
he cornered this young gay man."

Jensen sat staring at his hands, still shaking his
head.

"This defendant told you in the most sincere
tones that he never meant for his crime to happen.
Yet this defendant stated here in this courtroom that
he did not know if his victim was dead when he
finished stabbing him. This defendant made
absolutely no attempt to get help for a man he
claims he did not mean to kill. This defendant
stripped jewelry from his victim's bleeding body and
left a scene of horror not knowing if his victim was
alive or dead, slipping and sliding through his
victim's blood as he walked away."

Foster's gaze moved slowly over the jury. "By
every definition, this defendant has committed first
degree premeditated murder. This defendant has laid
claim to the cuts in his hands as proof of
self-defense. But in actuality they have been proven
to be a grisly part of a vicious act of premeditated

murder. Ladies and gentlemen, the People ask for
justice: the People ask that you find this defendant
guilty of murder in the first degree."

Linda Foster gathered up her notes. "Thank you,
ladies and gentlemen of the jury."

Rocking slightly on the thin soles of his highly
polished shoes, Kenneth Pritchard stood at the
podium, hands resting on a leather folder of notes.
He looked distinguished, Kate admitted — even
imposing in his power colors: black suit, snow-white
shirt, a tie with a striped pattern of subtle blues
and grays.

"Ladies and gentlemen," Pritchard began, his tone
soft, almost gentle, "I'd like you to remember back to
when we began these proceedings."

Pritchard paused but did not look around as the
courtroom door opened. Kate turned, and was jolted
to see Taylor. He nodded to her, made a thumbs-up
sign to the bailiff, glanced at Stacey Conlin and
rolled his eyes, then seated himself beside her.

Why was Taylor here? Curiosity about the
outcome of her solo performance on this case? Or
had Bodwin talked to him? Kate turned back to the
inner courtroom, pushing away thoughts of Taylor;
she needed all of her focus on Kenneth Pritchard.

"If you recall," Pritchard was saying to the jury,
"I promised lots of drama from the district attorney.
I promised you she would fill this room with as
much fog —" Pritchard's hands began to sculpture
clouds, "— as a special effects man in an old time

movie. And I asked you to keep an open mind. Do you remember that?"

Several jurors rewarded him with nods — juror number two, Robert Baldwin, number six, Dion Franklin, number seven, Victor Chen, and Eugenia Lowe, the older woman who was juror number eight.

"I told you that when all was said and done, this would turn out to be a very sad and very simple story. I told you that *why* Mr. Crawford died was the actual issue before us — and, ladies and gentlemen, it remains as the central issue the twelve of you must decide."

Pritchard leaned over the podium. "The State has laid passionate claim to this case as first degree, premeditated murder. *Passionate* claim, ladies and gentlemen, because they bear the burden of proof — beyond a reasonable doubt and to a moral certainty. And the State would like you to accept emotion in place of proof."

He raised both hands. "Yes, the State maintains it *has* proof. The State offers *claims* of proof. *Allegations* of proof. *Theories* of proof. What the State actually offers is a *veneer* of proof — the scenery they've painted to fit their case, like a salesman inventing virtues to sell his product."

Pritchard stepped out from behind the podium to stand before the jury box. "The State has made all kinds of claims about where blood is and where it isn't, they've trotted out their blood expert for your edification. An expert who described the scene where Mr. Crawford died as a massive pool of blood, yet who also tossed off opinions to a scientific certainty as to where blood from Mr. Jensen was and wasn't.

Ladies and gentlemen, use your good common sense. In a massive pool, blood from my client could be anywhere, masked by sheer quantity."

Pritchard extended his fine, supple hands, palms up. "The State makes much of the wounds to my client's hands, whether or not they're defense wounds. Two men were present at that scene of what has been aptly called a nightmare. No one else. One of those men is dead. My client has testified that in the altercation, in his words, he lost it. He doesn't know what happened. And that, I submit to you, ladies and gentlemen, is the simple truth of it."

Pritchard paced, stopped. "How did my client receive the wounds to his hands? My client says that Mr. Crawford came at him with a knife, its cutting edge up. The State has leaped on this as proof positive of his guilt. I for one believe my client, I have no problem that Mr. Jensen may have received initial wounds to his fingers instead of his palm as he reached up to try to disarm Mr. Crawford — and that those other wounds opened up as the entire incident escalated. Mr. Crawford may even have inflicted all those wounds on Mr. Jensen before my client got the knife away from him."

Pritchard nodded. "Yes, Mr. Crawford was the smaller man. But who can speak for his strength under such circumstances? We all know the story of the woman lifting a car off the body of her child."

Again Pritchard paced, stopped. "The State claims to know precisely what happened. But the State can only speculate. Ladies and gentlemen, all of us can only speculate. No one can say with certainty exactly what happened at Tradition, only the two men who were there. The State's own medical expert admitted that anything was possible."

Pritchard gestured in an arc. "The State has used two patterns of blood on the wall — what they mean, what they don't mean — to chart its version of the entire incident, like someone would use a poll to determine an election. Well, I for one believe in election results, not polls."

He pointed to where Kyle Jensen sat at the counsel table attentively watching. "The State has entertained itself by picking apart the statements of my client. But it's not difficult at all to understand the contradictions between Mr. Jensen's statement to the police and his testimony here. Kyle Jensen has never been in trouble, never been arrested. Never been in police custody. Never been in a police interrogation room. He did what most normal people would do in a situation that had turned into a living nightmare — he tried to protect himself. Ask yourself how you would behave in such a circumstance."

He turned back to the jury. "The State has also made great stock out of Mr. Jensen's statement about wanting to vomit all over Mr. Crawford and exactly when that particular emotion came over him. Mr. Jensen has been in Los Angeles less than a year. We who live here are accustomed to the diversity and tolerance for lifestyle in this city. We lose sight of the fact that others do not share our cosmopolitan sophistication. Sexual diversity may seem commonplace to us. Regardless of our opinions about it, we may have come to accept and even take it for granted. But it can be very foreign, frightening, intimidating, repugnant to someone else.

"The State trumpets that there was no reason for the young, good-looking Mr. Crawford to pull a knife. But why should anyone assume that Mr. Crawford, by any definition not a conventional man, was without a pathological side to him? Why is it less likely for Mr. Crawford to behave in a pathological fashion than it is for Mr. Jensen? Serial killer Ted Bundy was a good-looking young man. Why must we conclude that just because Mr. Crawford was good-looking, he was not pathological?

"At Wilshire Division and in this courtroom, Kyle Jensen was asked to remember a scene of horror. No, he didn't get all the details right. Kyle Jensen is a frightened young man. He was frightened then, he is frightened now."

Extending both hands, Pritchard said in a rising voice, "How could Kyle Jensen not know that Teddie Crawford was homosexual, the State thunders. Well, Mr. Jensen was brought up in a normal, conservative household. His father fought and nearly died for this country in Korea. Mr. Jensen has been brought up like most of us — taught that homosexuality is one of society's deepest taboos. I ask you to imagine yourself in his place. Here he is a stranger in Los Angeles, confronted by a man who embodies everything he has been taught to abhor. A man who makes an abhorrent sexual proposition — and backs it up with a knife. Need I mention the specter of AIDS?"

Kenneth Pritchard walked over to stand in front of juror number two, Robert Baldwin. "The violence of the incident at Tradition comes out of two elements: Mr. Jensen's drug intoxication and his revulsion. We are all products of our culture and upbringing. In the same situation, how much control would you have? If you were confronted by a coiled snake, aside from its threat to you, wouldn't you lash out at that snake from sheer, natural revulsion?"

A low, growling, angry murmur began in the courtroom; Judge Hawkins gaveled it down.

Kenneth Pritchard said quietly, "I said at the beginning of these proceedings that we all bear responsibility for our acts. If my client, Kyle Jensen, accepts that responsibility, so too, ladies and gentlemen, must the dead young man himself."

He stood back to address the entire jury. "The State bears the burden of proof — beyond a reasonable doubt and to a moral certainty. Clearly, the State has failed to prove its case. We cannot give young Teddie Crawford back his life. But we can give this young man . . ." He gestured to Kyle Jensen. "We can allow this young man, who will carry the scars of this incident his entire life, to go on with his life."

Kenneth Pritchard strode to the podium, picked up his leather folder. "Ladies and gentlemen, I ask you to find Mr. Crawford's death a justifiable homicide. I ask you for a verdict of not guilty."

* * * * *

As Kenneth Pritchard sat down at the counsel table beside a pleased-looking Kyle Jensen, Linda Foster ripped a page of notes from her pad and strode over to the jury box, disdaining the podium.

Kate, sickened by Pritchard's closing, forgot her nausea. *She's out of control.*

"Ladies and gentlemen," Foster said, and noisily cleared her throat. Juror number four looked at her in wonder. All the jurors looked disconcerted.

Kate watched in rising apprehension. *She's too angry, she's out of control, she'll blow the whole case.*

"The defense has correctly identified the nature of Teddie Crawford's death." Foster's voice was vibrating, her body rigid with fury. "Sexual diversity, the defense tells us, can be —" She jabbed a finger at the page of notes in her hand, "— quote, foreign, frightening, intimidating, repugnant. Unquote." Glaring down at her notes, she cleared her throat again. "Quote, If you were confronted by a coiled snake, aside from its threat to you, wouldn't you lash out at that snake from sheer, natural revulsion? Unquote. There is a word for this, ladies and gentlemen. The word is homophobia."

Foster slapped the paper with the back of a hand. "The defense claims the violence at Tradition came out of the defendant's drug intoxication and his revulsion. There is a word for violence coming out of homophobia, a word we haven't used yet in this courtroom. The word is gaybashing."

"Objection, your honor," Kenneth Pritchard said quietly.

"Your basis, Mr. Pritchard?" Judge Hawkins inquired.

"Inflammatory terminology. Drawing a conclusion without foundation."

Facing Pritchard, waving her notes, Linda Foster retorted, "The defense itself has established the foundation."

Judge Hawkins peered down at Pritchard through her half-glasses. "I must concur, Mr. Pritchard. Objection overruled. Proceed."

"The defendant," Linda Foster said, turning her back squarely on Pritchard and addressing the completely attentive jury, "is not the only gaybasher in this room."

Pritchard leaped to his feet. "Objection!"

Judge Hawkins looked at him expectantly.

"Your honor, I object!"

"Yes, Mr. Pritchard," Judge Hawkins said, "I heard your objection. I am waiting to hear your grounds."

Kate watched in pure joy. Pritchard was trapped. To explain his objection was to admit that Foster's statement applied to him. To not object meant that he accepted the statement without challenge.

Pritchard sank slowly back into his chair.

Kate thought: If we go on to lose this case, this may be our best moment.

"Mr. Pritchard," Judge Hawkins said, "are you withdrawing the objection?"

Kate thought: I love this woman.

Pritchard muttered, "Yes, your honor."

"Proceed, Ms. Foster."

Let it go now, Linda. You've made the point, don't dilute it.

Foster walked closer to the jury box, yanking off
her glasses as if they were a barrier separating her
from the jury. "Ladies and gentlemen, this crime is
not, as the defense terms it, an *incident*. It is a
crime. The crime of murder. Teddie Crawford made
no bones about the fact that he was gay, and he
died for it." She waved the glasses toward Kyle
Jensen. "This defendant knew Teddie Crawford was
gay. This defendant is so filled with the fear of
being thought homosexual that he lied about who
undressed him, he lied about having a girlfriend."

Vigorously shaking his head, Kyle Jensen glared
at Linda Foster. Pritchard put a hand on his arm;
Jensen shook it off.

"The defense says this trial is like an election
and the evidence the People have offered is a poll,"
Foster said wrathfully. "This is a court proceeding
about a man who is *dead*. The People have
presented concrete evidence of first degree homicide
to a reasonable scientific certainty. The defense
wants you to ignore qualified experts and take the
word of the defendant. If we could accept the word
of murderers about their crimes, we wouldn't need
experts."

Foster's body was no less rigid, but her voice had
calmed. "No, this defendant has never been arrested.
This defendant walked into the casino and went
right to the big game — and the defense says we
should all forgive him for it." Foster continued
bitingly, "The defense says we should just let him
have this one little murder."

Foster punctuated her words with shakes of her

glasses. "The People have proved their case beyond a reasonable doubt — so much so that the only avenue left to the defense is to scoff at the wall of evidence around this defendant. The defense has asked you to use your good common sense. The People ask you the same thing. Because your good common sense will tell you the defense wants you to ignore evidence of first degree murder."

Foster heedlessly stuffed her glasses and her page of notes into her jacket pocket. "The victim's body was mutilated by thirty-nine knife wounds. The People have demonstrated conclusively that the defendant did not act in self-defense — there was no blood from the defendant on the victim, the defendant cut himself in the act of killing the victim. There was not another mark on the defendant — not a bruise, not a scratch, nothing. But the victim was stabbed thirty-nine times. Thirty-nine times, ladies and gentlemen. Consider an act of homicide in which someone is stabbed thirty-nine times."

Foster lifted an imaginary knife in both hands and brought it down viciously, again and again:

"One . . .

"Two . . .

"Three . . .

"Four . . .

"Five . . .

"Six . . .

"Seven . . ."

Foster finally stopped her demonstration. "Thirty-nine times. This defendant stabbed his victim thirty-nine times."

She turned and looked directly into Kyle Jensen's blue-eyed rage. "This defendant has said he wishes he could change what happened. This defendant has said he never meant for any of it to happen. When did we hear this defendant say he was sorry Teddie Crawford is dead?"

Foster turned her back to him. Fishing her page of notes from her pocket and waving it, she said scornfully, "The defense claims other cities don't share our tolerance for diversity of lifestyle, our cosmopolitan sophistication. The people in the defendant's hometown of Pittsburgh will be interested to know they live in such a cultural backwater. Similar cities may be interested to know their citizens have a license to come to Los Angeles and kill gay people."

Linda Foster's voice rang in the courtroom. "The defense says the defendant has been taught that homosexuality is one of society's deepest taboos. If you agree with the taboo, then you avoid the taboo. You don't go into a bar gay men frequent. You don't stalk a gay man. You don't take that gay man to a secluded place and kill him in the most hideous possible way, you don't strip jewelry off his bleeding body. The defense says we're all products of our culture and upbringing. The People ask you: what kind of world do you want to live in?

"We complain about our society, we complain we're powerless to change anything. You have the power to change something. You have the power to tell this court, to tell the people who mourn young

Teddie Crawford, what kind of a world he had a right to live in."

Linda Foster crumpled her page of notes. "You can find this defendant guilty of murder in the first degree. Because he is guilty. And because it is right. I ask you for that verdict."

— 22 —

"Lots of fireworks," Taylor said, inclining his head toward the closed courtroom door.

Kate, still reverberating from Linda Foster's rebuttal closing, managed a smile at the understatement. Her entire life had merely been passing before her eyes in that room. Yet at her core she felt an indifference to Taylor and his remark that was separate from their conflict over this case.

At Taylor's signal she had come out into the hallway while Judge Hawkins read the jury instructions. She knew Taylor might have important information on one of the open homicides in their caseload. But, looking into his broad, slightly flushed face, she saw his purpose.

Taylor said, "Bodwin told me not to talk to you till he did — he's waiting till you finish up here. Screw him, we're partners, Kate."

He moved to sit on one of the benches built into the wall. The corridor was active with traffic — participants in other cases in other courtrooms. Kate joined him, wondering what Bodwin had said to Taylor.

"He calls me in," Taylor said heavily, "says we're getting all kinds of new people in the department, and he's gonna talk to you about working with different partners as a kind of training detective."

"Really," Kate said. She added in a more cautious tone, "I haven't heard a thing about it." She liked the idea. She hoped Bodwin had not invented it as a convenient explanation for Taylor.

"You couldn't pay me to work with a rookie," Taylor grunted. "Takes too fucking long to learn how to be a good homicide cop."

"It does take a long time," Kate agreed. Her investigative instincts had been honed over many years and many crime scenes.

"Bodwin says even if you're not interested, he's gonna give us new partners. It's fucking crazy, Kate. I mean, for chrissakes if it ain't broke, why fix it?"

Kate did not reply.

Taylor said, "I ask why and he just says it's time. It's time," he repeated in a sarcastic falsetto. "Must be the latest dipshit management theory."

He did not seem to notice that she had scarcely
reacted to his news. He picked at the crease in his
trousers. "I don't want a new partner, Kate. I don't
need the hassle. Me and Marie, we talked last
night." He looked up at her, his brown eyes
suddenly soft. "There's this place we've been looking
at in Fillmore . . . You're the first to know, Kate. I
really am gonna go raise some avocados."

"I'm glad for you, Ed," she said, nodding. "You've
been talking about it a long time."

He grinned. "I'll tell you something else, partner.
I feel good about it." Then he looked away, down the
hallway. "But all those years . . . there's a lot of
water over the dam."

She said sympathetically, "You're still part of the
police family, Ed — you know that. Once a cop,
always a cop."

He nodded. "We've had some good times together,
Kate."

"Yes, we have, Ed." She turned at an indefinable
sound from the courtroom. She belonged in there,
she needed to be back in there.

Taylor got up. "So I'll see you at the retirement
party." Injury was mixed in with his flippancy. He
had obviously noticed her divided attention. "Good
luck with your fag case," he said. "Looks like you'll
need it."

Reaching for the courtroom door, she paused to
observe his huffy march down the hallway. He had
pulled her out of proceedings on the major homicide
case on which he had forced her to go solo, had not
so much as inquired into her own feelings about
Bodwin's reassignment plans, had again maligned

her community. She thought: Go grow your stupid goddamn avocados.

Linda Foster picked up her briefcase and came out of the inner court as the courtroom emptied of spectators.

Kate said, "Wonderful job, Linda, the best."

"It's the best I could do, Kate." Her gaze was fixed on the men and women slowly filing into the jury room to begin their deliberations.

Kate beckoned to Aimee, who waved and began to thread her way through the benches. Kate watched with enjoyment the heavy swing of her dark hair, the sensuous grace of her body, the blue-violet of her eyes made more vivid by the royal blue of her silky blouse.

"Linda," Kate said, "I'd like you to meet Aimee Grant. My partner."

Ignoring the hand extended to her, Aimee reached to Linda Foster and hugged her. "You were fantastic."

Foster looked abashed, but pleased. "I hope I was fantastic enough." Inspecting Aimee in frank admiration, she said, "You two women have very good taste."

Kate said, "I think so too." Aimee grinned.

Foster glanced at her watch. "So. Let's get something to eat at the cafeteria, go on up to my office. The jury should be out a long time. I hope."

"Why do you hope so?" Aimee asked. "He's so obviously guilty."

"You're so obviously objective," Foster joked as they walked from the courtroom. "I've learned one thing from being a trial attorney — objectivity is a sometime thing with juries."

"Too true," Kate said.

"The longer they're out," Foster said, "the more chance they can work their way through their homophobia and get to a decent verdict."

The three women had settled themselves in Linda Foster's office. The Farberware coffee pot chuffed away, barely keeping up with their coffee consumption.

"Tell me something," Aimee said to Kate. "When that creep called you as a witness for the defense — if Judge Hawkins had allowed his questions, how would you have answered?"

"Kate may not want to answer that in front of me," Linda Foster said quickly.

"No problem, Linda," Kate said. "Police officers from any other minority group would never be asked such a question, never be challenged about their objectivity toward someone of their own culture — so why should gay or lesbian officers? Since no black or Latino or Asian officer would answer such a question, I decided I wouldn't either. I decided I'd refuse to answer."

"Right, absolutely right," Aimee declared.

"And absolutely the point I made to Hawkins," Foster said.

"Yes. I heard you."

"She was furious with Pritchard," Foster said

with a chuckle. "She was probably imagining her own judicial objectivity as a black woman judge being questioned."

Aimee mused, "Another judge maybe would have ordered you to answer, Kate. Sent you to jail for not answering."

"Yes," Kate said.

Foster nodded. "And I'd have —"

Her phone rang.

Foster looked at the instrument as if it had acquired unwelcome life. Gingerly, she plucked up the receiver.

"Linda Foster speaking." She listened for a moment. "Yes. Thank you." She hung up. "We have a verdict." She took a deep breath. "Fuck."

Kate looked at her watch. The jury had been out two hours and five minutes.

Cameras had been set up on tripods at the rear of the courtroom; a cameraman from KTLA waited near the door, a minicam on his shoulder. The room was crowded to capacity with spectators.

The jury filed in solemnly, looking at no one. Kate had taken her usual place, in the first row behind the counsel table; Linda Foster was studying the twelve grim faces, her own face tight with tension. Kyle Jensen sat rubbing his palms over his knees and staring at the jury. Kenneth Pritchard was leaning casually back in his chair, but he too watched the jury.

Looking regal in her judicial robes, Judge Alicia Hawkins waited for the jurors to settle themselves, then adjusted her half-glasses on her nose and asked evenly, "Ladies and gentlemen of the jury, have you reached a verdict?"

The jury foreperson, Eugenia Lowe, rose. "We have, your honor," she said in a firm voice.

The clerk, a studious-looking, plump young man, took the folded piece of paper from Eugenia Lowe, brought it over to the bench, handed it to Judge Hawkins. She unfolded it, looked at it, handed it back to the clerk.

"The defendant will rise."

Kyle Jensen and Kenneth Pritchard stood; Jensen's hands were clenched at his sides.

Amid the ritual of this ancient ceremony, Kate felt as if she too were standing to receive this verdict, that it would be as much a pronouncement over her as it would be over Kyle Jensen.

"The clerk will read the verdict."

Kate felt, rather than heard, a ringing in her head.

The clerk read in an uninflected voice, *"We the jury find the defendant, Kyle Thomas Jensen, in the above entitled action —"*

The ringing became a painful buzzing.

"— guilty of a felony, section one-eighty-seven of the penal code —"

Kate was dizzy with the ringing-buzzing.

"— murder in the first degree."

In the tumult of the courtroom Linda Foster sat frozen, then whirled to Kate; their gazes fused. Unable to speak or move, Kate watched Foster's eyes, her face, illuminate with joy, with triumph.

Kyle Jensen had sunk into his chair. Pritchard remained standing, leaning over, both hands flat on

the counsel table. Foster turned back to the bench
as Judge Hawkins gaveled and demanded order in
her court.

In the explosion of flashbulbs and the continuing
clamor, Kate looked around blindly, to see Carl
Jacoby, his face granite-hard, stalking from the
courtroom. Francisco Caldera and Gloria Gomez were
sobbing in each other's arms. Aimee was standing,
along with a sizeable contingent of the audience,
arms raised in exultation.

Kate's gaze settled on the jury. Juror number
four's face was again down in her PARIS sweater;
she was sobbing. Juror number three took her hand.
Eugenia Lowe met Kate's eyes with a swift,
gray-eyed glance, then took the hand of juror
number seven, Victor Chen, whose face streamed
with tears; he reached for juror number six, Dion
Franklin. All the jurors linked hands.

— Epilogue —

As Kate and Aimee pushed their way through a jam-packed Nightwood Bar toward Maggie Schaeffer, Kate noticed a forest of identical brown beer bottles on all the tables.

Maggie leaned across the bar. "Everybody, I mean everybody's ordering the same thing tonight." She winked at Kate. "Good thing I thought to get a lot of it stocked." She reached into a tub, opened two bottles of beer, and slid them across the bar.

Kate picked one up, and grinned delightedly at the label: Foster's.

Patton pushed her way through to the bar, salaamed to Kate and winked at Aimee. Kate pointed at the bottle of beer tucked into the belt of Patton's low-slung jeans and said incredulously, "You're actually contaminating the temple of your body with alcohol?"

"Shit no. This is just solidarity with my sisters. I'd as soon drink horse piss."

"This is real good horse piss, Patton." Tora, slinging an arm around Patton's shoulder, took a swig from her bottle, and waved it in salute to Kate and Aimee. "This fine horse piss came all the way from Australia."

Laughing, Maggie punched a button on the VCR behind the bar. "Hey, Kate," she exulted, and gestured with a flourish at the television screen. To deafening cheers in the bar, Linda Foster appeared, being interviewed by a KTLA reporter in the corridor of the Criminal Courts Building.

"The case is opening doors for her," Kate said, raising her voice above the din. "She's already been assigned another homicide case. And there's talk about forming a special hate-crimes unit in the DA's office."

"Is she interested?" Maggie asked.

Kate laughed. "She's told them she'll run it."

"I *love* that woman's style," Tora crowed. She flung her arms around Audie and Raney, who had made their way through the crush and up to the bar. "And I love *these* women."

"This is all great and everything," Patton said sternly, "but you know what we're celebrating?" She answered her own question. "That a guy got what he deserved for killing one of our brothers."

"It's more than Atticus Finch could do for Tom Robinson," Audie pointed out. She explained to Aimee, "That's the lawyer who defended the black man in *To Kill a Mockingbird*, honey."

"I *know* Audie," Aimee groaned. "I know how to read."

"Why, child," Raney said, "a beautiful sweet child like you knows how to *read?*"

And a number of other quite sophisticated things, Kate thought, grinning as the women teased and flirted with Aimee. Kate's gaze strayed over the swell of Aimee's thighs outlined in the tight denim of her faded jeans. Last evening had been filled with intimate conversation as Kate unburdened herself of all the anguish of this case; the intense evening had been followed by a night of intense lovemaking, its lingering memory filling her with hunger for the night to come. Had she ever — even at first — wanted Anne this much? Surely she must have . . .

Anne. She was still disturbed with Anne — disturbed that Anne was not here to explain her friendship with Kenneth Pritchard. But perhaps the explanation lay simply in the nature of the closed-in life she and Anne had led as lesbians in those days. Perhaps Anne, in her isolation and loneliness — and naivete — had confused prurient interest from Pritchard for sympathetic friendship.

The women were still bantering with Aimee, whose good-natured comebacks were picking up edges of impatience. Kate said, "I talked to some of the jury."

The women eagerly crowded around. Kate continued, "After they elected Eugenia Lowe, they spent a lot of time going over the jury instructions, making sure everybody understood them. Then they took the first ballot, just to see where everybody was about guilty or not guilty. The first vote was unanimous."

Kate reached into her shoulder bag. "Eugenia Lowe saved one of those ballots." She spread the small white square of paper on the leather cover of her notebook and held it up so that all the women could see the drawing: a stick-like figure, a hand held up, standing in front of a tank. On the body of the tank was printed GUILTY.

"Tian An Men Square," breathed Audie.

"I bet this was Victor Chen's ballot," Aimee said.

"Probably," Kate said, "but . . . who knows for sure?"

"Would you let me have it?" Maggie asked. "I'll frame it, hang it in the bar."

"A fine place for it," Kate said, handing it over.

Watching Maggie enfold the ballot in a napkin, Kate continued, "So then they had a discussion to be clear about the difference between first degree murder and voluntary manslaughter."

"What a conscientious jury," Audie said.

Kate nodded. "Having a leader like Eugenia Lowe had to make a difference. Then they took a second ballot — it was unanimous, too."

"Did they say anything at all about the why of all this?" Patton asked, hands on her hips.

"They mentioned various things. The evidence about the blood especially — Charlotte Mead's testimony. Mercer's explanation about the wounds on Jensen's hands was key. Stacey Conlin's conversation with Teddie. And Linda Foster," Kate said. "Mostly Linda Foster. Her anger." She shrugged. "They thought Linda Foster was a good person, they were all really impressed with how angry she was."

"God," said Patton. "What if she hadn't been angry enough."

"Linda says it's gay people who aren't angry enough," Kate said.

"I think some toasts are in order." Maggie reached for her own bottle of beer from under the bar.

"Do me a favor," Patton said, pulling her bottle out of her belt. "Let's propose all the toasts so I only have to take one sip of this horse piss. And I get the first toast." She raised her bottle. "To Kate Delafield. The best. Except at pool."

"We'll see about that, my friend," Kate said, touching her beer bottle to Patton's.

Maggie lifted her Foster's. "To Linda Foster — and good people who get angry."

Holding her own bottle aloft, Kate gazed into the caring faces surrounding her. "To Teddie Crawford," she said.

"A brother," Aimee added, looking at Kate, "who did not die in vain."

A few of the publications of
THE NAIAD PRESS, INC.
P.O. Box 10543 • Tallahassee, Florida 32302
Phone (904) 539-5965
Mail orders welcome. Please include 15% postage.

MURDER BY TRADITION by Katherine V. Forrest. 288 pp.
A Kate Delafield Mystery. 4th in a series.   ISBN 0-941483-89-4 $18.95

BENEDICTION by Diane Salvatore. 320 pp. Striking,
contemporary romantic novel.   ISBN 0-941483-90-8   9.95

CALLING RAIN by Karen Marie Christa Minns. 240 pp.
Spellbinding, erotic love story   ISBN 0-941483-87-8   9.95

BLACK IRIS by Jeane Harris. 192 pp. Caroline's hidden past . . .
ISBN 0-941483-68-1   8.95

TOUCHWOOD by Karin Kallmaker. 240 pp. Loving, May/
December romance.   ISBN 0-941483-76-2   8.95

BAYOU CITY SECRETS by Deborah Powell. 224 pp. A Hollis
Carpenter mystery. First in a series.   ISBN 0-941483-91-6   8.95

COP OUT by Claire McNab. 208 pp. 4th Det. Insp. Carol Ashton
mystery.   ISBN 0-941483-84-3   8.95

LODESTAR by Phyllis Horn. 224 pp. Romantic, fast-moving
adventure.   ISBN 0-941483-83-5   8.95

THE BEVERLY MALIBU by Katherine V. Forrest. 288 pp. A
Kate Delafield Mystery. 3rd in a series. (HC)   ISBN 0-941483-47-9   16.95
Paperback   ISBN 0-941483-48-7   9.95

THAT OLD STUDEBAKER by Lee Lynch. 272 pp. Andy's affair
with Regina and her attachment to her beloved car.
ISBN 0-941483-82-7   9.95

PASSION'S LEGACY by Lori Paige. 224 pp. Sarah is swept into
the arms of Augusta Pym in this delightful historical romance.
ISBN 0-941483-81-9   8.95

THE PROVIDENCE FILE by Amanda Kyle Williams. 256 pp.
Second espionage thriller featuring lesbian agent Madison McGuire
ISBN 0-941483-92-4   8.95

I LEFT MY HEART by Jaye Maiman. 320 pp. A Robin Miller
Mystery. First in a series.   ISBN 0-941483-72-X   9.95

THE PRICE OF SALT by Patricia Highsmith (writing as Claire
Morgan). 288 pp. Classic lesbian novel, first issued in 1952 . . .
acknowledged by its author under her own, very famous, name.
ISBN 1-56280-003-5   8.95

WILDERNESS TREK by Dorothy Tell. 192 pp. Six women on
vacation learning "new" skills.   ISBN 0-941483-60-6   8.95

MURDER BY THE BOOK by Pat Welch. 256 pp. A Helen
Black Mystery. First in a series.   ISBN 0-941483-59-2   8.95

BERRIGAN by Vicki P. McConnell. 176 pp. Youthful Lesbian —
romantic, idealistic Berrigan.   ISBN 0-941483-55-X   8.95

LESBIANS IN GERMANY by Lillian Faderman & B. Eriksson.
128 pp. Fiction, poetry, essays.   ISBN 0-941483-62-2   8.95

THERE'S SOMETHING I'VE BEEN MEANING TO TELL
YOU Ed. by Loralee MacPike. 288 pp. Gay men and lesbians
coming out to their children.   ISBN 0-941483-44-4   9.95
                                          ISBN 0-941483-54-1   16.95

LIFTING BELLY by Gertrude Stein. Ed. by Rebecca Mark. 104
pp. Erotic poetry.   ISBN 0-941483-51-7   8.95
                                          ISBN 0-941483-53-3   14.95

ROSE PENSKI by Roz Perry. 192 pp. Adult lovers in a long-term
relationship.   ISBN 0-941483-37-1   8.95

AFTER THE FIRE by Jane Rule. 256 pp. Warm, human novel
by this incomparable author.   ISBN 0-941483-45-2   8.95

SUE SLATE, PRIVATE EYE by Lee Lynch. 176 pp. The gay
folk of Peacock Alley are *all cats*.   ISBN 0-941483-52-5   8.95

CHRIS by Randy Salem. 224 pp. Golden oldie. Handsome Chris
and her adventures.   ISBN 0-941483-42-8   8.95

THREE WOMEN by March Hastings. 232 pp. Golden oldie. A
triangle among wealthy sophisticates.   ISBN 0-941483-43-6   8.95

RICE AND BEANS by Valeria Taylor. 232 pp. Love and
romance on poverty row.   ISBN 0-941483-41-X   8.95

PLEASURES by Robbi Sommers. 204 pp. Unprecedented
eroticism.   ISBN 0-941483-49-5   8.95

EDGEWISE by Camarin Grae. 372 pp. Spellbinding
adventure.   ISBN 0-941483-19-3   9.95

FATAL REUNION by Claire McNab. 224 pp. 2nd Det. Inspec.
Carol Ashton mystery.   ISBN 0-941483-40-1   8.95

KEEP TO ME STRANGER by Sarah Aldridge. 372 pp. Romance
set in a department store dynasty.   ISBN 0-941483-38-X   9.95

HEARTSCAPE by Sue Gambill. 204 pp. American lesbian in
Portugal.   ISBN 0-941483-33-9   8.95

IN THE BLOOD by Lauren Wright Douglas. 252 pp. Lesbian
science fiction adventure fantasy   ISBN 0-941483-22-3   8.95

THE BEE'S KISS by Shirley Verel. 216 pp. Delicate, delicious
romance.   ISBN 0-941483-36-3   8.95

RAGING MOTHER MOUNTAIN by Pat Emmerson. 264 pp.
Furosa Firechild's adventures in Wonderland.   ISBN 0-941483-35-5   8.95

IN EVERY PORT by Karin Kallmaker. 228 pp. Jessica's sexy,
adventuresome travels.   ISBN 0-941483-37-7   8.95

OF LOVE AND GLORY by Evelyn Kennedy. 192 pp. Exciting
WWII romance.   ISBN 0-941483-32-0   8.95

CLICKING STONES by Nancy Tyler Glenn. 288 pp. Love
transcending time.   ISBN 0-941483-31-2   9.95

SURVIVING SISTERS by Gail Pass. 252 pp. Powerful love
story.   ISBN 0-941483-16-9   8.95

SOUTH OF THE LINE by Catherine Ennis. 216 pp. Civil War
adventure.   ISBN 0-941483-29-0   8.95

WOMAN PLUS WOMAN by Dolores Klaich. 300 pp. Supurb
Lesbian overview.   ISBN 0-941483-28-2   9.95

SLOW DANCING AT MISS POLLY'S by Sheila Ortiz Taylor.
96 pp. Lesbian Poetry   ISBN 0-941483-30-4   7.95

DOUBLE DAUGHTER by Vicki P. McConnell. 216 pp. A Nyla
Wade Mystery, third in the series.   ISBN 0-941483-26-6   8.95

HEAVY GILT by Delores Klaich. 192 pp. Lesbian detective/
disappearing homophobes/upper class gay society.

                                            ISBN 0-941483-25-8   8.95

THE FINER GRAIN by Denise Ohio. 216 pp. Brilliant young
college lesbian novel.   ISBN 0-941483-11-8   8.95

THE AMAZON TRAIL by Lee Lynch. 216 pp. Life, travel & lore
of famous lesbian author.   ISBN 0-941483-27-4   8.95

HIGH CONTRAST by Jessie Lattimore. 264 pp. Women of the
Crystal Palace.   ISBN 0-941483-17-7   8.95

OCTOBER OBSESSION by Meredith More. Josie's rich, secret
Lesbian life.   ISBN 0-941483-18-5   8.95

LESBIAN CROSSROADS by Ruth Baetz. 276 pp. Contemporary
Lesbian lives.   ISBN 0-941483-21-5   9.95

BEFORE STONEWALL: THE MAKING OF A GAY AND
LESBIAN COMMUNITY by Andrea Weiss & Greta Schiller.
96 pp., 25 illus.   ISBN 0-941483-20-7   7.95

WE WALK THE BACK OF THE TIGER by Patricia A. Murphy.
192 pp. Romantic Lesbian novel/beginning women's movement.
                                            ISBN 0-941483-13-4   8.95

SUNDAY'S CHILD by Joyce Bright. 216 pp. Lesbian athletics, at
last the novel about sports. ISBN 0-941483-12-6   8.95

OSTEN'S BAY by Zenobia N. Vole. 204 pp. Sizzling adventure
romance set on Bonaire. ISBN 0-941483-15-0   8.95

LESSONS IN MURDER by Claire McNab. 216 pp. 1st Det. Inspec.
Carol Ashton mystery — erotic tension!. ISBN 0-941483-14-2   8.95

YELLOWTHROAT by Penny Hayes. 240 pp. Margarita, bandit,
kidnaps Julia. ISBN 0-941483-10-X   8.95

SAPPHISTRY: THE BOOK OF LESBIAN SEXUALITY by
Pat Califia. 3d edition, revised. 208 pp. ISBN 0-941483-24-X   8.95

CHERISHED LOVE by Evelyn Kennedy. 192 pp. Erotic
Lesbian love story. ISBN 0-941483-08-8   8.95

LAST SEPTEMBER by Helen R. Hull. 208 pp. Six stories & a
glorious novella. ISBN 0-941483-09-6   8.95

THE SECRET IN THE BIRD by Camarin Grae. 312 pp. Striking,
psychological suspense novel. ISBN 0-941483-05-3   8.95

TO THE LIGHTNING by Catherine Ennis. 208 pp. Romantic
Lesbian 'Robinson Crusoe' adventure. ISBN 0-941483-06-1   8.95

THE OTHER SIDE OF VENUS by Shirley Verel. 224 pp.
Luminous, romantic love story. ISBN 0-941483-07-X   8.95

DREAMS AND SWORDS by Katherine V. Forrest. 192 pp.
Romantic, erotic, imaginative stories. ISBN 0-941483-03-7   8.95

MEMORY BOARD by Jane Rule. 336 pp. Memorable novel
about an aging Lesbian couple. ISBN 0-941483-02-9   9.95

THE ALWAYS ANONYMOUS BEAST by Lauren Wright
Douglas. 224 pp. A Caitlin Reece mystery. First in a series.
ISBN 0-941483-04-5   8.95

SEARCHING FOR SPRING by Patricia A. Murphy. 224 pp.
Novel about the recovery of love. ISBN 0-941483-00-2   8.95

DUSTY'S QUEEN OF HEARTS DINER by Lee Lynch. 240 pp.
Romantic blue-collar novel. ISBN 0-941483-01-0   8.95

PARENTS MATTER by Ann Muller. 240 pp. Parents'
relationships with Lesbian daughters and gay sons.
ISBN 0-930044-91-6   9.95

THE PEARLS by Shelley Smith. 176 pp. Passion and fun in
the Caribbean sun. ISBN 0-930044-93-2   7.95

MAGDALENA by Sarah Aldridge. 352 pp. Epic Lesbian novel
set on three continents. ISBN 0-930044-99-1   8.95

THE BLACK AND WHITE OF IT by Ann Allen Shockley.
144 pp. Short stories. ISBN 0-930044-96-7   7.95

SAY JESUS AND COME TO ME by Ann Allen Shockley. 288
pp. Contemporary romance.   ISBN 0-930044-98-3   8.95

LOVING HER by Ann Allen Shockley. 192 pp. Romantic love
story.   ISBN 0-930044-97-5   7.95

MURDER AT THE NIGHTWOOD BAR by Katherine V.
Forrest. 240 pp. A Kate Delafield mystery. Second in a series.
    ISBN 0-930044-92-4   8.95

ZOE'S BOOK by Gail Pass. 224 pp. Passionate, obsessive love
story.   ISBN 0-930044-95-9   7.95

WINGED DANCER by Camarin Grae. 228 pp. Erotic Lesbian
adventure story.   ISBN 0-930044-88-6   8.95

PAZ by Camarin Grae. 336 pp. Romantic Lesbian adventurer
with the power to change the world.   ISBN 0-930044-89-4   8.95

SOUL SNATCHER by Camarin Grae. 224 pp. A puzzle, an
adventure, a mystery — Lesbian romance.   ISBN 0-930044-90-8   8.95

THE LOVE OF GOOD WOMEN by Isabel Miller. 224 pp.
Long-awaited new novel by the author of the beloved *Patience
and Sarah.*   ISBN 0-930044-81-9   8.95

THE HOUSE AT PELHAM FALLS by Brenda Weathers. 240
pp. Suspenseful Lesbian ghost story.   ISBN 0-930044-79-7   7.95

HOME IN YOUR HANDS by Lee Lynch. 240 pp. More stories
from the author of *Old Dyke Tales.*   ISBN 0-930044-80-0   7.95

EACH HAND A MAP by Anita Skeen. 112 pp. Real-life poems
that touch us all.   ISBN 0-930044-82-7   6.95

SURPLUS by Sylvia Stevenson. 342 pp. A classic early Lesbian
novel.   ISBN 0-930044-78-9   7.95

PEMBROKE PARK by Michelle Martin. 256 pp. Derring-do
and daring romance in Regency England.   ISBN 0-930044-77-0   7.95

THE LONG TRAIL by Penny Hayes. 248 pp. Vivid adventures
of two women in love in the old west.   ISBN 0-930044-76-2   8.95

HORIZON OF THE HEART by Shelley Smith. 192 pp. Hot
romance in summertime New England.   ISBN 0-930044-75-4   7.95

AN EMERGENCE OF GREEN by Katherine V. Forrest. 288
pp. Powerful novel of sexual discovery.   ISBN 0-930044-69-X   9.95

THE LESBIAN PERIODICALS INDEX edited by Claire
Potter. 432 pp. Author & subject index.   ISBN 0-930044-74-6   29.95

DESERT OF THE HEART by Jane Rule. 224 pp. A classic;
basis for the movie *Desert Hearts.*   ISBN 0-930044-73-8   8.95

SPRING FORWARD/FALL BACK by Sheila Ortiz Taylor.
288 pp. Literary novel of timeless love.   ISBN 0-930044-70-3   7.95

FOR KEEPS by Elisabeth Nonas. 144 pp. Contemporary novel
about losing and finding love.   ISBN 0-930044-71-1   7.95

TORCHLIGHT TO VALHALLA by Gale Wilhelm. 128 pp.
Classic novel by a great Lesbian writer.   ISBN 0-930044-68-1   7.95

LESBIAN NUNS: BREAKING SILENCE edited by Rosemary
Curb and Nancy Manahan. 432 pp. Unprecedented autobiographies
of religious life.   ISBN 0-930044-62-2   9.95

THE SWASHBUCKLER by Lee Lynch. 288 pp. Colorful novel
set in Greenwich Village in the sixties.   ISBN 0-930044-66-5   8.95

MISFORTUNE'S FRIEND by Sarah Aldridge. 320 pp. Histori-
cal Lesbian novel set on two continents.   ISBN 0-930044-67-3   7.95

A STUDIO OF ONE'S OWN by Ann Stokes. Edited by
Dolores Klaich. 128 pp. Autobiography.   ISBN 0-930044-64-9   7.95

SEX VARIANT WOMEN IN LITERATURE by Jeannette
Howard Foster. 448 pp. Literary history.   ISBN 0-930044-65-7   8.95

A HOT-EYED MODERATE by Jane Rule. 252 pp. Hard-hitting
essays on gay life; writing; art.   ISBN 0-930044-57-6   7.95

INLAND PASSAGE AND OTHER STORIES by Jane Rule.
288 pp. Wide-ranging new collection.   ISBN 0-930044-56-8   7.95

WE TOO ARE DRIFTING by Gale Wilhelm. 128 pp. Timeless
Lesbian novel, a masterpiece.   ISBN 0-930044-61-4   6.95

AMATEUR CITY by Katherine V. Forrest. 224 pp. A Kate
Delafield mystery. First in a series.   ISBN 0-930044-55-X   8.95

THE SOPHIE HOROWITZ STORY by Sarah Schulman. 176
pp. Engaging novel of madcap intrigue.   ISBN 0-930044-54-1   7.95

THE BURNTON WIDOWS by Vickie P. McConnell. 272 pp. A
Nyla Wade mystery, second in the series.   ISBN 0-930044-52-5   7.95

OLD DYKE TALES by Lee Lynch. 224 pp. Extraordinary
stories of our diverse Lesbian lives.   ISBN 0-930044-51-7   8.95

DAUGHTERS OF A CORAL DAWN by Katherine V. Forrest.
240 pp. Novel set in a Lesbian new world.   ISBN 0-930044-50-9   8.95

AGAINST THE SEASON by Jane Rule. 224 pp. Luminous,
complex novel of interrelationships.   ISBN 0-930044-48-7   8.95

LOVERS IN THE PRESENT AFTERNOON by Kathleen
Fleming. 288 pp. A novel about recovery and growth.
                                ISBN 0-930044-46-0   8.95

TOOTHPICK HOUSE by Lee Lynch. 264 pp. Love between
two Lesbians of different classes.   ISBN 0-930044-45-2   7.95

MADAME AURORA by Sarah Aldridge. 256 pp. Historical
novel featuring a charismatic "seer."   ISBN 0-930044-44-4   7.95

CURIOUS WINE by Katherine V. Forrest. 176 pp. Passionate
Lesbian love story, a best-seller.   ISBN 0-930044-43-6   8.95

BLACK LESBIAN IN WHITE AMERICA by Anita Cornwell.
141 pp. Stories, essays, autobiography.   ISBN 0-930044-41-X   7.95

CONTRACT WITH THE WORLD by Jane Rule. 340 pp.
Powerful, panoramic novel of gay life.   ISBN 0-930044-28-2   9.95

MRS. PORTER'S LETTER by Vicki P. McConnell. 224 pp.
The first Nyla Wade mystery.   ISBN 0-930044-29-0   7.95

TO THE CLEVELAND STATION by Carol Anne Douglas.
192 pp. Interracial Lesbian love story.   ISBN 0-930044-27-4   6.95

THE NESTING PLACE by Sarah Aldridge. 224 pp. A
three-woman triangle — love conquers all!   ISBN 0-930044-26-6   7.95

THIS IS NOT FOR YOU by Jane Rule. 284 pp. A letter to a
beloved is also an intricate novel.   ISBN 0-930044-25-8   8.95

FAULTLINE by Sheila Ortiz Taylor. 140 pp. Warm, funny,
literate story of a startling family.   ISBN 0-930044-24-X   6.95

THE LESBIAN IN LITERATURE by Barbara Grier. 3d ed.
Foreword by Maida Tilchen. 240 pp. Comprehensive bibliography.
Literary ratings; rare photos.   ISBN 0-930044-23-1   7.95

ANNA'S COUNTRY by Elizabeth Lang. 208 pp. A woman
finds her Lesbian identity.   ISBN 0-930044-19-3   8.95

PRISM by Valerie Taylor. 158 pp. A love affair between two
women in their sixties.   ISBN 0-930044-18-5   6.95

BLACK LESBIANS: AN ANNOTATED BIBLIOGRAPHY
compiled by J. R. Roberts. Foreword by Barbara Smith. 112 pp.
Award-winning bibliography.   ISBN 0-930044-21-5   5.95

THE MARQUISE AND THE NOVICE by Victoria Ramstetter.
108 pp. A Lesbian Gothic novel.   ISBN 0-930044-16-9   6.95

OUTLANDER by Jane Rule. 207 pp. Short stories and essays
by one of our finest writers.   ISBN 0-930044-17-7   8.95

ALL TRUE LOVERS by Sarah Aldridge. 292 pp. Romantic
novel set in the 1930s and 1940s.   ISBN 0-930044-10-X   8.95

A WOMAN APPEARED TO ME by Renee Vivien. 65 pp. A
classic; translated by Jeannette H. Foster. ISBN 0-930044-06-1   5.00

These are just a few of the many Naiad Press titles — we are the oldest and largest lesbian/feminist publishing company in the world. Please request a complete catalog. We offer personal service; we encourage and welcome direct mail orders from individuals who have limited access to bookstores carrying our publications.